This is a work of fiction. Similarities to real people, places, or events are entirely coincidental.

COVEN OF THE DEAD BOOK 2

First edition. October 31, 2022.

Copyright © 2022 B. D. Panthona.

ISBN: 979-8-9860174-5-7

Written by B. D. Panthona.

Coven of the Dead

Book 2

By B. D Panthona

To my sister,

Your existence is important to me. I'm so thankful you are in my life and I'll treasure you all of my days.

Acknowledgements

Thank you to all who have supported me!

Editor: Solace Zeta

Cover Art: Kawaii Cryptids

And to all my readers:

Thank You

Author's Letter

There are two guarantees in this existence; we will be born and we will experience death. Nothing else is guaranteed. Love is not guaranteed. Health is not guaranteed. Life is not guaranteed. Yet humans fear inevitable death because they don't understand it. What if it is only the beginning?

When I was a child, I read to escape. Heroes from fiction were the ones who would never let me down. Always doing miraculous things to change their world for the better, the best they can. Every time I was overtaken by grief, every time my soul would break, I would read a story. In those stories, the backstories of the characters were leaps worse than my own. Yet the characters overcame. They used their trauma to make them stronger, wiser.

Death has affected every soul, in one way or another. If all else, we all will die one day. It has become taboo to talk about it. Something to be feared because we don't quite understand death. Worse, the fear of the unknown has been made into a weapon of persecution. People use the fear of life after death to control others. So, I wanted to open a reality where death is not something to be scared of. Where it is just a step in a journey. I wanted to give a feeling of comfort to my readers as they think about the afterlife and not as a sentence of never ending torcher. Especially the people who just want to be their true selves. An alternate reality where there is acceptance for those who have been told that they will be punished in the afterlife.

I used the time I was given to do something that will hopefully make this world a better place. Hopefully, this work will at least be a safe haven for those who read it.

Thank you for reading.

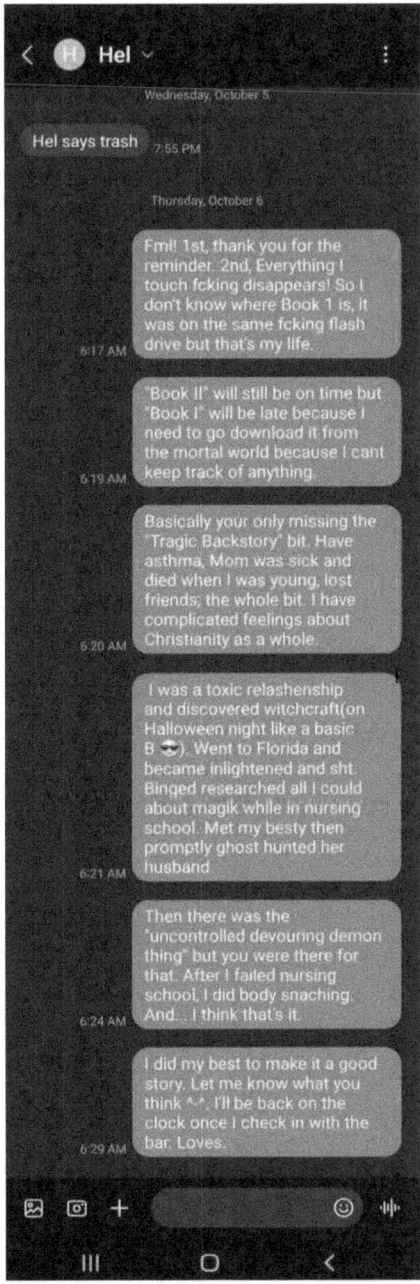

Book 2

Characters

Wendy- Main Character

Hel- Goddess of the Norse Underworld

Will- Wendy's Brother from Another Mother

Gunner- Wendy's Father

Neveah- Wendy's Besty

Gus- Friend from high school that is now a reaper from the voodoo realm

Regin- The all seeing Valkyrae

Venchi- Italian witch that can cross the vail

Makao- Reaper for Cthulhu

Lee- Reaper for Goddess Guan Yin

Chayya- A girl of the line of the God Karni Mata

Randi- Hel's Head Priestess

Sai- Bartender line of RāgarJacka

Lilly- Waitress Succubus

Fenrir- God Brother of Hel

Marty- Funeral driver

Amir- Investigator

Cernunnos and Adharcach- Celtic God of the Forest and his Big
Snake

Chapter Fifteen: Hel

Wendy started a rhythm for the day. She would get up early, exercise for a half-an-hour, then meditate for a half-an-hour, before dressing in a white dress shirt and black pants. She was on call from 6 PM to 6 AM, but her first call didn't always get in that early nor did she stay out that late most days. It was a taxing schedule, but each call was different. Within six months, she became comfortable with every type of body pick up. Going to houses, going to hospitals, and going to retirement homes quickly became an expert script. Bubbly short-talk became perfected with the time she spent with different people, all while doing her best to make the people who worked in such a depressing field have a pleasant experience.

During her six months, she learned that spirits rarely stay with their bodies. The old, who knew their time was limited, had no energy accompanying their bodies. Also, bodies that were picked up at a morgue hours after they died simply didn't contain the same energy as the dead she picked up at crime scenes. There were only two crime scenes where Wendy truly felt a spirit in the van that she drove.

The first experience came around her third week of working. She was sent to one of the many apartment buildings across the state. Like many apartments, there were only stairs. Wendy bantered back and forth with the coworker that was sent to help her, contemplating how they would get the two-hundred-and-fifty pound man down the stairs. Eventually, they decided to enlist two officers to help with the slope. All four of them headed up to the third floor.

It was the first thing she noticed when she walked into the residence. Little pink chairs accompanied by a pair of little pink shoes. A quick survey of her surroundings confirmed that this was definitely a family house, pictures showing a happy couple with a smiling pair of twins in their arms. Wendy's heart took another blow when the soft sobs hit her. The wife was doing her best to talk with the investigator as tears streamed down her face. Wendy quickly looked away to follow the officers into the master bedroom toward the back.

On the floor, medical equipment from the EMTs surrounded the still form of the father in those pictures. Considering the shock pads on the man's chest and the pills that had been lined up on the counter by the investigator, it looked like a heart attack. Within ten minutes, the team had

him bagged and on the gurney. In another ten, the team had successfully

hauled the gurney down the narrow flight of stairs. It wasn't until Wendy

was driving away when she felt it. A scream in her heart and mind. The

voice pleaded to her to turn around.

I can't leave my girls.

"I know, this isn't what you wanted." Wendy's voice soothed. "But

this is something we can't control. It can't be undone." she stopped,

centered herself, and then continued. "This coming from a girl from a

single-parent household, your little girls will be fine. They know you'll be

watching them, they'll work hard to make you proud. Save your energy for

the journey ahead. All there is for you now is to find your peace."

Stopping at a light, Wendy pulled up some of her favorite worship

songs. She let them run their course, soon moving on to bittersweet piano

songs that she had found a couple years ago. When those ran out, a

YouTube suggestion caught Wendy's eye. "Hel's Lullaby." Curious, she

clicked on it. A breathtaking, angelic voice accompanied steady drum beats,

words danced in a language unbeknownst Wendy. Short glances at the closed captions told a story of a gentle Viking woman who knew she wouldn't be going to Valhalla to fight during Ragnarök. So she was pleading with Hel, goddess of death that ruled a place called Helheim, to take her in. The words that wished for rest, and the heart soothing plea of the soft song, made it an instant favorite. With only two minutes until she arrived at the coroner's office, she decided to play the song for him again. All the while praying for him and his family to find a way to heal from this tragedy.

***

The second time was just as sad, though it came many months later. It was the first call of the day in the heart of downtown Denver. Wendy stood by the van parked on the street while the investigator took pictures of the one-person household. Delays with the family arriving (and with the discovery of prescription drugs in the household), caused Wendy to end up waiting for the better part of an hour. Any irritation of the wait left her as she got her first glimpse of the girl that had fallen asleep next to the toilet.

Pillow under her head, glass of water next to her, the small, mocha-skinned girl with beautiful braids looked peaceful in her never-waking sleep. She was a girl, the same age as Wendy. She had wanted for one night to forget about everything, only to end up overdosing. God, Wendy understood that. The temptation to lose herself in the green flower until she couldn't think about all the times she'd failed…

Wendy allowed the family time with their baby girl before she approached them. "Excuse me, I'm transportation and I wanted to offer my condolences for your loss. I like to play music on my way over, does she have any favorites?"

"AC/DC." A girl that looked like the deceased spoke. "Def Leppard, anything like that."

Wendy gave the warmest and most genuine smile to the family as she could, "I can definitely do that." In respect, she gave a slight bow. "I wish you peace today."

Back in the van, she put on her classic rock mix. Her heart breaking as she felt a smiling face rocking out to the music in the speakers. Keeping her eyes on the road, Wendy's head bobbed side to side as she sang 'Back in

Black' loud enough for the both of them. Though she did get a chance to send a prayer out for the girl, however, she wasn't sure if the Christen god would take an overdose victim. Hel's Lullaby came up in her suggested, giving her an impulse that she didn't expect a response from.

As she got close to the coroner's office, she played the lullaby and sent off a metered prayer. "Please. One mistake, one slip up shouldn't damn a person. Please someone take her and give her a good afterlife. Reincarnate her, give her peace, just please. Please let her exist in a better place."

With that prayer, Wendy let her heartache go. Knowing that she had done all she could.

***

Besides her work life and morning routine, Wendy didn't have much else going on. Wendy made sure she had time for Neveah and Jack, even if Nick called her the "Devil's bitch" behind her back. She visited the bar that Will worked at, doing her best to avoid the times when Ty was working. She did try to like the guy and could do a bit of small talk with him, but he just felt off.

Was Wendy happy? Not particularly, but she was existing quite nicely. She decided to take up learning how to scry and astral project. Scrying is a meditative state where the third eye has been known to see images of the future, or else visions that may help the practitioner. Astral projecting is the meditative state where one is supposed to be able to travel out of the body and travel to divergent places or realities. Though Wendy tried, spending hours in front of her enchanted mirror and seemingly doing every one of the guided meditations on YouTube, her mind kept holding her back. A part of her held her by a tight leash, repeating that what she was doing was ridiculous. There was no magik and no magikal realm that she could escape to! She couldn't even deny that she was trying to escape, because after every failed attempt came disappointment, and followed by losing herself in anime episodes.

Because the dresser in Wendy's room was cluttered by miscellaneous objects, her altar stayed in the living room. It wasn't much; her stones in an eye-catching design, her herbs in different baggies lining the outside, and the two mirrors propped up against the wall. It was nothing much to look at, but it was hers.

It was Friday night. Wendy lounged on her second-hand couch with a video game controller in hand. She spent hours online, with Will's voice radiating from the speaker of her phone as they strategize to win the matches. The higher the moon rose in the sky, the heavier her eyes felt, but it wasn't until she finally looked at her phone when she finally realized.

"Oh shit, it's 2:30 in the morning," she muttered as the match ended.

Will snickered on the other side, "So? I have my XP booster for another two hours."

"Well, you have fun with that. I will probably watch some videos and go to bed."

"Weak!" Will jokingly chastised. "Sleep is for the dead."

"Sleep is the best boyfriend I have ever had." Wendy laughed.

Will scoffed, "Considering your ex's, I don't doubt that."

"Hey, hey! Guess what," Wendy's voice filled with excitement and energy.

"What?"

Wendy hung up and turned off the game. She chuckled to herself as she changed the TV to the Youtube platform. She turned on an hour-long compilation of the Game Grumps as they played a dating sim that turned into a horror game. She made it through twenty minutes before her eyes were too heavy to open back up again, forcing her to embrace sleep right there on the couch.

***

Uncharacteristically, Wendy was herself in this dream. She knew who she was, but not where. It was pitch black, but the echoes of each step suggested a spacious cavern. She spun around, stopping when she saw a faint glow around a shaded corner. She hesitantly approached, cringing at each sound her feet made. She practically tiptoed as she glanced around the corner, squinting when seeing a torch propped at eye level. Past the torch was a figure. A black cloak that had its back to her. The arm was up, doing...something.

The arm fell and the figure walked forward until it was swallowed and disappeared. Wendy blinked, stepping out from behind the corner to see beyond the torch. As she stepped closer she realized that the wall she was facing wasn't a wall. It was a mirror. Oh God, it was her mirror. The unmistakable carvings on the outside matched the one in her living room. The only difference was that the one in front of her was double its usual size.

At eye level, there was a black symbol. The intricate swirls seemed to be burned into the glass. It was a face, one side smooth, while the other was drawn gaunt with her teeth showing. The hair was made up of beautiful crisscrossing artwork resembling Celtic knots.

Wendy reached out her hand, about to touch it when the figure appeared again on the other side of the mirror. Wendy wanted to recoil from the hooded figure, but found her body unable to. As she stayed frozen to the spot, the figure raised a hand to reveal skeleton fingers. The bone glistened in the torchlight as it began to write twelve symbols around the face. Each line seemed to be drawn in heavy charcoal, even though the pale bone never changed its color.

Wendy was frozen as the twelve symbols were completed. Once completed the finger dipped to the space underneath the drawings. The bone seemed to be writing backward but the letters appeared legible on Wendy's side of the mirror. Though, only two words appeared.

Call Me

Wendy was about to open her mouth to mutter 'what the fuck,' but Wendy's consciousness was slung back into her body. She immediately rolled off the couch and rushed to her backpack that was still lumped by the door from her last day of school. She retrieved a notebook and copied the symbols down as best she could. Then she went to the bathroom, taking the notebook with her. As she did her business, she struggled to wrap her mind around the experience. Most of her dreams felt real, but were obviously not. This dream…well, it seemed real. She tried to remember if she had seen any of the symbols before, taking her time to examine each one. The only one that seemed to resonate with her was the one in the center. The swirly eye face that split down the middle. Wasn't there a goddess who had a half-deformed face?

She finished up the drawing and went straight to her laptop. After allowing it to boot up, she began her search. Within minutes, she had her answer. Hel, the daughter of Loki, the trickster god, and Angrboda, the mother of monsters. She was the ruler of the underworld, receiving the dead who didn't die in battle, and thus did not earn their seat in Valhalla. She was said to have half of her body burdened by decay and rot, while the other half was a beautiful woman. Not much is known about the goddess, other than she kept to herself and that not even Odin, the main god of the pantheon, could tell her what to do.

The question was, did Wendy follow this to the end?

She worried her lip as her eyes drifted to the window. Light illuminated the curtains, even if the blinds blockaded most of it. Her mind was busy going over everything, analyzing all the possibilities. It seemed three things could happen; something good could happen, something bad could happen, or nothing could happen. If this was a trap, then it was a parasitic entity that would permanently attach itself to her. Possibly draining her energy, or giving her bad luck, or worse. On the other hand, if this was truly *the* goddess...

Well, she wasn't sure what to expect with that.

The worst possibility would be if nothing happened. If she got her hopes up and did all the work, and, assuming it was all just another one of her dreams, there was no magik or adventure awaiting her.

She wished she could talk to someone, but who would believe her? Plus, if she told someone and nothing happened she would feel like a crazy person. Hell, if she told someone and something happened, she may feel even more insane.

True, she could tell Neveah, but she worked during the weekend. She had enough to think of with her work, school, and marriage; plus she wouldn't be able to help anyway.

Wendy gave a heavy sigh as she shrugged. If she was going to do this, she was going to do it right. If something was wanting to contact her, it probably wanted her to do astral projection, a feat that requires lots of practice to complete and years to master. However, Wendy had been practicing almost every day for six months. She reasoned that she wouldn't know unless she tried. With this in mind, she started researching. She went about finding books and websites that were dedicated to the art of hypnosis, meditations, and astral projection. She listened to audiobooks while she

worked and took notes. Once she had a good understanding and an idea of

what techniques would work for her, she started to practice.

She got comfortable, sitting cross-legged on her bed. She started by

entering into a meditation, cleansing her mind until her mind was blank.

Imagining a stairway that she felt in the center of her brain, she delved

deeper into her mind. She kept this up, her mind only filled with taking each

step deeper, until the stairs were gone. She was in a room. Four gray walls

surrounded her, nothing around but knowing she wasn't alone.

The walls turned gold, flowing shimmers crawled down until it

encompassed her.

"Aw, you came to visit?"

Wendy knew that voice, even if she believed she had never heard it

before. It was a deeper, colder mimicking of Wendy's own voice! She

turned to see a reflection of herself that was completely different; the eyes,

her body language, and especially her aura. Wendy could see it. If the gold

of the walls were true neutral, the rippling gold that cloaked around Eabha

was colder, deeper than the energy of the room. Wendy could also feel her own energy, sedated rapids that gleamed with energy. Though she was different, she was Wendy. Though Wendy held Eabha back, they did not hate nor did they fear one another. In fact, Wendy was ecstatic that her meditation was working.

Words flew out of Wendy's mouth before she could register that she was talking. "Yes, I came to ask you something."

A tip of Eabha's lips perked up, "Hel?"

Wendy nodded, "What do you think about it?"

She put an arm around her waist and the other under her chin, her eyes unfocusing. "The dream was indeed... different. As for answering the call, I believe we will be ready." Her eyes focused on Wendy as she bared her teeth in a ferocious smile. "At least, I'll be going in ready."

Wendy's eyebrows knitted and she felt her neck bend to the left, "How will you be ready to take down a possible Goddess?"

Her arms dropped. She closed her eyes as her face hardened in concentration. A purple circle started at her feet, colored mist rising from the light. It quickly enveloped the room. When the mist had covered Wendy's eyes, a whip-like force slapped over Wendy's brain. She doubled over in pain, her arms feeling her crossed legs. Registering the soft cotton sheets that contacted her skin. As if waking from hibernation, Wendy pried her eyes open just a bit.

Yep, she was definitely back in her room. She'd been sling-shotted back into her body in the most painful way possible.

"Yeah, I guess I deserved that…" She muttered as she uncrossed her legs and laid back.

It worked. She had a way to protect herself, all that was left now was simply to do it. Maybe a little bit after her head stopped pulsing, that is.

Like a migraine, Wendy ended up taking a nap to get rid of the pain. Waking up in the late afternoon. Feeling like pampering herself before meeting a goddess, she went all out: vanilla bubble bath, lavender bath salts, and all the other products her relatives gave her at Christmas, the year before; 432 Hertz cleansing music playing over her phone speakers as she mentally composed armor for her spiritual self, while praying this wasn't the biggest mistake of her life.

When the water started getting cold; she got out, put on a sundress, and headed out to the living room. Only the soft glow of yellow light from the bathroom illuminated the enchanted mirror. The tones that radiated from her phone still played as she grabbed the very last bit of oil she had left over from when she first drew symbols on the mirror. She carried the Tupperware around with her to fetch the notebook with the symbols from her dream. As she walked she realized something as she studied the oil. It was clear. That wouldn't work, the symbols were too detailed to blind eye the drawing.

She took the notebook and the oil into the bathroom, setting them both on the sink as she rummaged under the sink. She brought out her practically new makeup bag and pulled out a charcoal eyeliner pencil that she had had for years but had only used half of. Since she only really wore makeup when she was cosplaying, her makeup tended to last for years before she was forced to throw it away. Taking the pencil sharpener, she spent a good ten minutes adding enough charcoal to the oil to make the mixture stand out. Satisfied, she brought the needed items back over to the mirror, retrieved one of her fold out chairs that were used if she ever had friends over, and started finger painting.

Wendy wished she had a knack for free handing an art piece, but she did her best at coping the symbols on the upright surface. Taking her time to make every stroke of her fingers not drip down and ruin her work. It seemed to take hours, but Wendy didn't mind. She found the act soothing as she dedicated all of her brain power to the task. When she was done, she smiled at her work. Taking a moment of pride before wondering what to do next. Shrugging, she began to meditate. She found it surprisingly easy to open the stairwell into her mind. Though, this time, it did not lead into a room. It led into her spirit.

If one had never had an out of body experience, it could be difficult to understand the description. It's almost like a combination of the feeling of falling and the fuzziness of a head-rush. Her skin prickled under heavy weight. The electricity of limb sleep coursed with every movement, but her physical limbs did not move. Stinging and shocking pins and needles plagued her discarnate arm as her energy lifted into the symbols. Unthinking, she channeled her heart energy to force down her fingers, specks of her ember-light floated to each of the symbols, powering the sigils until they glowed. The unease of paranoia washed over her, along with the undoubted of knowing that she wasn't alone as she instinctively leaned out of her own body. Stretching a bit farther, her phantasmagorical hand reached through the mirror. The shocks of electricity dimmed by the cool feel of entering water encompassed the area. Some of the weight lifted as she passed through the portal. Leaving her body behind, she fully entered the mirror.

Though her form moved as if it knew where to go, her mind registered a few things. First, she had completely lost her sense of smell. Not even the subtle familiar smells that her nose had since become blind to, as not even the smell of air registered. The second thing was that she couldn't see, per se. Her heartbeat created a type of energetic sonar that was interpreted by her third eye. She knew she was in a deep, tall hallway. Curious, she drifted to the wall. Static pinpricks raced up her fingers, indicating the barrier as her energy made contact. Though she didn't feel the same sensation with her feet touching the floor. Was she floating?

As her mind raced, her form kept moving down the hallway. Traveling deeper into the cavern until the radar picked up something. As she got closer, she registered a heavily enchanted door. Dark, powerful purple and green energy pulsed from the decorative carvings which seemed to fill the door with ancient runic sigils that were surrounded by snowflakes, leaves, and rivers. In the middle was Hel's sigil. The face cut in half by the doors opening at her approach. Wendy felt blue and purple shimmers of energy surrounding her form. Eabha's protective energy enchanted the premade armor Wendy had created prior. This shield seemed to keep the foreign colors from touching Wendy as she felt no change when the energy seemed to surround her. Confident, her spirit continued into the room.

The room was cluttered. With what? Wendy didn't really know. The energies of the piles were too conflicting to make out just one item, and the piles lined a slightly curving pathway.

She was tempted to stop at one of the piles, to discover how all the energy's felt whilst in her new form, but an energy presence stopped her curiosity. It was an overwhelming power. Wendy was bombarded with the same energy as she felt when next to a decomposing corpse that she had to move for work. It was the sense of rot, and death. Its thick, imposing energy seemed to suffocate her until it was reflected by her armor. The energy burned away before it could touch her, making her want to let out a relieved breath.

Then she realized she didn't have to breathe. Though her lungs felt like they were inflating, there was no sensation of air moving down her throat and of her chest expanding. *Weird.*

Letting the energy of death lead the way, she steadied herself. Instead of butterflies stirring her stomach, she could feel the energy in her core starting to ripple frantically. She took a moment to calm the energy before she turned her attention to the goddess, and there was no doubt that it was the energy of a goddess. Though Wendy couldn't breath, she was suffocated in the sludge of her power. It was like navigating through a lake of mud, Wendy having to fight the weight of the power with each movement closer. Wendy got close enough to register the form on top of the throne that the massive purple and green energy sat on.

"I was wondering if you would answer my call. I was starting to consider contacting you again."

She didn't speak in a physical voice for Wendy's ears to pick up. It was as if her words were transferred directly into Wendy's mind, each word filled with power and commanding energy. For a moment, Wendy panicked. How did she communicate back without her voice? What did she say? However, her panic disappeared before it consumed her. Eabha's energy reminded her that she wasn't alone, reminding her that she had seen this type of scenario played out multiple times in the books and manga that she consumed. Heroes meeting gods in order to achieve their favor and complete the quest. Just talk like a main character and things would work out. Hopefully.

Steeling herself, Wendy did her best to bow in her energetic form. Imagining her words floating over to the energy. "I have never entered this plane of existence. My apologies, but I had to prepare."

"Yes, I see your shields. Distrusting of the immortals, are we?"

"Unsure, goddess Hel. I have never spoken with one. I was only thinking of protecting myself if it were not truly you who was contacting me."

She nodded, "I understand. From what I hear, you have been making quite the enemies."

Wendy froze, her composure slipping. "Wh-what?"

"Yes, human, I know the story of how you decapitated and devoured a fragment of Beliar. Not only is that an embarrassment to his line, but would make you a target of attack if others knew how much of a threat you were." Wendy felt Hel examine her, her senses doing a top to bottom. "Though, it has been generations since a mortal has been able to enter our realm. Even if the call was not answered immediately, the fact you had been able to enter at all is a testament to your strength."

"I assure you, I was only acting in self-defense. He attacked me after escaping his demon box." Wendy just stifled a flinch, was that the right thing to say?

"And I suppose that you were the one to put him in there?" at Wendy's nod, the energy seemed to flair up with… amusement, if the tone was conveying right. "Strong but not well learned, a dangerous combination at the best of times."

Eabha's anger flared in the pit of Wendy's stomach, but Wendy was able to keep it contained. "I am young and have only scratched the surface of my learning. To be honest, I mostly make it up as I go along."

The energy around the goddess seemed to slow, as if in thought. "So, you were not certain if anything would have worked? You defeated the Beliar fragment on impulse? You made it to this realm on sheer chance?"

Wendy felt her core as it began to agitate in worried ripples. Should she have lied, played up her knowledge and experience a bit more? In her hesitation, the goddess had her answer.

Hel laughed, an echoing snicker rolling over Wendy. "Well, well. You've met with a terrible fate, haven't you? "

Wendy froze. Her eyebrows shocked as they furrowed in confusion. The reference completely disrupted her act and seemed to throw any sane thoughts directly out the window.

"Hold up…" Wendy straitened as she studied the goddess, "Did- did you just make a *Legend of Zelda* reference?"

The energy around the goddess froze as if completely caught off guard. Her voice lost her authority as she stuttered. "Wh-what, no."

Wendy's energy lit up, "Yes, you totally did! That's the words the Mask Salesman said to Link in *Majora's Mask*. I wasn't able to finish it, got stuck on the gorgon ice level. If anything, the Ben Drowned / Creepypasta is my absolute favorite."

The goddess aura started retracting back into the goddess's body. Her own energy lightning up at the new change in topic. "Right? It was so well made. I think Jadusable was the one who created it. Do you know about the grief and purgatory theory?"

Wendy started talking with her hands, "Didn't Nintendo debunk that theory?"

The goddess waved her hand, "Psh! You know how many times they have redone the timeline? They are just mad that they didn't think of the idea when it surfaced."

Wendy drifted a bit closer, "Well, and it makes sense if you link it to the dead warrior in twilight princess-"

The goddess held up a hand, "Wait, are you talking about MatPat's theory?"

A surge of brightness showed through Wendy's area, "You know the Game Theorist?"

She shrugged, "I have it on as background noise, but I prefer the Game Grumps."

"You have internet *here*?"

"Well of course, what's the use of being a goddess if I can't get someone to hook up the Wi-Fi for me?" She stood from her throne, "Have you ever played Overcooked?"

Wendy shook her head, "Never had the money for the consol."

The goddess started walking down the stairs, her energy completely retracted into the hooded form. "Some of the last levels are hard to do by yourself. Persephone plays with me sometimes while she's at Hadis's palace, but he hates letting her out of his sight. Males, you know."

"Well, she is gone half the year. I can see why he gets possessive."

Hel started talking with her own hands, "Oh please, they have ruled together for-ever. He could let her have at least one month. He always demands her back just after a week, not enough time if you ask me."

Wendy shrugged, "Yeah, I guess, to gods, a month would be a blink of an eye."

Hel gave what appeared to be a genuine chuckle, "Yes, it is." she stared for a moment before nodding, "Yes, I like you mortal. You are exactly what I need."

Wendy blinked, "Wait, what."

The hazy energy waved for Wendy to follow as she turned around and headed deeper into the room. "What is your name human?"

"Wendy."

"Well, Wendy. To tell you the truth, I have been looking for you for a while." She traveled to a pile of energy and started rummaging around as if she could see the contents. "About six mortal months ago, an unexpected soul turned up in my realm. Not concerning by itself, but when more souls showed up at my door I became intrigued." Hel pulled out an ember. The same flowing ember that Wendy recognized as her own energy. "When they all were sent with this unique energy, I started discreetly asking around. It wasn't until Medusa whispered a story of a mortal that didn't exercise a demon, but devoured it, that I found you. It took a pretty penny to pay Medusa to use her mirror to contact you."

Wendy groaned a bit in embarrassment, "She saw the whole thing?"

The goddess turned back to her, the other hand falling on her hip. "What did you expect? I was told that you practically set off a bomb of energy in front of a portal, it would have been impossible not to notice. Even if the demon realm seemed to throw a hissy-fit afterwards. Demonic energy hasn't been destroyed in generations. Exorcized, sure, but it's hard to ignore a disappearance. Though, it was fun seeing them scramble like bugs for answers."

Hel flicked up her hand, sending the flame back to Wendy. The ember was absorbed as soon as it touched Wendy's aura. As Wendy watched the flame, Hel continued. "I brought you here because of that power. I would like you to join my realm and collect souls for me."

Wendy blinked, her mind railing through the information. Though, if she was going to consider anything…

"Well, I have to have the lore breakdown first."

Wendy couldn't see it, but she felt a flash of confusion from the goddess. "The *what?*"

"The lore. How this new world runs. The breakdown of the rules and workings of the realm. You know, the fine print before I agree to anything."

Silence. Uncomfortable...stunned silence.

Hel snickered, its sonorous, low-song dissipating Wendy's insecurities. "Such a smart human. We may as well become comfortable. Come, follow me."

Wendy followed behind the goddess. As she did, she concentrated on truly seeing her. Now that Hel had drawn in her power, it was easier to distinguish the base form. However, Wendy could only make out a full-length cloak with long sleeves and the hood pulled up. The purple and green of her aura seemed more like mist that clung to the darkness of the fabric, moving in contrast with the float walk that they seemed to do.

Wendy's attention snapped to the new room they were in. Though she didn't remember moving rooms, the entire surroundings had changed. She spun, seeing the blue-gray energy of stones that completely surrounded her. Wendy turned in a complete circle, instantly surmising that she was in a fairytale-cottage made of stone. A warm fire blazed under a thin slab of rock which held an unusual looking kettle upon it. In the middle of the room was a beautiful carved table and matching chairs, all in front of an old-fashioned window. Wendy floated closer to it, scrunching her eyes to try and see past the aura. She got right up to the window, the pinpricks accompanied with winter cold. A subtle ice-blue sheet steamed from the blanket outside, the brown auras of what Wendy assumed were trees peeking out from the cover. She wanted to see it, but couldn't make the details out. Her only thought was whether or not this was what being nearsighted was like…

"That's right. You mentioned that this was your first time to this plane of existence. You probably cannot see as we do."

Wendy turned back to the goddess who was by the fire, seemingly pouring a tea of all things. Wendy moved to sit at the far seat as Hel continued. "I have never conversed with someone like you. Tell me, exactly how do you experience this world?"

Wendy involuntarily gave out a short moan as she placed her thoughts, focusing on the table as she moved her hand over it.

"I… I see the auras of everything. I don't think I necessarily see the wood, I think I'm seeing the wood's energy. It's not completely brown, it has streams of happy-yellow, content-blue, and a bit of pink. Whoever made this for you did it out of love, but I can't make out the carvings like I could on the massive doorway I walked through. I can't really feel either. Everything kinda tingles."

She chuckled as she glided over, taking the seat across from Wendy and setting the two mugs on the table. One she set in front of Wendy, the other she cradled in her hands. Wendy tried to make out the details, seeing if she could see the skeleton fingers from her dream, but only seeing the masses of aura.

"That's not surprising," The goddess said before she slurped at her drink. "Your form hasn't gotten used to our side of the veil. Most would enter after they have shed their mammal skin and can fully immerse in the world. You have a barrier, per se. The more time you spending staying and consuming on this side, the clearer everything should become."

Panic flashed over Wendy, "Over time, right?"

The goddess seemed to stare for a moment before she barked a genuine laugh. "Silly mortal, you will not be stuck here if you drink the tea. You are my guest and I won't destroy your trust."

Wendy smiled in relief, chuckling as she picked up the mug, whispering, "Just making sure," before taking her first sip. It was sweet like honey, strong like a well-deserved drink at the end of the day, and so warm that it seemed to settle in her core. It wasn't hot chocolate, but it had just become her favorite winter drink.

Wendy gave Hel her warmest smile. "This is amazing! Thank you."

She seemed to smile back, "An old mead recipe that has been lost to your world. I make sure to serve it to all the newcomers of this realm. However, I didn't bring you here for the drink." Hel waved her hand, bubbles of energy floating from her flicked fingers. "As is with the humans, we do not remember the beginning of the universe, but our two planes of existence were not so separated. Few remember a time where everyone was the same, but it existed, surely.."

The bubbles combined into one big ball, the patterns suggesting that it was earth, back when the land was all connected. A sheen cover surrounding the planet. Pangea.

"However, time changes all things and humans eventually became energy wielders as their minds grew in scale."

The land broke apart, separating and spreading until it looked similar to the earth she knew. As it did, small bubbles started branching off the land, still connected but growing.

"As energy beings, we fed off the energy that the mortals would throw away. Becoming what they wanted as gods. Every song, every sacrifice, every altar and prayer gave us power and identity. Every soul that died could join their god or goddess side and bring that energy into the realm as their expectations molded and shaped their afterlives. The ones who had not become popular or were forgotten joined the lines of those who were still relevant. The joint power in the process started creating the realms."

The bubbles that connected to the continent became bigger, more defined. Some symbols appeared on the bigger bubbles. She recognized a few, but she could only name the symbol for Rah covering Egypt.

"As power passed through the veil, the more powerful entities found it harder and harder to pass through and interact with the mortals, making the need for lines more prevalent. Some demanded human sacrifices, the trauma rendering a soul more complete, and creating more complete energetic creations to do their bidding. Some influenced their humans to conquer other lands, making more people that gave power to their realm. All the while, the gods changed their image to satisfy the newest generation of humans."

Some of the smaller bubbles were swallowed by others, feeding the bigger bubbles around the world.

"Then the wars happened. First were the entities which fell from Yahweh's line and had aligned with Lucifer Morningstar. They had used the Europeans to twist the word and culture of the Jewish slaves to create the Catholic Church. Though Lucifer brought many people to seek Yahweh, every mortal who believed that they would be sent to the burning cage that Lucifer was kept in, ended up sealing their own fate. Lucifer quickly got strong enough to leave his cage and make his own realm. Around the same time, Bai-Ulgan and Esege Malan, gods of a small nomadic tribe named the Mongols, made a fierce warrior named Gagus Khan. The conquest wiping out many smaller deities and creating a realm powered by fear."

Two bubbles grew, the one covering Asia and one covering most of Europe.

"Thankfully, Bai-Ulgan and Esege Malan's champion's legacy didn't reach the World conquering influence they were reaching for, but the European Christian conquest did something we never expected. With the colonization and expansion of one power, plus the movement and mixing of cultures and ideals... well."

The bubbles that were left, even the two mounds that had encompassed most of the planet, broke off. Wisps of energy connected the bubbles to the planet, the energy moving like the smoke of incense as the wisps moved and reached around the planet.

"This separation made it practically impossible for our kind to influence the other world, even weak fragments of lines have problems manifesting on that side of the veil. All that, and the war is still raging on." She took another long sip before she ended with, "Any questions?"

Wendy took another sip, thinking of something smart to say in lieu of all the new information.

"So basically, Christianity ruined everything. And it was invented by Lucifer to get back at his father for locking him in Hell... not you Hel, but the Christian Hell."

She smiled, "Gehinnom is the name of his realm, but yes."

"Okay, and what is that?" Wendy pointed to the shimmer that floated above it all. A cloud of energy that encompassed everything in a protected shell.

Hel seemed surprised as she crooked her head. "I believe the mortals call it Nirvana, or some refer to it as the 'void,' where being and unbeing coexist, and yet do not exist. It's the runoff, mindless energy that makes up the two worlds. If a soul of a mortal is not claimed by a realm, or a forgotten god does not join a line, they defragment into Nirvana. That energy is then dispersed and used to keep balance in any way it needs to."

Wendy nodded her head, "Energy is not made or destroyed, it only changes forms."

"Exactly," Hel finished off her drink and stood, heading to the stove. "Any other questions?"

"Well…" Wendy fiddled with her cup. "I'm still a bit confused on how souls are… I mean… What makes a soul destined for one place or another? Is it based on heritage or where their soul originally came from? I assume that reincarnation is a thing-"

Cutting Wendy off, the Goddess turned her head and said one word, "Frequency."

Wendy stared. "What?"

"The *frequency* of the aura. Just like sounds and color run on frequencies, so does a soul. This frequency, or wavelength determines what realm the soul is compatible with. Though blood does make a connection with a person's ancestors, it definitely doesn't guarantee anything. As for the reincarnation question," she finished pouring her mead and headed back over to the table. "I don't know how the mortals view reincarnation, but it's not like body-hopping or anything like that. If a soul is just water on a spoon, and the spoon is put into a bucket and then brought out again, would it be the same spoonful? But," she pointed at Wendy as her voice rose an octave, "that's not the question you want to ask."

Wendy blinked as Hel set down, "What question?"

She scoffed then stated cheerfully, "The correct question is, 'how does death work'?"

Wendy blinked again, opened her mouth to say something but Hel waved her off.

"Don't worry little human, this is your first day so I won't hold it against you. Now, there are three scenarios. First one is when a soul is already claimed by a realm. Whether the death was planned or unplanned, a member of that line will be notified and they would collect the soul. The second scenario happens when the soul isn't claimed or the soul rejects the offer to join the predestined realm. Then, it becomes a race by the other realms to convince the soul to join a compatible realm. Usually the first representative that shows up gets it because mortals will believe almost anything in that state. Then there's the last scenario."

"When no one takes them?" Wendy guessed.

Hel's energy sparkled, "Very good, you're right. The last happens more now than ever before. Usually it happens when a person dies unexpectedly and alone. When the person had no belief and lived their life... averagely." She took a sip of her drink then continued, "This also happens when a soul is rejected by their belief or rejects all of the offers to pass on. If they are strong and filled with emotion, they can pull energy to them. Creating an energetic entity on your plane of existence."

"Ghost?" Wendy asked, doing her best to arch an eyebrow.

Hel shrugged, "If that's what you're calling them nowadays. These spirits usually have something to prove or something goes wrong and they get stuck in a loop. If they didn't get visited or if they don't draw energy to them... well, they deteriorate into Nirvana, or void. Cycled into the world energy. This happens more often than not with those that take their own life. Because of free will and all, sometimes Gods don't get warning and the souls don't have the energy of a traumatic death to become a 'ghost' so," she sighed, "they fall through the cracks, so-to-speak."

Wendy looked down at her cup. The drink sparkled with a honey-yellow glow, the energy specks dancing quickly with the warmth. She didn't see the dancing lights though, her mind was too full at just processing the information. A small, mocha-skinned girl that liked classic rock flashed in her mind. Unrealizing that she did, Wendy muttered, "Or drug overdoses."

"Medeah." Wendy looked up at Hel's word, seeing her energy move slower and the purple become softer, more predominant "The young girl you sent to me. To tell you the truth, she was the reason I decided to find you. Not only did she appear without my knowledge, but, based on her story, she would have been one who would have fallen through the cracks."

"Her… story?"

Hel's energy sparked again, "Yes, the last step in accepting souls into the realm. Every underworld has a different method to their refinement process. Getting the souls to their most base frequency. The Egyptians have a journey, then a trial; by the way the feather was rigged centuries ago, the Greeks have the boat man, I have story time." At Wendy's blank stare, Hel sighed. "Look, when my grandfather became a war god, he wanted me to separate the warriors from the common folk. However, my refinement process is through a story-based process, for what is a lifetime, but a collection of experiences that mold a person into who they are? But all of the warriors had the same exact story; trained since they were a child, started pillaging, then died. It was boring, so I stopped doing it. Odin threw a hissy-fit and created the Valkyries to take his warriors to his crowded hall and left me to collect all the 'weak common folk.' But joke's on him, because my realm can accept way more frequencies than his warriors-only club. Not saying that my realm is the reason the world tree is so strong, but I've accepted I'll never get any credit."

"So for clarification," Wendy mumbled while reflecting and absorbing, "when a... fragment of a line brings a soul to you, the entry price to enter Helheim is to tell you their life story?"

"Yep! The entry price to enter Valhalla is to die as a warrior, and so on and so forth."

Wendy looked down, taking a sip of her mead. "Wow."

"So you're in, right?"

Wendy stopped the cup when it was halfway to her face. "What?"

Wendy couldn't see it but she knew Hel just rolled her eyes, "To be one of my reapers. Why did you think I summoned you from the mortal realm? To give you a job offer as part of my line. I even set up the throne room to make a huge show of it."

"Well- I- I mean-" Wendy sputtered. But Hel waved her off.

"I understand that you are invested in the mortal realm, and I have thought of that. I don't know if you know, but the longer you stay here, the weaker the physical body becomes. But I have found a way for you to live in both worlds for a time. I am able to give you somewhere between twenty to thirty mortal years, give or take, if you equally spend time in both worlds.

And you don't have to give me an answer right away, you have my sigils now so you can give me your answer anytime."

Wendy nodded, then drained the cooling liquid in her cup. She set it on the table and tried her best to smile. "Thank you, this is a, a lot to take in."

"Of course, I can see how this could be much for a living mortal." Hel stood, taking both of the cups back to the stone slab. "In the meantime, do you have a steam account?"

Wendy chuckled in disbelief, "The gaming platform?"

"Psh, of course. It's the best thing that you mortals ever created. I had to call in a lot of favors to keep getting computer parts here and I will use it to its full capacity."

Wendy laughed, "Good point."

Wendy gave Hel her information, having a short conversation on the games they liked to play. Soon, Wendy was on her way back down the long hallway to the mortal realm. Walking more and more into the darkness until she entered the realm of sleep. Embracing the familiar feeling and drifting off into the warm blankets of her dreams.

***

Wendy woke up in a puddle of her own drool. The cold liquid formed the only barrier between her cheek and the table. Heavy light battled the shades to enter the room. She looked back at the mirror, the black symbols gone and her drained-pale face looking back at her. She tried to stand, but a headache, the likes of which she had never before experienced, made her sit back down. With a moan, she slinked to the floor and crawled to her laptop. She wanted for its boot-up, groaning as she debated what would take the pain away. As the computer booted, she noticed that it was well into the afternoon of the next day, confirming Wendy had been out for around sixteen hours. Once the computer was fully booted, Wendy immediately booted up steam, a gaming platform that Hel said she had an account on. If that was all a dream…

In the corner of the screen was a notification of a new friend request. Wendy maneuvered her pointer and clicked on it.

NorticHel1Goddess has sent you a friend ⁶request.

Nope, wasn't a dream!

Sighing, Wendy accepted the friend request before dropping her head on the carpet. Closing her eyes as she processed everything all while wondering if she could handle it.

She waited for it, the freak-out at everything she had learned, for it to hit her that she now had confirmation about different...dimensions? The nervous breakdown freak-out about how she used a mirror as a portal and traveled outside of her body? That gods and goddesses existed and one of them had sent her a request to play videogames with her!?

She winced as she tried to get up off the floor, clutching her head as she managed to make it to a sitting position. Nope, she was in too much pain to care. Grinding her teeth, she made her way to the kitchen, got ibuprofen from the tea shelf, popped two in her mouth, swallowed, and made a beeline to her room. After she made it safely to her mattress, she promptly went to sleep. Promising to deal with it all tomorrow.

***

The next day, Monday, Wendy was sent on a long drive first thing in the morning. Two hours one way into the mountains by Colorado Springs to drop off a body at a funeral home in Cañon City, and she definitely didn't mind, as she had plenty to process and think about. As she drove, she stole every glance she could get at the mountains towering next to her on the highway. It was well into fall, but the snow had only dusted to sacred peaks of her mountains. The calming beauty that she had been looking at all her life, the anchor to her homeland. Whenever she would start to enter the dark well within her thoughts, the very sighting of her mountains brought her into the clouds.

By the time she started making the journey back to Denver, she decided her decision rested upon one main, central issue. Would taking this position be a betrayal to mother Holy Spirit and her own upbringing? Sure, this whole, 'only live on this plane of existence for twenty more years' thing was a hurdle, but that didn't really seem too bad. Everyone has to die eventually, and Wendy would be lucky enough to know where or when she was going. Perhaps it would be less stressful to know when she would pass, as it would keep her priorities straight.

Wendy sighed as her eyes soaked up the red cliffs and dark trees lining the serpentine road back to Colorado Springs. Part of her wanted to stop the car and disappear into the forest, to keep walking until blisters started forming on her feet and feeling her muscles screaming at her. When she walked, she could think clearer. The blood circulation kept her mind from wandering.

She thought back to a long ago concert with her youth group, embers of energy floating in the sky as the people sang. The overwhelming feeling of connectedness as she promised her loyalty to that perfect moment. Though it wasn't as strong, she still had a tie to that promise. She did her best to draw on the Holy Spirit and Christ in most of her rituals, she still prayed and meditated to the hum of her savior, but would this position cut that connection? Most importantly, did the 'no other gods before me' rule count if she joined another line?

Wendy sighed again, wishing for the hundredth time she could speak to Christ as easily as she spoke with Hel, especially now that she was just a text message away.

Hey God, should I take the job? Y or N.

Wendy shook her head. Nope, she didn't think that would work out.

Then another thought popped up in Wendy's mind, a memory of a voice that she had heard as clear as day. This wasn't the first time she had spoken to a god. No, there were two other times. One was in Florida, on the bank of a lake that remained an oasis of her dreams. The other was in a bathtub when she was deciding if she was going to break up with Sato. Back then, Wendy just accepted that she understood the voices and didn't question it too much. Now, those interactions held so much more context. Then she thought back to the night her mother passed, the sight of the Holy Spirit, and the kiss that was placed on her forehead.

She stopped her thoughts before emotions bombarded her, taking a moment to glance at the mountains outside her driver's window. She took a few deep breaths to cast out the last memory before returning to her thoughts. Concentrating on the last two memories, she replayed as much as she could remember. If she remembered correctly, both times she just… asked. Both the bath meditation at Sato's house and at the lake, all she did was meditate and ask to speak with them. Was it that easy?

Of course, she would have to test this theory when she had the time to dedicate her full attention to it. A part of her was frustrated that she would have to wait for answers, but she had no choice. Instead, she shoved all of those thoughts into a corner in her mind in order to come back to it later. There was nothing she could do while she was driving, so she concentrated on that, promising to figure it out by the end of the week. She turned up her jazz music and continued with her day.

***

Wendy pulled up to Will's bar two hours before she was technically off-call. She didn't feel like she would be called, but she didn't want to get comfortable at home just in case. As she pulled up, she caught Ty talking to a group that were sitting in a car. Wendy didn't pay too much attention, doing her best to slip by without being noticed. She probably should have at least greeted the hulking male, but she felt like that was asking too much at the moment.

When she got inside, she made a direct line to one of the open stools that were scattered around the main counter. A short Latina Wendy had spoken with a couple times manned the bar. When she saw Wendy, she quickly finished her conversation and walked to her side of the bar.

"Hey 'Lizabith. Is Will in the back?"

She scoffed as she rolled her eyes, "No, just the mistake. Will doesn't start 'til six."

Wendy pointed her thumb toward the front door, "Know who Ty is talking to out there?"

She scowled as she turned, peeking into the kitchen. She spun around back to Wendy, "No, but the bitch is supposed to tell me if he takes a break! Is it too much to communicate just a bit?"

Wendy chuckled, "Well, mind if I get a ginger ale, and I'll be out of your hair."

She smiled, expertly filling up a glass with the bar gun. "You're good. You know Ty, right? Has he always been like this?"

Wendy muttered a thank you as she took the glass that was set on the counter in front of her. "No, I didn't hang around him much. Will went to elementary school with him so that's why they're so tight. He got caught

being a mule for someone in middle school. He went to juvie for a bit but

that's all I know. "

'Lizabith's eyes narrowed, "Think he's still doing it?"

Wendy averted her eyes and shrugged, "Will says that he's cleaned

up, so I have to believe him."

She nodded, seeming to understand. "Thanks girly, soda's on the

house."

Wendy gave her thanks before 'Lizabith ventured off to serve other

customers. After a moment, she pulled out her phone and texted Neveah.

Wendy: Wanna hang out after class? Your house?

Neveah: Sure, not my house though. Nick is

being an ass. Meet you at yours?

Wendy: Sure. Door will be open.

Wendy finished her drink and hopped off the stool. She gave the bar

patrons a wave farewell before she walked out to the parking lot. Ty was nowhere to be seen, meaning he walked to the back before going back inside. Wendy couldn't help but wonder, but it really wasn't her business. Instead, she went straight to her car and drove back to her apartment.

***

Wendy had just gotten into comfortable clothes when Neveah walked through the door. She dramatically slid her bag to the floor just inside the door. With a groan, she walked over to the cheap couch and flopped face down on it.

Wendy did her best to hide her smile as she walked over and crouched in front of her. "Tough day?"

Another extended bemoaning came from the couch cushions.

"Want some tea? I have chamomile."

After a beat of silence, a softer grunt of agreement emitted.

Wendy couldn't stifle a chuckle making her way to the kitchen, then throwing over her shoulder, "Wanna talk about it?"

From the other room, Neveah practically yelled. "Fuck birthing shit!"

"Well, if you're fucking the right anatomy-"

"NOT what I meant!"

Wendy giggled, "Unless your *shit* is big enough to be considered a *birth*!"

She gave a frustrated, muted scream from the living room. Laughter twinkled her voice as sounds of her rising from the couch and following Wendy into the kitchen. "No, we had an OB test today. If that wasn't nerve racking enough, Nick was calling all throughout it. I guess he wants to put my boy in a Christmas play that his mom's church is putting on."

Wendy froze a second, pot halfway to the sink, before she continued with her task. "Isn't Christmas still like, four months away?"

"It's supposedly a big production. Honestly, it may be good for him to have new experiences. What I'm mad about is my phone was going off nonstop in the hallway and we all got a lecture on phone educate. Like, he knows I had a test today. Yet he can't wait thirty goddamn minutes when I don't answer the first time." she sighed, "Is there a chill-the-fuck-out jar that we can do?"

Wendy smiled, putting the filled pot on the stove. "I'll see what I can find, but how is all that going anyway?"

Neveah put a hand on her hip. "You mean how Nick is locking me in the broom closet? Just dandy. It's been upgraded from devil worship to the reason for all of our problems. Because putting up my altar is the reason we don't have any money."

"Oh, and how many times has he called in sick to work?" Wendy asked.

"Three, and only because I worked for him last Friday," she sighed, her shoulders slumping with the action. "So, how is your life going?"

Wendy's heart tightened. There was so much she wanted to tell her. She wanted to spill everything, to have someone help her decide what to do. She wanted to show her, but then she remembered the massive headache it caused. Plus, it didn't seem like the right time. So, she gathered all of her feelings and tucked them away.

"I think the bartender thinks one of the cooks is selling drugs at the bar."

Neveah turned her head somewhat quirkily, "At Will's bar?"

At Wendy's nod, Neveah scoffed, "That boy doesn't deserve that drama. I've only met him once, but I like him."

Wendy nodded as she made the tea, "Yeah."

The conversation continued on, flowing from topic to topic, with the mirror and Hel topic never making an appearance. Even though it seemed like it was burning her to keep it all in.

Hel,

Who do you tell your secrets to? I guess as one of the immortals, you have much more to lose if your secrets ever got out. I don't even know why I was worried; whether she believed me or if she would have thought I was crazy. I guess I felt if she didn't believe me, then everything I experienced wouldn't have been valid... or something like that.

You're right, human emotions are confusing.

Chapter Sixteen : Sounds of Silence

"No, no, no, no no no. Damn it!"

Wendy sat with the laptop on the table, her giant mirror in front of her propped up against the wall. The black symbols were painted and Wendy could see a wisp of the purple and green spilling out from the mirror as a small laugh played across her mind.

We can play something else. I told you, I have been consuming mortal entertainment since its invention. There are not many who may best me. Hel's voice played through her mind.

Wendy looked at the clock on the bottom of the screen. She sighed and spoke audibly. "Can't, I picked up a shift at work tomorrow so I should be getting off anyway. Saturday is usually when they have road trips scheduled. With my luck, I'll get a call to go to Nebraska at six in the morning."

Well... the goddess dragged on the word. *If you became one of my minions, I would make sure that you had a schedule you preferred.*

"I know, and it's an amazing offer. I'm just…still thinking it over." she said as she went about shutting down the laptop.

You know, some humans have literally killed their fellow humans just to get a message from a god, while you have been thinking about this for three months. So, I can't help but wonder what thoughts are crossing the mind of my little human friend? Your existence in this consciousness will be extended considerably, and furthermore I have already offered to set you up with magik tutors, so why the hesitancy?

Wendy lowered the black screen and looked into the mirror. She only saw her reflection around the strokes of black oil. Her green eyes looked beyond as she released her feelings. "The truth is…when I was little, I had an encounter with the reaper who took my mother to the other side. I believe that she was the Holy Spirit from the trinity, and… I feel… I'm wrestling with the feeling that if I take this job, I'll be betraying the ones who helped me through my childhood."

It was quiet on the other side before the Goddess asked, *What trinity? What realm do you speak of? And tell me of this Holy Spirit.*

Wendy's eyebrows frowned in the mirror, "You know; the father, the son, and the Holy Spirit. Yahweh, his only begotten son, and the part of god that lives inside his followers? She looks like she is on fire without the actual… fire part?"

Though she couldn't see the goddess, she could feel the energy on the other side still as the goddess appeared deep in thought, only to hear her respond in solid, unmistakable confusion, *What?*

Wendy's head reared and her body recoiled backward a bit.

"Is that *not* how it works?"

No, the goddess said a bit aghast. *No, Yahweh rules his realm as most high, and wouldn't share his throne. I guess he may be powerful enough to connect to the hearts of his devoted followers, but it is not a fire being. And who is this son?*

"Umm...Jesus?" Another silence, "Born in a manger? The son of god? Died a brutal death on the cross for all our sins so we have a chance to go to heaven?"

Yeshua? The one of his line he sent to possess a baby? Only to become a martyr to save his precious Jews? Didn't they reject him? I heard he tried it again hundreds of years later with a different prophet called

Muhammed, Mohammed, or something...

Wendy stared at her reflection. Processing the information that had just slapped her across the face. It wasn't so much that the stories in the bible were a bit skewed from the truth, Wendy had taken enough world history, religion classes and enough personal research to realize that Jewish farmers and travelers couldn't handle certain concepts. No, what froze Wendy was the image of the female figure made from flowing embers escorting her mother away. The single tear on her mother's turned-face as Wendy told her that she loved her.

Wendy leaned closer, "This entity has hair that can consume a room, she has a female form that is made up of embers that seem to flow over her, she can enter our world in a physical form. Anything ringing a bell?"

Enter the mortal realm? In **this** *time? I was dumbfounded that you were physically attacked by the demon a couple months ago. It's been generations since an energetic force has been able to be in a physical form on the mortal plain so far as we know.*

Wendy pressed her fingertips to her forehead, closing her eyes as her fingers glided across her skull. "Well, then." Her brow furrowed with consternation.

"Sorry Hel, I'm going to go."

Okay, sleep well little human.

The black markings didn't go away as it had the first time, instead they dripped. The power seemed to drain from the symbols, allowing the oil to reconnect with the gravity around it. Wendy didn't pay it the same attention she did only a few weeks ago. The wonder of her magikal life was suffocated by a new question that seeped into every thought, ultimately thinking back to her interactions with the entity who took her mother.

It never gave a name, or any indication as to who, or what, it was. Wendy had just connected it to the Holy Spirit because… well, what else could it have been? She had no reason to doubt the energy. Hell, the energy had actually reassured her multiple times. It helped with Eabha, it helped with Sato; didn't it?

Wendy let it go, as she was standing up, and mindlessly got ready for bed. She let her mind mull over her thoughts, but she didn't let her mind question anything at the moment. It was too much, she had to have time to process this. She had to let everything settle.

She had tried to contact the spirit those last three months, but it had been fruitless so far. Wendy wasn't surprised, she knew deep down she wasn't trying as hard as she could. A part of her was holding back, a part of her didn't want to get the answer, as she knew that she would get: The Christen God. The one she had grown up with, who was a particularly jealous God. A part of her deeply, and somehow instinctively, knew He simply wouldn't approve of her working for a Nordic goddess!

Plus, the more she learned about the realms beyond the veil, the more she became unsure. The realm of Yahweh had become isolationist from the other realms during the Catholic crusades In other words, Yahweh was completely disillusioned based on his own personal experience. He was so appalled that the words meant to lead the Jews toward his wavelength were instead being used as an excuse to pillage and kill, that Yahweh, God barricaded his realm and had not appeared since. A good thing too, considering how many other gods had sworn to attack anyone, from either Yahweh's or Lucifer's line, on sight. The thing about Lucifer's demons, they rose to the challenge. Surviving demons became a formidable army who were not afraid to show it. Though this was all very interesting, this new information about Wendy's Holy Spirit not being of or from that realm was a major car crash destroying her reality.

Her mind spun as she silently got ready for bed. She would usually have a YouTube video playing, but the silence was better company tonight. She got into bed, doing her best to sleep, eventually succumbing to the cradling darkness.

***

Next day was a busy one. First call came in at 6 am and the calls continued to be one, right after another. Normally, Wendy didn't mind and would have appreciated time moving so quickly. However, she wasn't having it today. She wanted to be home, she wanted to curl up in a blanket and watch the December day through her window, a hot drink in hand as she pondered her decisions, and weighed her options. Instead she smiled and made small-talk with the security guards, nurses, and morgue staff she came across. The manners her father drilled into her covered the turmoil storming in her heart.

Wendy looked down at the glowing clock on the van radio. The screen read 2:18; two more hours and she should stop getting calls, she thought, and I will finally be able to go home. She sighed as her stomach growled. She was debating going through a drive-through when a very powerful sensation hit her.

An icepick ripping out a bit of Wendy's heart through her own chest is more what it felt like. The cold knife twisting in her stomach making any thought of food causing bile to travel up her esophagus, which was such an overwhelming feeling of dread and loss, it ultimately forced Wendy to immediately turn off the main road and find a safe place to park.

When she was safe, she leaned back, only then realizing how much she was panting. Though startled at her body's reaction, the lack of wheezes accompanying her breaths was a comfort. It was as if she had been split in two, one part screaming about a fire and the other still looking around for the smoke. An unknown part of her emotions wanted to sob uncontrollably, and to hold her legs to her chest and disappear from the world; but why?

73

The worst part was having felt this sort of disparaging panic before. Last time she felt it she had jumped out of her bed to discover her mother being taken away by an unknown entity. It was the same feeling when she felt her mother die.

God, was she giving herself a panic attack? Was this feeling some sort of PTSD attack brought on by getting lost in her own thoughts? Such a thing had never happened before. She honestly thought that her having asthma attacks made her immune to panic attacks in some way.

She looked at her phone and a text message arrived as soon as she checked the screen.

Marty: This is going to be a crime scene, just tell the officer
you're transport and they'll show you where to go.
Unfortunately, you'll be picking the two bodies up alone.
But Amir will help you.

The address and information came in next, sending Wendy's stomach through the floor.

It was the bar. The bar Will worked at. Oh fuck, there were two bodies at the bar that Will works at.

Everything clicked into gear. Her heart began to race in her chest, her mind scrambled to respond to the text, her fingers danced as she navigated through the phone. Thankfully, she was only ten minutes away. Once the text was sent, she flipped around to go back on the main road. Driving like a road-raging asshole, Wendy swerved in and out of traffic to gain even a second over the drivers around her. At each approaching light, she flicked a bit of energy from her heart space through her third eye at the light. Though, normally, this would work for Wendy about a third of the time, but all lights were green on this drive.

In the five minutes it took to get there, Wendy's mind was blank. Only emotions ruled her senses; panic, sorrow, frustration, and worst of all, a bit of hope. Even as the flashing lights came into view, she hoped that her gut was wrong. She hoped he was just injured, she hoped he didn't work today.

She slowed as she pulled into the crowded parking lot, a police officer immediately walking up to the vehicle.

Wendy rolled down the window, a plastic smile painting her face. "Mortuary transport."

The officer's face softened as he looked her over, "Oh, the coroner is out-back. You'll have to back up at an angle," his finger pointing to the adjoining side road that Wendy knew led to the employee parking lot. The gray afternoon clouds were busy ingraining the moment into her nightmares. She thanked the officer, leaving the window down as the cold gnawing upon her face was the only thing keeping her aware. As she entered the gaggle of police cars, officers and witnesses, she crawled the van forward, searching all of their faces. There were waitresses she recognized, familiar regulars...

It took all of thirty seconds for her to know who was missing.

She mindlessly parked the car, the muscle memory guiding her. She turned it off and stepped out, not closing it as she walked towards the low-strung tarps blocking the bodies from the world. She didn't rush, she couldn't. She was on autopilot as her muscles casually walked to the flashing camera.

Just as it had all those years ago, all she could remember was time slowing. The curse of remembering every moment as she turned the corner.

Dark-blue material-perspective peeled back to reveal the only two people missing from the crowd.

She didn't see everything at once, part of her training. First was the terrain; could the gurney get up to the bodies? The concrete carnage crumbled all over the ground. The little holes were going to be trouble when there was weight on the gurney. The next on the checklist was general positioning of the bodies. The two figures were slumped to the ground. The larger caucasian sat as if he used the wall to slide to a more dignified position. The next was a darker body that was facing towards the wall, Amir and one of the officers already placing a body bag underneath.

Seconds extended as she finally saw what was left of him. Blood had just congealed, red streams still flowing with every movement, including exploded holes blotting his honey skin with the red and white of skull, his face destroyed by a spray of bullets.

She felt the tear as she stared, transfixed. His voice, his smile, his laughter, his humor, his ideas, his mother.

She had seen gunshots from suicide victims before. The worst was a splattered room with brains and shotgun shells. The skull and eyes were missing from the victim. The visual before her would be the only one she would remember on her deathbed.

"Wendy, are you okay?"

Wendy's eyes moved to the source of the question. Amir's eyebrows furrowed as he studied her.

Wendy inhaled a shaky breath. "Mind if we load the other one first?"

"Wendy, do you know them?" concern started flooding his face.

"Yes, I-I may have information on what probably happened here."

Amir stood up, "Need me to call Marty? We can wait for someone-"

"No" she cut him off, "No, he was my brother. It's the least I can do for him."

Amir and the officer's faces paled as shock flashed through them. But they both nodded and headed to the other body.

The job was silent. Not silent as in the lack of noise, but silence between people. The three humans worked in efficiency as they took the necessary pictures of Ty's body. Then loaded him in a bag, put him on a gurney, and loaded him in the van. Wendy didn't remember the interaction.

Instead her memory captured kneeling down to Will's side. Brushing his thin black hair away with her gloved fingers.

He was gone. He went to the other side. He's gone. He's gone.

Was his death unexpected? Maybe a reaper hasn't come for him yet?

Wendy straightened, her eyes unfocused on the destroyed wall. If she hurried…

Wendy zipped up the bag. She stood, brought the second gurney and dropped it to the ground. Amir and the officer helped her place the bag on the gurney and strapped him in. Wendy rose the gurney, nodding her head in thanks before taking Will back to the van. She loaded him in the van before closing the trunk door then quickly shuffled to the driver door. As she got in and closed the door, she had already pulled out her phone. She punched in her map's route to the coroner's office, texting Mardy ten more minutes than the ETA that was on the screen. When completed, she left the crime scene. Immediately going to a back road and parking safely where she wouldn't be interrupted. She turned off the car, locking the doors so as not to be disturbed. Her determined gaze stared back at her in the rearview mirror, where a pink-rimmed the cornea and the tear streaks still glistened off her cheeks. She looked around the van for something to draw the sigils on the mirror with. She had a permanent marker but she didn't want to pay for a new mirror. Her saving grace was a tube of ChapStick. She used the sharp sides of the cylinder to hastily draw Hel's symbols in the small mirror. When done, she closed her eyes. Adrenaline made stillness quite difficult. It took a few tries, but Wendy eventually felt the pinpricks from leaving her body. She forced herself through the small mirror, arriving in the black hallway with a powerful entity in front of her.

The purple and green energy lazily flowed around the hooded figure. The distinct aura of confusion surrounding her. "Wendy?"

She cut the goddess off, "I'll do it. If you save my brother, make him part of your line. I'll work for you. I can't give my soul to you but I will do whatever you want. Just please, save Will."

The goddess's power grew, the size of her form growing twice the size of Wendy. "One thousand years of service is what I will require for saving his form. However he will have the choice if he joins my line."

Wendy didn't have to think, "Agreed. Will is the Native American next to my body. I don't care what happens to the other one."

Hel seemed intrigued, but didn't push. "Since you hold it so precious; vow your commitment to your soul. If you go back on your word, your soul will be forfeited and I will make you regret it."

Wendy's heart skipped a beat…but she nodded. "Agreed."

Hel's energy flashed and a flowing hand raised toward Wendy. She only hesitated for a moment before collapsing her own hand in the goddesses. When they touched, a lightning bolt of electricity brought Wendy down on a knee, the burning shock traveling through her body, resting in her heart. By the time her ears recovered from the wounded scream, her panting held a sharp edge with every inhale. Hel let go of Wendy, ignoring her as she caught her breath. The goddess turned, lifting both of her hands out to an empty corner.

Slowly a brown whirlwind rose up from the ground. Orange swirls lined in pink, snaked through the earthy tone. Wendy could feel it, with her energy glowing at the recognition. She didn't know how, but she knew that this was Will. He was shorter in his spirit form, the energetic mass nowhere close to the intensity of the goddess or even Wendy. He seemed to recognize Wendy as his form began to move apart from the summons.

Feeling the need for haste, Hel started, "Greetings Will, friend of Wendy. I am Hel, Daughter of Loki and ruler of Helheim. Wendy has bought you an opportunity to join me in the afterlife."

He seemed to give himself a once over, still processing his situation. After a moment, a whisper floated across Wendy's mind. Will's voice sounded wispy as he asked, "What?"

"The offer is that you can become part of my line, grow your power and live in the realm of gods, or you can pass on. Your consciousness will be lost to be part of the cosmos. What will it be, mortal?"

Wendy could almost see the confused caution on his face as he answered carefully. "Well... Like, what would I be doing? Will I be torturing people? Poking them with pitchforks? I mean, I won't mind but I should know what I'm getting into."

Wendy couldn't see Hel's face, but she could have sworn the goddess rolled her eyes before one hand rested on her hip while the other waved in circles as she spoke. "What was your occupation, human?"

Will shrugged, his voice still unsure. "Chef technically. I practically ran the bar I worked at. I can't mix a drink but I did do my part making sure the books lined up."

The purple and green of Hel's aura sparkled, "A barkeep. There may be some use to you after all. No mortal, if you join my line I will make you my secrets master. Gathering knowledge from the long list of entities that can not hold their tongue along with their liquor and then reporting it back to me. In return, you will have the protection of the Nordic realm and live among us as part of my line."

A moment of silence hung in the air. Wendy was about to get worried when Will held up his hand, "Hold up! So, what you're saying is that I'm not rotting in a lake of fire but instead I get to run a bar that gods go to?"

Hel nodded, "Helheim is in an eternal winter, the only fire you will find will be in the structures. Though, the tavern will be in a pocket dimension, so I don't know for certain if it will be hot there."

The pinks and oranges around Will became brighter, the swirls dancing quicker around his form. "Well, today didn't start out the best but it has definitely turned around. Yeah, I'll take the job."

Wendy let out a breath she didn't realize she was holding. With it, all the tight stress seemed to be eased in the pit of her stomach. As if feeling her relief, Hel turned to Wendy.

"Rest now my little witch, he has accepted and will not be lost to you. With your new responsibilities, you will see him often."

A surge of panic spiked through Wendy. "May I have two weeks?" at what suspiciously looked like a raised eyebrow, Wendy quickly continued. "It's typically considered rude to leave a job without two weeks' notice."

The wisps of her aura moved slower and glowed with a comforting warmth of a loving embrace. She floated to Wendy's form, crouching down even though Wendy never registered falling to her knees.

In a reassuring whisper, Hel stated, "Two weeks is a blink of an eye compared to a thousand years. I have no problems with you finishing your earthly duties."

She hand patted Wendy's head, sending her falling. Her heart dropped and everything became blurry as the sinking feeling consumed her. She fell back into her body, crashing without the whiplash that Eabha had given her. Instead her entire body tingled uncomfortably as her vision came back. She took a moment to steady herself, sitting in the thick silence. When she was safe to drive, she made her way to the coroner's office.

The drop off at the coroner's office was quick. Amir was already there to help transfer the bodies off her gurneys and onto a slab. Once everything was where it was supposed to be, Amir brought her back to his small, gray cubicle. She sat in the stiff chair used for guests and mindlessly told him all she knew.

When she had thanked Amir, she walked back to the van and wrote a long text message to Marty. Explaining her relationship and using it as an excuse to give her two week notice. She froze after she sent it, the van in a quiet sleep as her mind buffered. The ringtone of her phone broke the spell. Of course Marty understood, telling Wendy to sleep in the following morning to recover.

She smiled, a bittersweet burn in her heart at leaving the people she had become comfortable around. She deeply inhaled as she turned the key, not needing maps to get to her destination. She drove in silence, the quiet was the only thing holding her emotions inside, armor she needed as she turned into the familiar apartments, parking in the first available spot. She turned off the car, the dam of emotions cracking as she got out and dragged her feet to the door. Two knocks and ten seconds later, it opened. Red, puffy eyes; angry, dripping nose; and the loss of all spirit in the saint of a woman.

A bit of Wendy sighed in release as she thanked God that Will's mother already knew. Though the sight cracked the dam open as tears dropped down her face.

"I picked them up. I saw them, they-"

Wendy was cut off as she was embraced. The woman sobbing on the porch as they held each other. When they could go inside, Wendy fretted over Will's mother. Making tea, picking up the mess the boys had left that morning, and listened to every rambling word she had to say. Wendy offered to spend the night, a bit relieved when she said that church members were on their way. In a bit over a half an hour, older women and men came with an array of different foods and prayers for Will's safe passage to heaven's gates. Wendy's stomach turned with guilt, but not at taking Will's favorite gaming controller. As soon as Will's mother was safe and surrounded by comforting friends, Wendy made her escape. Giving the older woman one last hug before slipping out the door.

She wasn't ready to tell anyone else yet. She had stared at her father's contact while she was at Will's apartment, but didn't have the strength to press the call button. He worked nights, he didn't need the grief right before he went to work. She would call him in the morning. Neveah had met Will for a few brief conversations, but she wasn't who Wendy needed to talk to.

Wendy made her way to her apartment, the silence again cloaking her as she made the journey. When she entered her apartment, she went immediately to the mirror. She sat in the fold-out chair, grabbing the water bottle holding her mixture of blackened oil within it. She dipped a drop on her finger. She closed her eyes and connected to earth and sky. When she felt the flowing, bright energy fill her; she followed her heart.

She brought the bead of oil to the controller, connecting Will's essence to the oil. She left the bead on the handle on the controller as she dipped her finger in again and began writing Will's full name on the mirror. Each stroke burst with energy as Wendy's empty concentration perfectly directed the energy coursing through her. To finish it off, she wiped up the drip of oil from his controller with a clean finger. She underlined the letters, connecting his essence to the mirror.

In a soft whisper, she called to him. Summoned him the same way she summoned Hel for the LAN parties. She was about to lose hope when a familiar voice boomed across her mind.

"Holy fuck was that weird! It's like having a vibration in your skull, now I know what my phone feels like."

More hot tears flowed down Wendy's cheeks as she coughed out a strained breath. Her face tightened at the sound of Will's voice. "Fuck you," she replied hoarsely, "I didn't even know if this would work. Give me some slack."

"Hey!" he barked with an edge of humor to his voice. "I literally <u>died</u> today. If anyone deserves to get a break, it's me."

"Aw, poor baby. Is Hel putting you through the ringer?"

"Nah, She's actually pretty nice. Gave me the whole rundown on how this side of the veil works over a cup of this bomb-ass mead she made."

Wendy rested her head on her hand, elbow resting on the table. "Did she do the whole magik-hologram-earth-realm thing?"

"Oh yeah, blew my fucking mind! I just wish those judgmental asses at mom's church could have seen it."

A pang of sorrow at the remembrance stabbed her, but she didn't want to touch that now. "Do you have a place to stay? She doesn't have the bar she was talking about fixed up yet, does she?"

"No, I'm staying in Helheim until she has the...*pocket dimension* set up?" his voice in an upward inflection as a question. "I'll be honest, some of the stuff she said went right over my head."

Wendy perked up, "what does it look like? I couldn't see shit last time I was there, Hel said that I saw things differently than the dead do."

"Oh," he paused. "Think of all the winter hallmark cards. You know all the fancy mountain ones? It's like that. Plus, the snow is warmer than the snow at home, like you could go out barefoot and still be okay. It's peaceful and, honestly, the fucking best."

"That sounds amazing."

"Yeah," he paused again, the tone in his voice taking a serious edge. "She also told me what you did for me…what you would be giving up."

"I went to your mother's," she interjected. Unable to hold it in anymore.

Will's voice dropped a bit, "How is she?"

"Um… well, she's…" When Wendy couldn't finish, so she tried a different approach. "She is probably going to move to Arizona after the funeral. She said that there was family out there she could stay with."

"That's good," he sighed, "she'll be happier there."

"Yeah."

Anger filled his voice, "She's not doing anything for Ty, is she?"

Wendy shook her head, even though he couldn't see it. "No, no his fuckers of a family are dealing with it from what the investigators are saying."

"Good. I hope that bastard pays for getting me killed."

Wendy's voice went soft, "What-what happened Will?"

"Well, walked in the door to get bitched at by 'Lizabith about Ty messing up orders and acting like a junky. I go back in there to find out that he is on coke, even finding some on his fucking face. So I drag him out back to beat the living shit out of him, getting out of him that he has been selling out of the bar for the past few months. I was yelling so loud that I didn't hear the car crawl up behind us and-" he was practically screaming by the time he cut himself off. When he spoke again all the anger had left him. "I woke up alone, looking at our bodies as 'Lizabith found us… I watched as the police showed up and started taking statements. Sure, everyone was crying and in shock, but when you were the one who came. God, your face broke me. I tried to get your attention. I was yelling and screaming at you… and… well, you know the rest."

Wendy sniffed out a small laugh, "Well, what was I supposed to do? You have been the only one to stick by me all these years. You're the only one who hasn't stabbed me in the back, pushed me away, or left me after we graduated high school. Even after I went to Florida, you still found time for me in your life. You're part of my pack, I would do everything to make sure you came out of that okay. Lucky for you, I had the right connections."

He scoffed, "Lucky for me is right. Speaking of, when the fuck were you going to tell me you knew gods? I thought witchcraft was just lighting candles and dancing under the full moon."

"Would you have believed me?"

He paused, "Fair enough."

Wendy giggled, then sighed as she stayed herself for the last question. "What… what do you want me to tell her?"

Wendy had never tried to be a medium and wasn't sure if his mother could hear him as Wendy could. Though, for him, she would try.

There was silence, broken by a heavy sigh. "Don't tell her anything."

Wendy was a bit stunned at first, but she understood. "You sure?"

"Yeah, I don't think she could handle the truth. Let her think she will see me in heaven, it's probably better that way."

Wendy smiled hollowly, exhaustion trickling passed the carnage from the day's emotions. "Okay. I won't tell her."

"Okay." he echoed, "Get some rest, turns out that the dead don't need it."

Wendy chuckled, "Fine, if you're kicking me out."

In his mocking cry, he yelled, "Get out of my room!"

"I'm not in your room!" Wendy retorted, dropping the link as she would have hung up on him. Leaving her alone in the dark room.

Her mind blank, she eventually made her way to her bed, stripping down first before slipping under the covers. She snuggled her pillow, relishing the feel of cool softness around her. As the trickle became a river, she followed exhaustion into a dream-filled sleep, her unconscious mind taking her to a beautiful land of snow.

Hel,

And thus, my adventure began.

Chapter Seventeen: New Job

The next two weeks were hell in Wendy's world. The days were busy, Wendy seemed to get home later and later. Whenever she wasn't working, she was helping Will's mother with funeral preparations. Not only gathering up enough money, but finding a funeral home and a grave site. Wendy used every connection she had made in the past six months, Marty giving any advice he could. Wendy called Gunner the morning after, catching him before he went to bed. He took half of the vacation time he was saving for Christmas to be there for his friend. As someone who had lost a loved one, he seemed to know exactly how to console Will's mother.

As the bustle of preparation consumed the people around her, Wendy suffered. Every time Will's mother broke down in sobs, she wanted to scream. Wanted to tell her that her son wasn't lost, she had talked to him every night to give him updates. She even played an online game with him on Hel's account, but she kept her word to Will and said nothing about it. .

94

Will was right though. With the small interactions Wendy had with the church fanatics squawking around Will's mother; not only would telling her the truth hurt her, but she probably would never believe it, and so, Wendy stayed quiet. Her tears of frustration and empathy made her seem like a grieving friend. This made some of the church people try to talk to her, saying it was some sort of plan. Wendy typically had to walk away before punching them in the face.

Wendy found a few moments to go over to Neveah's, telling her about the shooting and the funeral before being called to work. She was planning to tell her everything, but one thing or another always seemed to get in the way. Neveah offered to go to the funeral, but she had a test and Wendy convinced her that she would be fine. Neveah was so close to a nursing degree, she honestly felt she didn't need the distraction.

Two days before the end of her two-weeks' was the funeral, and Wendy didn't remember a single word of it. She remembered the small church, backlit by stained-glass windows as the preacher talked. She remembered seeing old faces, Shone and his mother coming to pay their respects. They talked a bit, but it was very apparent that Shone wanted nothing to do with her now that he had become a pastor. His eyes not only looked through her, but also his entire demeanor outright suggested he was completely fake as he asked about her life. A member of Ty's family made an appearance, but they were escorted out by an uncle that Wendy only met in passing. She wanted to leave, but she stood firm for her oldest friend's mother.

After the group had put the closed casket into the ground, Wendy said her last goodbye to Will's mother. There were promises of going to Arizona to meet her and her coming back to see Wendy, but they both knew that it was all words. Wendy held her a bit tighter knowing that this was likely the last time.

"Thank you for looking after my boy." Will's mother breathed in her ear. "I did my best but you're the reason he turned out so well. I don't know what would have happened if he didn't have a friend like you keeping him on the right path, so thank you Wendy."

Wendy squeezed tighter as she shook out a cry. She couldn't say anything, but tried to convey everything in that embrace. All the gratitude, all the remorse, all the emotions she couldn't name.

Eventually everyone went home. Gunner slept the night on Wendy's couch as he did every time he came down. They didn't speak much and barely ate the Chinese food they picked up on the way. Instead their eyes glazed over a sci-fi drama that Wendy put on and went to bed early. By the time Wendy had gotten home the next day, her father had gone. Leaving early to get back to Nebraska so he could be at work that night.

She stood in the deafening isolation of her apartment. Nothing to distract her, nothing left to do. With a sigh, she resigned herself to sit in the hard, fold-out chair. She picked up the black water bottle hidden underneath the table in a box with all of her other occult tools. She sat up straight, putting a bit of the oil on a finger and started drawing Hel's sigils. Once done, she poured magik into it until a familiar voice tuned into her mind's eye.

"My favorite living human! Is your two-weeks' up yet? I thought I set an alarm-"

"No, no." Wendy reassured, "I still have two days left. I just wanted to talk. Do you have a bit?"

"Oh!" the goddess muttered, seemingly a bit taken back. "Yes, just give me a moment."

Wendy smiled a bit at the silence, finding it funny that she was being put on the magikal equivalent of a hold.

Within a few minutes, Hel's voice rang across her mind again. "Gods, sorry. Who knew that trans dimensional real estate was such a pain-in-the-ass to get ahold of! Then again, if it were easy everyone would be doing it. Dealing with these self absorbed, greedy barbarians reminds me why I hate leaving my realm. I even had to change out of my comfy cloak."

Wendy held back a snicker, "Sorry you're having issues."

Hel sighed, "It will be worth it in the end. I just have to remember that. So, what can I do for you Wendy?"

Wendy leaned forward, crossing her arms to hold her weight on the table. "I just wanted to get some more information on what's going to happen. Like, is there a ritual that I have to do or some sort of test? Plus, I know that I'll be collecting souls for you but how is that going to work exactly?"

"Yes and yes. As for the last question, I have arranged for someone from your time to train you."

Wendy blinked, "Someone from my time?"

"Yes, my priestesses are from a time before the Norse traveled the seas. I figured you would feel more welcome if you had someone from your century to guide you."

"Well, uh - thank you."

"Though appreciated, there is no need. I would hate for a cultural barrier to escalate into a misunderstanding. This is a completely new existence for you, it would be better to dip a toe in the waters instead of throwing you to the deep." The goddess chuckled, "You'll get the joke when you meet him."

Wendy shook her head, "I'll take your word for it."

"As to what to expect on your first day," Hel continued, "I have arranged for a guide to take you to Portunus and Papa Legba. They will give you the keys to your new home and, after you get settled, you'll begin your training."

Wendy crooked her head, "I've never heard of Portunus and isn't Papa Legba part of the voodoo religion?"

"Very good!" Hel's voice beamed. "He has become good friends with my brother. Portunus is the Roman god of gateways. Portunus and Papa Legba created a working relationship after the veil became too thick to travel through. They are one of the easiest ways to gain access between the mortal world and the realms, even if they are bloody expensive."

Panic and exhilaration started whirling in Wendy's stomach. "Hold on, I'm going to meet them. Like, face to face?" She paused, "And what do you mean 'my new home'?"

Hel made a sound of dismissal, "You'll do fine and yes, you'll be getting a new home. What did you think, that I was going to pay you in mortal currency? That would be inefficient."

"Do I get paid?" Wendy asked slowly.

Wendy could almost see the shrug in the goddesses voice. "Eh, I can get you anything you need so there isn't much of a reason. Also, that sounds like another thing I would need to keep track of. Trust me, I'll forget."

The whirlwind became a tornado in her stomach, "Okaaay."

"Is there anything else? I do so love speaking with you, but at this very moment I need to get a few more things ready-"

"Is Will okay?" Wendy asked before she made the decision to speak.

"Why don't you ask him?" obvious confusion in the goddesses voice.

Wendy sputtered. "Well, he's a guy, you know. He could be just putting on a front to make me feel better."

"No, he seems fine to me." Hel answered. "He's been exploring Helheim with the residents. Plus, with the time difference I don't believe he has had time to be depressed."

Wendy's eyes widened, "Time difference?"

"Yes, in most of the realms twelve hours here is sixty minutes on earth. I thought you knew that?"

Wendy dropped her head to the cool table. "Nope, but thanks for the clarification."

"Of course!" the chipper voice splitting through Wendy's mind, "see you soon my hired human!"

The presence left, leaving Wendy with overwhelming anxiety. She sat with her head on the cool table for a moment more. Mind made up, she silently pushed herself up from the table and made her way out the door. She went down to the company van, hopped in, took it to the nearest dispensary, bought some THC gummies, took the van to her boss's house with a text message apologizing for leaving a day early and how she just couldn't do it.

With all that done, she ate fifty milligrams of gummies, figuring that would be enough for her clean system. With that done, she began to walk back to her apartment. It was an hour walk, but she arrived back without incident. When back, she turned on her computer and navigated to an anime streaming site. She drowned herself in fictional worlds the entire night, falling asleep just as the sun was beginning to rise. When she woke up, she took the other half of the gummies and avoided thinking for the day. She kept the door locked and escaped into the world of the internet. She was not allowing her thoughts to drift into contemplation about what her new life might be like. For that one day, she was a child again. She had no responsibility, nothing to do but enjoy the colorful worlds in front of her; the worlds where good always won, where everyone smiled easily, and where the hero would always live happily ever after.

Follow the dog.

Wendy jolted awake, almost knocking her laptop off the couch. She whipped her head around, as if the owner of the voice was in the room with her. It was dark, only the light of the street lamp outside, poorly illuminating the living room with what little light seeped through the blinds. Wendy turned on the laptop, squinting as her eyes adjusted. It was two forty three in the morning. Usually she would go back to sleep at such an early hour, but hearing Hel's voice in her dream seemed to inject energy right into her.

Following her instinct, she got dressed in a warm black outfit, grabbed a coat, and slipped on her shoes before going out the door. She ran outside, the frigid air forcing a gasp from her.

A canine whine drew Wendy's attention downwards. On the asphalt in front of the door to the apartment building was a medium-sized dog with big pointed ears. Shades of white, gray, and black glistened in the streetlight as the heeler sat, light-brown fur dressing his mask and socks while big brown eyes looked straight at Wendy.

For a moment, Wendy stood there. Conflicted with the competing urges to either go back inside or else try furiously cuddling the dog.

Hesitantly, Wendy asked. "Are… are you with Hel?"

The dog huffed, standing up and turning to walk out of the parking lot.

Wendy shook her head, bundling her arms to hold in the warmth. As she walked, she muttered to herself. "Follow the dog… treading out in the middle of the night in goddamn December… I must still be high because this is fucking ridiculous."

Dutifully, Wendy followed the canine down the back streets for a good ten minutes. From her knowledge of the area, they were heading for a section of the green belt. This was confirmed when the small dog crawled under the decorative post-fence that marked the trail's perimeter. Wendy followed, swinging her legs over the fence to step in the wild grass. Though it was harder to see, she still followed the movement ahead of her until the dog came to a stop at the stream's edge. The dog looked back at her, as if checking to see if she was still there. Satisfied at her presence, the dog leaned down to the slowly moving tidepool.

From the very touch of the dog's snout to the water it seemed to hum. It didn't glow, per se, but it seemed to radiate the glow of the moon. Her body felt as if she were back in her astral form. As she stepped closer, her skin became more static with her entire aura buzzing at the nearness of the power.

The dog looked back at her one last time before silently jumping in, his entire form swallowed by the deep pocket. Wendy stared dumbfounded.

"You've got to be kidding me…"

When the dog didn't surface in five seconds, Wendy groaned. She quickly took off her shoes and hid them in a bush for later retrieval. She turned back to the water, resigning herself to her fate, as she took two quick steps before jumping in herself.

This wasn't the first time that Wendy had done an ice dip. However, it had been so long that a slew of curses flew across her mind when her body became enveloped by it. Her eyes were closed, so she didn't see the moment when the chilling waters turned into the feeling of a warm, sunny day.

Her eyes snapped open, blinking a few times against the light. At that moment, she registered a few things. First, she wasn't wet despite just jumping into a body of water. Second, she was on farm land, the soil under her feet soft with small yellow sprouts lined up all in rows around her. Stringy grass lining the tilled ground in the distance. Lastly, Wendy realized that she felt awful, as if she were in the throws of the flu. She had shakes, she was cold despite feeling the warmth on her skin, and bones inside her were replaced by granite.

Hugging her arms around her waist, she bent over as she absorbed the shocking change of condition, releasing a small gasp at the pain.

After a moment, a huff of air directed her attention behind her. She turned her head to see the dog, quietly staring at her. Another moment of staring before his cold nose nudged Wendy's leg before he turned and pranced away. With a long sigh, Wendy straightened and followed. Each step was agony on her limbs.

The dog led her to a wooden cabin at the other end of the field. It wasn't big, possibly a two room cottage with a large, covered deck looking out towards them. On the deck was a table with five people sitting on wooden chairs and benches. As she got closer, she realized that they were playing cards. More interestingly, each person was wearing completely different and outrageous outfits: a beautiful brown-haired woman in an ivory cloth, clasped at the shoulders by brooches; a very old woman, white hair contrasting with her dark gray dress; a wispy man with a green tint to his skin, dressed in only a white cloth wrapped around his hips and legs, and with the only hair on him being a black goatee; a bronzed-skinned man with puffy brown hair and a beard, dressed in a toga; and the last was an elderly man with a straw hat, his skin the color of coffee under worn brown pants and a loose maroon shirt.

There was no doubt in Wendy's mind that these were gods as she felt Eabha stirring in her soul simply from the raw power leaking outward from the group. The different energies created a bouquet of power threatening to crush her.

Wendy slowed as she approached the stairs leading to the deck, watching the dog walk right up to the elderly man. There was no sound of nails to indicate the dog's presence, making the dog need to make a high pitched grunt that seemed like it was from a badger. The group looked down, a gleaming smile rested upon the elderly man's face.

"Well, hey there friend," the man's southern accent sounded slow and soothing. "Been a while since you've come to visit. Last time I saw you, you were a Dachshund. Sadly we are well into the cards, do you want to be dealt-in the next round?"

Another squawk came from the pup, the tail wagging as the man petted behind his ears.

"Escorting?" The man muttered to himself before he looked up. Meeting eyes with Wendy. As soon as he saw her, emotions flashed over his face too fast for Wendy to name every one. The main thing Wendy gathered at the widening of his eyes was recognition. As if he was seeing a long-missed friend. Sadly, Wendy felt too horrible to question it. Instead she put on her best smile, her coat squeaking as she raised her hand to give a small wave.

"Bridget? Darling girl, is that you?"

The entire table turned to her at the man's words, varying forms of interest on their faces.

Wendy cleared her throat and shifted her weight under the gazes. "Uh, no. Sorry, my name is Wendy. I've been sent here by Hel?"

"Oh! Oh, yes child. Come here, let me get a good look at you." he waved her up.

With a cautious glance at the table, she stepped up the stairs. Fighting her body and Eabha for dominance. When she reached the top, the man studied her. Comparing her to whomever this Bridget was.

Feeling like she was intruding, Wendy cleared her throat again. "I'm sorry to bother you. I was just told to follow the pup-"

"When did you cross the veil, girl?" Wendy's eyes snapped to the elderly woman, a scowl on her face as she waited for her answer.

Wendy sputtered. "Well- I mean-I don't."

"What she means is, when did you die, mortal?" The brunette woman clarified with a smile.

"I-I haven't died yet, mam."

"Sold your soul then." the green tinted man interjected, Wendy focused on his coal painted eyes. "Joined a line?"

Guessing their question, Wendy answered in an unsure tone. "Today?"

The older woman shrugged, "That must be why she doesn't have an aura."

"Papa?" the bronze skin man asked, concern on his face as his hand rested on the elderly man's shoulder. The older man seemed to be broken out of his musings, leaving a bright smile.

"My apologies, welcome to the other side of the veil Wendy. I'm Papa Legba or sometimes known as Saint Peter. This is Portunus, Roman god of the gateways." he gestured to the bronze man, his long face expanding with a greeting smile. "The lovely lady is Hecate, goddess of magik and the crossroads." The brunette nodded her head, a small smile on her face. "Our dashing green man is Khons, Egyptian god of the moon and travel." The man stroked his goatee, raising his nose at the introduction. "And the old crown is Baba Yaga, she's just here because she cheats."

The old woman gave a toothy grin, an eye patch crinkling at the movement. "What do the mortals say? 'Don't hate the player, hate the game'?"

Wendy returned back a genuine smile, the acceleration of the situation making her feel lighter. "Nice to meet you all."

Portunus stood from the table, making a point to put his cards face down on the table. "Papa, make sure none of these sore losers cheat while I get Hel's order. I'll just be a moment." He got up, the tension of the screen door closing it behind him. As soon as the door slammed shut, it was Papa Legba that snuck a peek at his cards.

Khons rolled his eyes before he focused on Wendy, "I'm surprised that the Nordic hermit communed with…anyone, let alone the mortal world. How did she come across you?"

"Well…" unsure of what to say, Wendy looked down at the dog. The unhelpful bastard just stared up at her, head tilting to the side. Resigned to her fate, she continued. "I used an old lullaby one of her priestess made while I was transporting the dead. I guess that somehow made me a reaper candidate."

Baba Yaga's eyes narrowed, "If that is true, then you must have some strong spiritual energy to reach through the veil. Stronger still if you can hide it so well."

Hecate slapped Baba Yaga arm. "She said that this was her first day, so be nice." Beautiful bright purple eyes looked back at Wendy, a polite smile on her face. "For all we know, her mortal body is shielding it from us."

"Very true," Khons muttered, leaning back while continuing to stroke his face. "I have never met a living one on this side of the veil. It could be possible."

"I met Merlin, but she had already been on this side longer than she had been on the mortal plain. Therefore, I can not say." Hecate shrugged.

Wendy's heart jumped as she was about to ask more, but her musings were cut off by the door opening again; Portunus grinning as he walked over to Wendy. "Freshly made, two portal keys." Wendy instinctively held her hand out, Portunus clasped it and dropped a warm metal piece inside. "She should know how to enchant them, but if she has questions, contact me."

Wendy smiled and nodded, mesmerized by the handsome god, just then realizing his eyes were different shades of blue; colors swaying like the ocean. Their hands parted at the groan Papa Legba let out as he stood.

112

"I believe it is your turn, Portunus. Don't worry though, I'll walk the young lady to the portal."

Portunus nodded, taking his seat and picked up his cards. "It was very nice to meet you Wendy. Feel free to come by at any time."

"Thank you for the offer." And because it seemed polite, Wendy gave the group a small bow. "It was very nice to meet you all."

Baba Yaga turned up her nose, but the others tilted their heads down in acknowledgement. That done, Wendy turned to follow the spry old man with the medium-sized dog following right behind.

Once they were a bit away from the cabin, Papa Legba snorted a laugh. "I hope you know how much of a wave you are going to make. Gods don't usually like to stick their noses where it doesn't belong, and I know that they-ill be sniffing around a living mortal hanging around on this side of the veil. Keep your ears up and your head down until you find your place, I'd hate to hear that something bad happened to you."

"Because of the person I look like?" Wendy softly asked, making the older man give her a blinding smile.

"That and the fact you're connected to the Nordic realm. The fact that you're holding a set of keys that can give any god a free pass to the mortal realm. Depending on who it is, they may just attack you for sport. Just as a kindly warning, lay low until you know how this world works, and who you can trust."

Wendy smiled, "Thank you."

"My pleasure, darlin'." The man stopped, pointing to the distance. "There will be a door in one of the first trees you see. Let the dog touch it first before you go through, and it will take you back to Hel."

Wendy looked where he pointed. Sure enough, just a bit farther down was a large tree. On it was a door, outlined by the natural bark markings with a branching handle. She turned back to the man, giving him another smile. "Thank you for everything Papa Legba. If there is anything I can do for you, please let me know."

He sighed, putting his hand on Wendy's shoulder. Brown, green, and gold swirled in his eyes as he stared at her. "The only thing you can do at the moment is to stay away from the voodoo realm. You won't be able to avoid them forever, but stay as far away from dealing with them as long as possible. If you can do that for me, I will definitely be grateful."

Wendy frowned her eyebrows but nodded, "I'll do my best."

His hand patted her twice before falling to his side, "That's all I can ask. Safe travels, Wendy."

Wendy smiled and waved before following the dog to the tree. He was already looking at her over his shoulder, eyes calculating her pace. When he was satisfied that she was close enough, he turned and touched his snout to the aged bark. At his touch, the rugged outline of the door began to glow, the light winding to the natural lines of the tree. Wendy's eyes fixated on a sturdy broken branch. Her hand followed and latched on to the branch, pulling the handle to open the door.

Darkness greeted her on the other side of the door. Darkness, but not emptiness. Wendy wanted to study it more, but the dog forced his way in, eager to move on. As he entered, he became enveloped by the darkness as if it were sludge that was swallowing him. Once Wendy couldn't see the white fur of his tail, she took a deep breath. Just as with the river, Wendy leaped in, the door closing behind her.

The sensation was as if she was being enveloped by a mud bath. The thick energy coating every inch of her. Before she could react, it was over. She opened her eyes to see a small, well-kept kitchen. Gray stone walls surrounded a medieval fireplace, a gray slab jetting out a bit. Shelves carved into the stone held mugs, herbs, bottles and cooking supplies. In the center of the room was a hand carved wooden table that overlooked a window.

The dog went straight to a blanket that was hidden underneath the table. He spun around three times before plopping down with a grunt, his brown eyes still watching Wendy as his ears twitched.

Wendy looked behind her when she felt the doorway close. Instead of a door made of bark, there was a well-made carved door that seemed to be built into the stone.

"Brother?" A voice coming from an open archway a bit down from the wooden door called. In the next moment, a beautiful woman entered from the archway. Ethereal pale skin with thick snow hair possessing quite a bit of curl to it. All of that however contrasted with the heavy-hooded wool-cloak reaching to her feet. Peeking out from the bottom was teddy bear slippers, small heads bobbing on the top of her toes.

The woman's eyes fixated on the dog's as she fully entered the room, "Oh, that was quicker than I thought. I thought Papa Legba would try and keep you there all day."

The dog made a sigh, resting his head on his paws.

The woman nodded, making a noise of agreement. "I forgot about their card days. Oh well, there is always next time." the woman turned towards Wendy, her eyes swimming with a familiar purple and green. She held out her hand, "You got the keys?"

Mindlessly holding them out by the ring that connected them, Wendy got her first good look at them. First, she noticed that they were not keys as in the literal sense. Instead, the two long wisps of metal narrowed and wiggled out before the end. The only differences between the two metals is that one seemed to be made of bronze and one of platinum. Wendy dropped them into Hel's hand.

Unable to stop herself, she asked, "Hel?"

The goddess's eyebrows knitted even while her mouth perked up in amusement. "Who else would I be?"

"And.. you called him… brother." Wendy pointed at the blue heeler dog.

"Yes." she answered as she made her way to the table and bent down to scratch the dog behind the ear. "This is Fenrisúlfr or Fenrir, also a child of Loki."

Wendy looked at the dog, his eyes closed in enjoyment as his head leaned towards the scratches. "This is the beast that tore off Tyr's arm? The one that was so ferocious that he had to be chained?"

Hel rolled her eyes at Wendy from over her shoulder. "Yes, this is obviously not his original body. It is still chained in Asgard along with most of his power. No, I rescued him a millennium ago. Now he hops from dog to dog, possessing them until Ragnarök comes. That is why he is able to physically manifest in the mortal plain."

"Because he is possessing a mortal being?"

"Exactly." she rose and looked at Wendy as she gestured toward the table. "Might as well sit down while I get these keys ready for you."

Obediently, Wendy walked to the seat in front of her and sat down. Wendy leaned down, brushing her fingers through the fine fur of Fenrir's coat.

"Hey, I'm sorry if I was a bitch during the trip. First day and all that. I hope you'll forgive me."

In response, the dog leaned back and dainty licked her hand. Rewarding him with a big smile as she went back to petting his neck.

"He's honestly really gentle unless backed into a corner. If you ask me, I think it's because he is secretly lazy. I know from experience that terrorizing the other Gods can be exhausting."

Fenrir sighed, looking at his sister from the corner of his eye. Wendy laughed, straightening her back in the chair while Hel sat in the one across from her. Wendy watched the goddess lay the two keys away from each other, the metal ring still attached to the thickest part. She then pulled out a knife from a pocket on her cloak, separated a lock of hair from the nape of her neck, and started to braid.

Not looking at what she was doing, Hel looked at Wendy. "So how was meeting other gods? Hope they didn't bother you too much."9

119

"No," Wendy said, fixated on the creation of the braids. "They did say I don't have an aura though. Which is weird because I saw it whenever I traveled through the mirror."

Hel took another look at her before shrugging. "Maybe your other side is keeping it hidden? Maybe it's because you're in your flesh and blood? I honestly couldn't tell you. As for when you were astral projecting, you were all spiritual energy, so it's a 'no, duh' that you were able to see your own spirit. Don't worry, it will probably seep out as your body deteriorates into this side of the veil."

Once she had finished the creation of two thin rope braids, she pulled out the knife and cut them off of her head. She set one aside and started to wrap the remaining braid around one of the keys.

Wendy leaned forward for a better look, "I guess I also look like someone named Bridget, any idea who that is?"

Hel glanced up from under her lush eyelashes, "I know it seems like I know all of the other gods, but I assure you that I don't. I literally do everything I can to avoid other gods." She paused her eyes, drifting off in thought before she reemerged. "I talk to around twenty entities a year, other than for work."

"What are you doing?" Wendy pointed to the intricate knot Hel made around the key.

Hel looked back at her work. "Knot magik. Instead of using words or ingredients to influence the energy, I am twisting the energy to program the key. This will be the key that will allow you to enter the mortal world and back," she nodded to the other one. "That one will take you to unclaimed souls."

"That's amazing."

Hel shrugged, "The Celtic Gods are better at it."

Wendy watched for a bit before her eyes were drawn to the window. Her breath was caught up in the amazing cliffside view. About five meters from the house was a ledge, misty mountains expanding on both sides, the snow tops covered in forest greens reminding Wendy of her old mountain home in the winter. In the middle was a gigantic tree reaching even higher than the mountains, the upper branches peeking through the clouds. Though there was no sun, light ribbons jutted through the mist in the sky, painting the clouds in yellows and pinks of an early sunset.

"There we go." Hel's voice snapped Wendy's attention back toward her. Each of the keys had different, but equally intricate, knots of the white braids surrounding them. Hel raised both of her hands over them, her eyes closed as she started to softly chant in an unknown language. From her palms, Wendy could see mist of the same purple and green she was used to seeing from Hel. The colors dropped to envelop the keys, mist shadowing the braids until the hair began to boil, almost as if the dead rot of skin had developed on the hair follicles, expanding until they popped and rotted into black craters. Not only did Wendy get wafts of burnt hair, but the potent stench of decayed flesh escaped with each pop. Wendy held back a gag, holding her breath as she watched the hair be devoured by Hel's magik. Sizzles of the rotten goo burned into the metal. The chanting ended when the smolders had all been soaked up by the keys, leaving imprints of the twisting knots on each key.

Hel held the platinum one up. "Your room key," she said knowingly as she switched to the bronze, "And your work key. Don't get them lost or

I'm adding another thousand years to your sentence." She looked like she was half-joking, but half-serious.

Wendy took them from Hel's outstretched hand and nodded. "I promise."

Hel's face lit up in an unworldly smile as she stood, "Good, I have one more thing before you go."

She left the room through the dark, open doorway. Wendy bent down to escape the lingering smell to see Fenrir's face curiously tilted up at her. She cooed at him as she scratched his favorite spot on his neck. His leg kicked with the timing of the scratches. By the time that Hel came back, the pair was both smiling.

"Here you go, your shiny new uniform."

Wendy looked up only for a thick, black wool cloth to cover her face. Wendy straightened as she pulled it off her and held it out to get a look. It was a cloak, black as Hel's own. Instead of being a cloak that would have to be pulled over her head, it was one that clasped in the front with a silver brooch matching Hel's sigil insignia interwoven with gold on the back of the cloak. What excited Wendy the most was the seams of deep pockets on either side of the cloak, just under the arm holes lined in silk.

"It doesn't have a hood, but I can get one put on for you if it bothers you."

"No," Wendy breathed, "No, it's amazing. Thank you."

Hel waved the compliment off, even as she looked away from Wendy. "Don't thank me, it's your uniform. You have to wear it while on this side of the veil to have my protection. I really don't want to get into a war because someone decided to pick on my newest minion."

Wendy giggled, "I'll do my best to stay out of trouble."

"You *better*." She headed to a door that was hidden behind Wendy's seat. she opened the door, greeting a refreshingly cold breeze creeping in at the invitation. Hel leaned herself around Wendy, focusing her eyes on Fenrir.

"You want your ball?" At her words, the dog's eyes sparkled as his body lifted and tightened in readiness. This made the goddess smile as she gestured out the door. "Will has it! Go get him!"

At her words, Fenrir raced out the door, fluffs of snow kicking up from his speed.

Hel flicked her head at the door while locking eyes with the unmoving Wendy, "You'd better catch up with him or you'll never learn where Will lives."

Wendy jumped up and wrapped the cloak around her as she rushed after the dog. Realizing the keys were still in her hands, she placed the keys into her cloak pocket. Once it was secure, she concentrated on finding Will. She still wasn't a runner, her lungs seeming to work hard in the high mountain air, although her experience kept her from slipping on the snow as she followed the footprints. The day was warm, Wendy debated taking off her coat as she ran.

Fenrir's footprints lead to a town embedded in the beautiful forest. Wooden houses lined a main street where different people talked, laughed and played. All were in wool clothing that looked handmade, Fenrir slowed to greet the people that called out to him, but kept going. Wendy slowed a bit as she entered the crowded street, those who noticed her waved and smiled politely as she passed. Wendy's eyes bounced around the quant

village until a familiar laugh grabbed her attention.

Will stood in a doorway, throwing a brown ball mass for Fenrir. The

dog's tail wagged until he sprinted after it. Wendy talked to him every night,

but that didn't stop her eyes from watering. The memory of seeing his body,

the emotions from his funeral. She didn't stop her movement towards him,

tackling him in a fierce hug when he buffered her stop. Will only laughed,

hugging her back just as hard.

"God, Wendy, you would have thought I died or something."

Wendy drew back and punched him in the shoulder, "Fucking

jackass."

Will laughed as he rubbed his arm. "Did you expect anything less?"

Wendy rolled her eyes then gestured to the massive wooden building

he was in front of. "Keep up that attitude and I'll burn your house into the

ground."

Will's brows knitted, "This isn't my place, this is Helheim's

equivalent of a YMCA." He motioned inside, "Here, I'll show you around

before we go to the bar."

Wendy followed him into the cabin. Recreation center was a good word for it; multiple TVs were placed on the walls with large couches facing them, a large fire rawred in the open kitchen allowing more than ten people to feel comfortable doing their own thing, and in the middle was a large table that could sit a good fifty people.

"This is nice." Wendy said.

"Right, This is the only place that gets the internet so it's always monitored. Kinna sucks but I get it. Don't want anyone getting on social media from beyond the grave."

Wendy scoffed, "I'm sure that's the *only* reason."

Will rolled his eyes, "Get your mind out of the gutter! Besides, supposedly there are brothels called Nymph covies, so there isn't any need for porn. Plus, succubi are always down to party, and good at it too."

Wendy's eyebrows jumped to her hairline, "You serious?"

The bastard only shrugged, "I've already met one."

"Nymph or succubus?"

"Succubus, Lilly is my front of house manager. Come on, we gotta take a pegasus to the world tree." Will casually threw over his shoulder as he walked to a door on the other side of the room.

Wendy stayed in her spot, frozen.

Until she burst out, "We get to ride a Pegasus!"

He laughed, the sweet music dancing with all the other sounds of the room. Wendy ran to him, filled with newfound energy as she bounced around him. They made it back outside, the cold was not even touching Wendy as she interrogated Will. As they talked, he took her to a large stable that was just as big as the other building. They walked to the doors, pulling them open. It wasn't like a normal horse stable, more like a bird emporium. There were no stalls, only open space. The high ceiling bordered by planks so the pegasus could land. Shelves lined what could be considered a second floor. Multiple hay troughs, water basins, and nests were strategically placed around the area. Fauns were learning how to fly while others played with beach ball-sized balloons they bounced and kicked to one another.

"Well, well, if it isn't the new guy. Already up for another round with Sca?" A very large middle-aged man called out. He was massive without a shred of fat on him. Tattoos made up for the lack of shirt, as he was only wearing brown pants and boots. His blond hair braided back with a large beard covering his face. Wendy would have guessed that he was a bodybuilder and guessed that most would be scared shitless of him.

"Definitely not, but Wendy and I *do* have to go to Yggdrasil though."

The man looked around Will to look at Wendy. When Wendy gazed upon his smile, she only saw her father. Her heart cried a bit at the stray though.

His swirling orange eyes glittered when they met hers. "Ah, this must be the famous living girl that Hel was talking about. Pleasure to meet you, I'm Baldur."

He stuck out his hand, Wendy quickly taking it in her own. "Pleasure to meet-" she stopped herself, tilting her head before asking, "Baldur? Like the God that got killed by holly?"

He barked out a laugh as he dropped her hand, "It was mistletoe, but I am one in the same. My mum, Frigg was so livid when Loki killed me, I still remember the sound of her screaming."

"Well... that's good?" Wendy said with a questioning tone.

Baldur shrugged, "Can't complain. Now," he clapped his hands together. "Do you know how to ride a horse?"

Wendy shrugged, "I know the concept. I'm confident I can figure it out."

His face lit up with a gorgeous grin. "Well, I wish I could put you through the ringer as I did with Will, but I figure you are in a hurry so it will have to wait for another day. Let me just saddle up one of the more docile mares and get you on your way."

He strutted away, giving a short whistle as he did. Wendy turned to Will. "So, are you going to tell me who Sea is?"

Will looked around until he pointed into the rafters. "See the black stallion?" When Wendy spotted the beautiful stallion, she nodded and he continued. "Fucker almost bit my hand off when I tried to get near him. Turns out pegasus's are temperamental Basterds, only Baldur and a few others can get near the meaner ones."

Wendy's eyes moved over the flying beasts. She, like most girls, went through a horse phase. That was, until she met a boy that had almost died because a horse stepped on him, an indent permanently deforming his chest. After that and learning just how expensive they were, she finally decided horses were not her thing.

Wendy sighed, "Well, you have fun with that. At least they can't kill you again."

"Yep, they can't."

Wendy turned to look at him. The way he said that statement brought to mind a whirlwind of questions. She opened her mouth to voice every single one of them when Baldur returned, a soft, paint mare in tow behind him. Its wings were so large they dragged on the ground, and fully dressed the beast such that it was noticeably taller than Wendy. Instead of being scared, she was in awe. Her heart soared at the beauty of the beast.

Reading Wendy's face, Baldur smiled and patted the muzzle. "This is Ruen, she'll take good care of you. Plus, she's an old girl. Perfect for new riders."

"Thanks so much for your help, Baulder. I'll bring you back a drink when I'm off." Will said, taking the reins from the hulk of a man.

Baldur gave a hardy laugh, "Bring two and share the drink with me. Maybe I can get Hel to let me pop in the Bar soon."

"Looking forward to it." In an obviously practiced step, Will ducked under one of the wings and swung himself onto the saddle. He motioned at Wendy, "You coming?"

Shaking her head, she made her way over while muttering under her breath, "Now how many times before you got that one right?"

"Three." Baldur volunteered, "not the worst I've taught. At least he wasn't scared of them."

Ignoring the interaction, Will gave Wendy a hand and pulled her onto the horse. Once secure, Will gave his thanks before guiding the horse to a trot out of the barn. It was a rough ride, Wendy not having any stirrups on the back of the horse to lessen the blows coming from each bounce. Before she could complain, Ruen began to gallop. The hard bounces became a continuous bumpy road. Her wings expanded, each one expanding farther than Ruen herself. She took a few warm-up flaps before she lifted them into the air, Wendy felt nothing but wind. It reminded Wendy of being on a motorcycle; the rushing wind tugging on her hair, the feel of freedom as the world and its problems blurred.

Though it was thousands of times better because she was *fucking flying*!

The only downside was how strong the wind was, stealing the air right from out of Wendy's lungs, making it difficult to breathe. She boxed her arms around her face to make a pocket of air, stealing glances of the view before it could literally take her breath away.

It was about a twenty-minute fight, ending with a graceful landing despite such a bustling pace. Once Ruen came to a stop, Wendy took deep gulps of air as she dismounted on shaky legs.

"Wendy, you're breathing hard. You okay?" Will asked as he dismounted.

She nodded, "Just… exciting, that's all. I'm fine, promise."

Satisfied with her answer, Will walked to stand in front of Ruen. Petting her snout he talked to her in a soft voice. "Thank you for getting us here safely, good girl. Think you can get home safely?" When the horse nodded, Will rewarded her with a kiss. "Good, thank you again Ruen."

The horse huffed in his face before walking off. Will turned toward Wendy and waved her over as he began walking towards the tree.

Wendy huffed as she ran towards him, "Hey! Wait up."

***

The base of the world tree was an actual city. Carts and tents danced with the noise of the crowd. Though there was one thing for sure, they were definitely not human. Wendy couldn't explain it, but she could feel the power coming off of each person she passed, the hum of electricity that crawled on her skin with every close pass. She realized she felt it when she was around the other gods she had met, but not at this level. With so many around her, she felt small. The need to hide was almost overwhelming, like a mouse avoiding human eyes. She held onto Will's shirt, studying the surroundings as Will led the way. Once they were out of the crowd, she walked beside him as they approached two gigantic doors carved into the tree.. Like Hel's, these doors were expertly carved. Beautiful depictions of battles, magikal creatures, and titans covered the wood.

Though it only looked cracked, the five-story-tall doors left a crack big enough to allow people through. Guarding the entryway was a female entity that radiated the same ash color as the tree. A blindfold covered her eyes even as she seemed to watch the two approach.

"Hello, we're here on behalf of Hel." Will started, but she didn't face him. Instead, her face never turned away from Wendy.

"Are you ready to face your destiny?" The being's airy voice asked, catching Wendy off guard.

Wendy blinked, glancing at Will for direction. "Umm…Yes?"

The entity smiled, "It will come for you whether you are ready or you are not. As long as you make your greatest weakness to your benefit, victory will be yours." She then stepped aside, waving them both inside.

With a confused word of thanks, they both entered. Wendy watched the entity until it became uncomfortable. Once she made it inside, she took a heavy breath. It was something out of a fairy tail. The hollowed out tree wasn't as busy as the outside, but it had a lot more squirrels and birds. Cawing of the black birds and chittering of squirrels echoed up the massive tree as they made their way up and down the tree. Stairs carved into the cylindrical walls curved up the tree only to disappear from sight. About every ten steps, doors followed up the tree, each with its own carvings.

"Now here comes the fun part." Will's tone filled with sarcasm as he pointed up. "Our door is about half way up.

Wendy's eyes bulged, "Is there an elevator?"

"Not for us lowly mortals. Only those who are of a line get to use Ratatoskr's pulley system. Even then, I'm not sure I'd trust the bastard." Will muttered.

Wendy held up her hand, "Wait, what are you talking about?"

Will squinted his eyes and gave her a look of utter confusion. "What has Hel told you?"

Wendy shrugged, "Honestly, not much."

He let out a big sigh as flicked his head towards the stairs, "Come on, we will talk on the way."

Wendy followed close behind to hear him as they climbed. "From what I understand, there are three classes in the world beyond the veil. There are the mortals or souls. Those who die and are brought to the underworld of a realm. They don't carry much energy and end up either reincarnating or being absorbed into the realms energy within sixty year or so. If they join a line or are a lesser deity as we technically did, they are considered the middle class. Depending on who rules them, how old they are, or how they get their energy dictates their standing and how they are treated. Lastly are the immortals, all the gods that we know and love. They got to a point where they could siphon power off the realm itself. However, that means that they can't leave. Requiring them to need people in their line to do the traveling for them."

"So, other than us, how do people join a line?"

Will snapped his fingers, "Good question, the only ones I have met were former priests or priestesses. I don't know if you could just ask."

Wendy shrugged, "Guess the rat race is being played no matter where you go."

"Right!" he spared a glance back at Wendy, "Though I don't think our situation is that special."

"No? Why do you think that?" Wendy responded.

"Well, first off, you're going to be training with a guy who was taken for the mortal world to work as a reaper."

Wendy almost tripped, "What?"

"Yeah," Will snickered after she recovered. "Met up with him yesterday at the bar. Cool guy if a bit weird."

"Weird is my language." Wendy laughed. "So wait, you've already been to the bar? Is it open?"

"Not yet, it opens in about a week or so. It's been a pain getting all the types of liquor. Every realm having their own favorite, and everybody is so fucking stingy about giving it up. It's been hell in a handbasket getting trade agreements settled."

"If anyone can do it, you can."

He fist pumped the air in response, then pointed up. "Almost there."

Wendy let out a breath, the air carrying the brisk freshness of the forest. When they reached the door, he pulled out a thin piece of metal that looked like Wendy's keys. He put it in the ancient lock, making a hard clunk as it opened.

***

It was a club. Even if the lights weren't on and there was no music in the air, the large room was decorated with plush couches, an LED dance floor, and a glass bar. The high ceilings seemed to have floating tables with glass pedestals holding the tables up.

"Come on, the chill part is upstairs."

Wendy followed Will up a set of glass stairs that went to a second floor. Compared to the first floor, the second was the equivalent of a dive bar. Everything was made out of honey colored wood. TVs lined the walls next to large targets much too big for darts. The only glass was behind the bar, backdropping unlabeled potent bottles from an array of different colors. With them was a large-breasted blond, her hair as voluptuous as the rest of her, complete with short shorts and a thin t-shirt paired up with high-top boots. Her cherry-red lips turned up at their appearance.

"Well, hey darlin'." A sultry and risqué American southern-accent greeted. "Sai said the balche brue from the Mayan god Acan will be late…Oh, well, who did you bring with you, sugah?"

"Lilly, this is my living sister, Wendy. Wendy, this is the front of the house, manager, Lilly." Will introduced her very business-like.

Wendy walked forward and shook the woman's hand. She smiled despite just now remembering that she was only wearing pajamas under her coat and cloak.

Without giving Wendy any time to respond, the woman latched onto Wendy's hand and began talking. "So you're the one that saved little Will from the river of death! When he told the story, I was so touched that you sold his soul to help him. Brought me to tears what you did. I nearly flipped backwards accepting this gig. With people like you around, my entertainment will never be threatened. Plus, with my kind, places like this is certainly the easiest way to find food. You know?"

Wendy blinked, "I-I'm sorry?"

Lilly dropped her hand, "Gosh, I forgot. You're mortal. I'm a *succubus*. Tried being a vampire in the early days but I couldn't handle it. The energy always tasted bitter, while sexual energy has a kick to it that I just can't stay away from."

Wendy held up a hand, "You were... going to be a vampire? Aren't vampires and succubi like... completely different."

Lilly tisked, "Has that Hermit goddess told you nothing?"

Wendy sputtered, looking away. "No, not really. This is my first day."

Lilly put her hands on her hips and sighed, "Aegir left some of his Mead in the back. I'll bring out Sai and we can all give you the basics. 'Bout time for a break anyway."

Without another word, she sauntered into a door behind the bar. Wendy turned to Will, who was obviously watching the succubi leave.

Wendy slapped his arm. "Succubi are off the menu."

He rubbed his arm, "Says who?"

"The bitch who saved your ass. Now who is Aegir, or Sai for that matter?"

Will looked at her for a moment before asking, "Rough morning?"

Wendy let out a breath along with all of her tension. "You could say that. Let's just say I wish I could have taken a shower before all this craziness."

Will chuckled, patting her back a few times. "There, there. It's definitely thrown me for a loop too. Aegir is the Norse god of liquor. Supposedly he tried opening this bar first, but would end up drinking most of the supply. Hel offered a business arrangement, he had the connections to all the other gods of intoxication, and I make sure it actually does well. As for Sai, he's one of the guys helping me out."

Wendy gave him a sheepish smile, "Thanks Will."

"No problem, you should have seen the panic attack Hel helped me through after you left that day. Definitely not pretty."

"Well, you did *die*."

Will shrugged, "Still, this is all definitely a culture shock. What I'm saying is I'm here if you need me."

Wendy leaned over and rested her head on his shoulder, "Thanks."

"Found it!" Lilly shouted, making Wendy snap up as her and a short, but ripped, Asian man entered from the back. Gesturing with a dark bottle, Lilly introduced. "Wendy, this Sai. Sai this is the girl that brought Will to us."

Wendy shook the man's outstretched hand. His hands were hard from years of hard work. His short, raven hair spiked up from his scalp, and his smile, made Wendy feel safe.

"It's very nice to meet you, Wendy. I am Sai of the line of Rāgar Jacka."

Wendy's head crooked in confusion, "I've never heard of him."

"He is the protector of taverns, mostly on the eastern side of the world. I was a Chao Thi or a household guardian spirit until they were all killed. Rāgar Jacka took me in soon after when I was about to fade. I'm helping out as my last step before I am sent to protect a new tavern in Rāgar Jacka's name."

Wendy leaned forward. "That is fascinating."

"And a really good opener!" Lilly said, setting down glasses in front of everyone. "But, ;et's start out with what you know, Wendy. What have you been told?"

"Well." Wendy looked into her glass, gently turning the liquid as she spoke. "Almost no one remembers the beginning, just that the humans and the energetic beings were made at the same time. Slowly, the humans…formed the energetic beings. Like made them into the gods they needed. The humans would give them energy in the form of worship and the entities would help them. Over time, the most popular entities became too powerful to leave their realms or the veil became too thick to go through, or something like that. Then there was the war that shattered the realms connection with the earth, that plus human migration has messed up humans connection to this side of the veil. Then Will just told me about the class system you have going on with the human souls and the lines. Other than that, I know that the Christian and Muslim God are not only one in the same, but have the most power in all the realms at the moment."

"Because of the Great War." Lilly nodded, taking a swig of her drink. "You've got all the basics down so we aren't starting from scratch. You see, the rule of this world is to adapt or fade. When we all form, either as a strong human soul, or formed by a more powerful deity or whatever, the rule is to find what can keep you alive. Jinn, poltergeist, vampires, succubus; we are all energetic entities that pick up jobs which keep us alive. We just have different ways of getting that sweet, sweet energy."

"Is it hard switching? Like going from a house guardian to part of a line?" Wendy asked, finally taking a sip of the strong honey-spice. Though the bite was strong, it was still something Wendy wouldn't be nursing for long.

Sai chuckled, "Better than the other way around. Being part of a line is secure and definitely easier than being on your own."

"How does working here help you, Sai." Will asked then pointed to Lilly. "I get how boosted up guys make her job easier but how does it give you power?"

"Not only guys." Lilly smiled as she drank deeply. Wendy took another drink to hide her own smile.

"Recognition." Sai said, ignoring them. "If I do well keeping this place in check, I will get to go to Hong Kong or Tokyo to a big inn with lots of employees that will pray to me in Rāgar Jacka's name. If this place burns to the ground, I'd be lucky to get sent to a small town."

Wendy eyebrows knitted, "Hey Lilly, why are you glowing deep red? And why is Sato a blue with yellow on the edges?"

All three slowly turned to look at Wendy. Wendy hesitated, looking at the half filled cup. "Maybe this drink is too strong."

"Wendy, how long have you been on this side of the veil?" Sato asked very slowly.

"Just today." Wendy stated.

"Think it's because she is still alive?" Will asked, making Sai's head snap to him.

"She hasn't died! How'd she get here then?"

Wendy sighed, "Fenrir made me jump into a river by my apartment and Hel gave me dual citizenship for the moment."

Sai glared at Lilly, "And you didn't warn her."

"Don't get testy with me. I don't know what you're going on about."

Sai sighed and took away Wendy's glass. "Have you heard the saying that you are what you eat. Well, the same goes for this situation. Anything that you have to eat or drink on this side of the veil will anchor you here. If any of us eats or drinks offerings from the mortal world, it connects us to their energy. Make sense?"

Wendy took a moment to process before she nodded.

"Good, as for the colors, you were seeing our auras. You were just unable to see them because of your mortal eyes." Sai finished.

"Oh, that's good to know." Wendy muttered before her eyebrows drew together. "Wait, how do you guys eat mortal food?"

"Mostly through it rotting or returning to the soil." Lilly clarified. "Some send animals to eat it on their behalf. If it was left on an altar or something."

Wendy nodded. "Makes sense."

"Does it though?" Will asked through a laugh.

The sounds of lumbering up the glass steps made everyone turn around. They all watched as a large man walked through the door. He wore a midnight=black cloak, a hood framing his round cheeks. Cocoa skin almost glistened under thin glasses-frames, glassy black bangs poked out from the hood. He froze in the doorway when he realized that he had everyone's attention on him.

"Umm, I'm looking for Hel's new reaper."

Wendy hesitantly raised her hand, "That's me."

"Oh," he lowered his hood and began to mutter. "That would probably help." He walked forward to fully stand in the room. He was a giant, over two meters with the bulk to match it. However he did not have the intimidation of the size. It could have been the glasses or his obviously awkward demeanor, but she couldn't help but smile.

He was a teddy bear.

Sudden nervousness crept through her. It had been one bombshell after another and she wasn't sure could deal with everything all at one time. In the end, she could only sigh as she turned towards Lilly and Sai. "Thank you both for everything, If you ever need anything I'll make sure to help."

Lilly waved her hand at her, "Don't be silly darlin', jus' take care of yourself."

Sai smiled, bowing his head before moving towards the back room.

"Well," Will slapped his hand on Wendy's shoulder. "Guess we both better start our new lives."

In a soft voice, Wendy muttered, "Guess we should." She began to stand but Will's pressure on her shoulder stopped her. Will held her eyes, the swirls of his aura seeping from his eyes.

"Thank you... You have done so much. I know you can handle this." Will shrugged and smiled.

Wendy took a deep breath and smiled back. "So can you. We've got this.

He let her go, using the momentum to push himself up. "Yeah, but now I got to see what's going on with the balche brue."

With Will making his exit, Wendy directed all of her focus on the giant patiently waiting as she stood. Giving her best smile, she looked the man in the eyes before extending her hand. "I'm Wendy and I'm Hel's new minion. Pleasure to meet you."

The man gave a tilted smile as he morphed her hand in his. "Well how-yah-do? My name is Makao and I am a reaper for Lord Cthulhu."

Wendy snickered until she realized that he wasn't joking. The smile faded as she dropped her hand. "Are you serious?"

He snapped his fingers and pointed at her, posing. "Actually, yes." he turned around and, in black, was a familiar monster with tentacles expanding from its face. Low and behold, it was Cthulhu.

"What the hell?" Wendy muttered in awe as she reached out and touched the embroidered fabric.

Makao turned to wave his arm for her to follow. "Come on, I'll tell you everything on the way."

They walked down to the first level and to the front door. Just as the outside, the inside also had a lock. His had reached into his cloak pocket as he pulled out a set of keys looking just like Wendy's. He put the copper one in the key ring and twisted it. It unlocked, opening the door to a hallway of darkness. Makao walked in, giving Wendy no choice but to follow. When the light of the empty club was gone, all that was left was dark.

It wasn't complete darkness though. It was the darkness of eyes which had already become accustomed to it. She could still see Makao and she could still make out her surroundings. She was in a hallway. Doors lined corridors which didn't seem to end in either direction. Wendy could tell that each one seemed to be from different buildings, though she could only make out the first four doors in front of her.

Makao outstretched his arms, "Welcome to the doors of death, Hel should have given you a copper key that was infused with her frequency?"

Wendy patted her cloak before reaching for the keys that were buried into her cloak. When she held them in front of them, he nodded. "Good, grip the silver one." Once done, he clicked his tongue on the roof of his mouth as he chopped the air in front of her with his hand. "Now this is tricky to explain, but you need to feel the door that leads to your home. Just close your eyes and think of home. It will... tingle when you're close to your door."

Her lips tipped up at his description as she closed her eyes. It was different than in the mortal world. In the living world, she felt the energy flow through her like a physical touch. She could even tell what the energy was by the emotions that came with it. She felt the colors, saw them through her mind's eye by using her imagination to give form to what she was feeling.

If such centering was somewhat what it was like to sense the energy using feeling, then grounding on the other side of the veil was like seeing the flow in a third person view. Wendy could indicate the exact veins the energy flowed through. She could point out the exact locations of each small bead that whirlpooled the energies and changed it throughout her body. The arch of each foot pulled in the rainbow of energy from that found around her. It filtered out the chaos, the power her body could not handle, and sent the filtered nerves up her legs to another bead that rested right behind her knees before moving upwards. From here, the energy started moving slower, colors separating to go to their designated chakras on the spine. The intricate system converged on the major pulse points which Wendy was forced to remember for her head to toe. The energy didn't mirror the vascular or nervous system, it was a flow that was all its own as it weaved and swirled around her body. With barely a thought, she sent the energy flowing to her hand. She watched, fascinated when a bit of every color traveled the necessary pathways to reach the tips of her fingers. Once there, she could feel the energy bolt over to the key until it practically glowed.

She thought of home, but quickly discarded her first thought. Instead she brought up a mental image of her little apartment: the small one-room in a cheap building she had made her own. Down the hall to her right, a door seemed to respond, glowing with the same energy that the key held.

She opened her eyes to find Makao staring at her with wide eyes, but he quickly recovered. He adjusted his glasses as he looked away, "Guess Hel picked you for a reason, huh?"

"Wait," Wendy took a step back. "Could you see that?"

"First you didn't have anything coming off of you, then you burst into flames for a second. I've never seen anything like it, but I have only been dead since the eighties, technically."

Wendy crooked her head, "How can you be 'technically' dead?"

His head bobbed with mock frustration as he pointed at her. "I would tell you the entire story if we could only get out of the hallway."

Wendy chuckled as she held up her hands with palms up. "Okay, okay. This way."

She led him to the door that hummed with the same energy radiating from the key. She slipped the key in as she had seen Makao do, the knob turning with the disengagement of the lock. She opened the door leading to her apartment.

Her dark apartment.

When she took her first step into the room, her entire body felt heavy, as if she was recovering from a hard workout. She rushed to the clock that glowed in her microwave display. She gaped, only forty minutes had passed.

"Um, Wendy?" Makao called from the doorway.

She walked back over to the door. Puzzled, she waved him in. "You can come in if you want."

He chuckled and muttered, "Better for you to learn this now."

He glided into the room. As he passed through the doorway it was as if it coated him in fog. He became a mist, the hymn of his robes seeming to disappear as he became a shadow. Wendy blinked, her hand going to the light switch. With the click, the light erased him. Making him dissolve completely.

She waved her hand where his body should have been, but there was only the open doorway. The light not able to puncture the other worldly darkness.

"That is my belly." a whisper of Makao glided through the air.

Wendy pulled back her hand, completely speechless.

"Close the door." Makao whispered. Wendy obeyed and he continued. "Put both keys in."

Hesitantly, Wendy complied, putting both of the thin pieces in the lock. It took a moment, but the door handle did smoothly turn. She pulled the door open to reveal her apartment. Though it wasn't hers, it was the same layout but it was empty. She felt a chill crawl down her spine before Makao materialized in the doorway.

He took a deep breath, walking farther into the space before turning to her. "It is so uncomfortable talking audibly when in ghost form. It's like talking while driving." When Wendy didn't move he prompted, "Well come on, get some chairs and I'll explain everything."

"Okay." Wendy blinked, "Do you want tea?"

He beamed as he shrugged, "Sure!"

Wendy set some water to boil before bringing two chairs across the doorway. Once across the doorframe, Makao was able to grab hold of the chairs and sit them where Wendy directed.

"So… this is what exactly?" Wendy asked, standing in the mortal world to keep an eye on the water.

He motioned to the empty apartment. "Your pocket. Because you're still alive, having your room in the network of the underworlds is close enough to the mortal realm to stave off the side effects of being on the other side of the veil."

Wendy nodded in understanding, "The becoming a literal ghost thing that you just did?"

His mood became serious as his eyes softened. "Wendy, why do you want to stay in the mortal world?"

Her mind blanked, after a moment she wrapped her arms around herself and shrugged. "My dad. My best friend, and her kid…"

The silence stretched on. When Wendy didn't break it, Makao did. "I grew up smack-dab in the center of Honolulu, Hawaii. We lived off my grandmother whose family owned one of the hotels. We weren't super rich, but rich enough for my parents to waste their lives high on meth. I saw what it did to them, what their actions did to my sister, and wanted nothing to do with it. I had a few friends who would play dungeons and dragons with me. It had only been out a few years, meaning we had to make our own campaign every once in a while. It was my turn and I wanted to run a Cthulhu campaign because we were studying Lovecraft in school-"

Makao was cut off as Wendy held up a finger, "So sorry, one second."

Without wasting any more time, Wendy ran to pull the boiling water off the stove. She poured the water into a ceramic teapot painted with cherry blossoms. Grabbing two mismatched mugs, he set the tea set on the counter in the small kitchen in the empty apartment. Within a few minutes, Wendy had pulled over two chairs and brewed tea for them.

"Okay, so you were making a D&D campaign about Cthulhu..." Wendy trailed off as she sat down in her seat.

"Happen to know anything about hula dancing?" Makao asked, raising an eyebrow.

Wendy shrugged, "I'm a belly dancer and there was a Youtuber I watched that had a hula workout. It's beautiful but I had a hard time with it. Other than that, everything else I learned was from Lilo and Stitch."

Makao staired, not blinking as his mouth opened just a bit. Wendy let a bit of concern show on her face. In response, he muttered, "Nope, didn't understand a word of that."

Wendy's eyebrows slammed together as she jolted back in disbelief. "When did you get Cthulhu-ed?"

"Nineteen eighty six!" His back straightening at the declaration.

Wendy relaxed and waved her hand between them. "Oh. Well, Yeah. Guess you would have no idea then."

Wendy leaned forward and poured the drinks. She handed one to Makao before sitting with her own. He nodded in appreciation. Though it was a full-sized American mug, it looked like a child's as he soaked in the warmth.

He took a sip, continued, "Basically, a hula is the history of our culture. It is the way we told our history and how we passed down our legends. The type of dance that I made for my debut was a hula kahiko with an oli or chant that I made myself. There was an old book at my grandmother's about different hulas and I based mine on a hula dedicated to Kanaloa, the god of magik and the underworld. You know, now that I look back, the book kind of just fell into my lap..." Makao shook his head and took another sip. "Anywho, I performed it the day before the game to practice it and next thing I knew I was transported to the middle of the ocean. It scared the crap out of me. In a flash, I had fish all around me and Cthulhu in front of me. And trust me, he's not a small guy either. So, while I was pissing myself, Cthulhu gave me a similar offer that Hel gave to you. He told me that I could stay in my world when I wasn't working... but I would eventually fade with time. I agreed and six months later, mortal time, I was diagnosed with Osteosarcoma, a bone cancer. Six months after that I had signs of Leukemia."

Out of need, Wendy laid her hand on Macao's arm. He rewarded her with a smile, "Thanks, but it wasn't a hard decision. My family was a mess, my friends were drifting apart and I didn't have much of a future because of all the setbacks. I told my grandmother and moved to the akua realm. Turns out the entity that is now Cthulhu was once high up in Kanaloa's line and graduated to the position. His presence allows more frequencies into the aqua realm."

He took another sip before leaving her eyes on Wendy , "To answer your question; Yes, the ghost thing will eventually be a consequence for being a reaper. Because your pocket is on the outer rim of the veil, it will take longer than six months. The question will be if the reasons you stay are worth the suffering." He held his palms up, the handle of the mug secured around his thumb. "Just wanted to put it out there. I have found that gods can be clueless to what they think humans should know."

"No, I appreciate you telling me." A weary smile pricked up Wendy's lips.

In a cheery voice, he nervously laughed, "I mean, I can guarantee it's worth it. You manifest powers for one thing. Also, because we are low on the food chain, we can visit other realms, but you'll feel extremely weaker outside your home realm. Plus, you get to travel all over the world. It doesn't matter who they were in life, if they match up with the frequency then they get the option. Even if they have no idea who anyone in your realm is, you give them the pitch and let them decide. Pretty cush job for a stable afterlife."

Wendy sipped her tea, "So, that's what Hel meant when she said this side of the veil will drain my life force?"

Makao nodded, "Yep."

Wendy let out a breath as she looked into her cup. Only a thin layer of tea coated the bottom as she gently swirled the bottom. She knew she was going to die, and had thought about it quite a bit. Now she knew she was probably going to die of cancer. She knew from seeing it first-hand in her clinicals that it was not a quick or painless death, and now she knew that it would be her fate if she continued to live in the mortal world.

"Speaking of," Makao stuck his hand into his pocket. "Ah, here it is! I'll give you this to keep for the trip. It's my invisibility talisman I had to make when I was alive. Since you're not dead and all, you'll have to make your own." He pulled out a necklace with a wooden talisman hanging from the hide rope. He put it in Wendy's outstretched palm. The dark-brown wood was shaped into a tribal looking flower, two sets of two petals standing vertically on a bed of senpai . In the center was a small circle with a line connecting heaven and earth.

Wendy ran her hand over the carvings, "What is it?"

"It's an heirloom from my grandfather. It's a lotus flower."

Wendy smiled up at him, making sure to capture his eyes. "It's beautiful."

He smiled back. "Well," Makao sighed, putting his glass down. "Now that that is out of the way. How about we show you how to guide a soul?"

Wendy put the necklace on then glanced up to see him stand. She quickly polished off her drink before setting it down. "Do I need to change? I don't think people expect to see the grim reaper in pajamas."

He shrugged as she got up and moved her seat out of the way. "You can but you should be fine if you just tightly wrap your cloak around you. I'll be the one talking so they shouldn't pay much attention to you."

"Better not waste time then." Wendy nodded as she saluted. "Lead the way, captain."

Makao chuckled, lumbering past Wendy towards the door. He stuck his key in and opened the door to the hallway of darkness. Wendy followed, closing the door behind her.

"So the key is connected to the frequency of the realm. Give it some energy and it will act just like the other one did." he held up his bronze key. Wendy could vaguely see deep navy energy radiate from the key as Makao fed it. In another moment, he was walking. Wendy followed him down the hall until he turned to a door. Without a word he opened it. Turning the knob and walking in, Wendy right behind him.

She stepped into an emergency room. Alarms going off, people talking over other people as the medical team fluttered around the medical bed. A long constant tone bleeding through it all.

"He's gone, there is nothing else we can do." A voice said, making everyone else in the room slow down. The air froze as the room became cold and the orderlies began to shut monitors down.

"Damn." a dirt-gravel voice floated in the heavy air. "My ex-wife was right."

Wendy couldn't see him very well. To her, the voice was just a haze. Reminding her of how the demon looked outside of Neveah's home.

As if realizing her dilemma, Makao pushed back at Wendy's scalp until it was in the hallway. Once past the threshold, her eyes changed. The man in the room looked down at a battered mirror image of himself. He was short, with long, gray-hair thinly tied down his back. A thin gray beard covered a metal band tee shirt.

Makao stepped farther into the room, bending his head and making his raised-hood bend to cover his glasses. As if slipping into character, Makao's voice came low, crisp, and slow. "The journey is not over, even if the chapter has ended."

The ghost jumped at the statement. The ghost took a step back as his eyes bulged at the size of the massive man, but the reaction didn't slow Makao. "Through life you have suffered, loved, and experienced life to the best of your being. Your heart has proven itself, and has called to our lord, the old one." He paused for effect. "Lord Cthulhu. He has sent me to go bring you to his domain so you may begin the next step in your journey."

The man just stood there for another moment, jaw dropped as he processed the dramatic statement. Eventually, he swallowed, "You're saying a tentacle-faced monster is what is waiting when we die?"

"No," Makao leaned down, "Just for you."

The man raised an eyebrow, "You got a drum set down there? Maybe an electric bass?"

Makao straightened up, turning around, and coming toward the door. "Many musicians have made their homes in Cthulhu's realm. The question is whether you have the courage to follow them?" When Makao came to the door, he gently pulled Wendy into the waiting room and closed the door. There was no lock, but the sliver of metal glided into the door handle just the same. It turned and Makao framed himself next to the open doorway, dipping his hand towards the dark. Wendy turned towards the ghost, only seeing the hazy outline.

The man took a hesitant step as a nervous chuckle escaped his lips. "So, no eternal hell? No suffering in damnation?"

Makao shook his head, "Not for you."

Wendy couldn't see him, but could feel his excitement as he got closer. "Fuck yeah! I'm not passing this shit up."

"Go through this door and begin your next adventure." Makao declared.

With another chuckle, the haze bolted through the door. Once through, Makao raised his head enough so Wendy could see his glasses. He smiled at her as he nodded towards the open door. Wendy nodded, following the man through the inky black. When she stepped through on the other side, she stepped into an underwater city. Masses of glowing rocks lit up the amazing coral towers. A rainbow of colors glistened off of every fish scale meandering around them. There was no glass of an aquarium nor anything looking man made. This Atlantis was made into the natural terrain and flora at the bottom of the ocean. It was indescribable beauty that froze Wendy, Makao needing to physically push her so he could fully close the door behind him.

"Welcome to the aqua realm!"

The entire group looked down to find a small child-like creature? The ears looked like fins but the creature had a stocky body that was less than a meter tall. Warpaint from reds and whites seemed to be tattooed on its cocoa face. The dreadlocks seemed to be made of the same threads decorating a guppy. The colorful and glistening strands seemed to float in the swaying tides. It had donned a dress that seemed to me made of scales, an array of changing colors sparkling off it.

The little being had a child's smile as it stared up at the ghost. "We have been waiting for you. Please." It stretched a small hand out to grasp the much larger hand of the dead man's. With an energetic pull, the being began to pull the ghost towards the coral city, egging the older spirit on with unbridled excitement.

Wendy stepped a bit closer to Makao and stood on her tippy toes. She couldn't get close to his ear but he bent down when he sensed what she was doing. In the slightest whisper, Wendy asked, "Does the Hawaiian underworld have water Elves?"

He flinched and whispered back, "Don't ever let one of them hear you say that. That is one of the Menehune. An ancient race of beings that can harness the energy of the veil. They are expert craftsmen and practically built the framework for our ancestors' success. Built underwater caverns that travel throughout all the islands. Most of the Menehune came to this side of the veil when James Cook came to shore. Eventually, all of them came to this side, one way or another. They are respected gardens of this realm and will get really pissed off if they think they are being disrespected."

"So, they're dwarves then?"

Wendy's eyes bulged from her head. She didn't mean to say that. It just flew out of her mouth. Makao turned his face to stare at her, total astonishment leaving his mouth slightly open. He closed his mouth, opened it, then closed it again.

"Well, yes." He admitted, standing up straight and pointing at her. "But don't let them hear you say that."

Wendy gave a short salute, "Roger, roger, captain."

Shanking his head to hide his quirked lips, Makao sighed before turning back toward the door. "Come on, there's one more place that I've got to take you."

Wendy watched him go to the door, closing and using his key to open it again. Wendy took one more look at the city, ingraining the soft-green tinted-glow against the deep waters, and the sights of the unusual fish swimming around the colorful reefs. She wanted to ask to stay, but was unable to form the words. Instead, she turned when she heard the door open, following Makao into the sludge of the gateway.

***

Wendy stepped into the hallway filled with doors and followed Makao down the halls. They went farther than before, though they never took a turn.

"So," Makao stated, breaking the silence. "You wouldn't happen to know of the seven valleys, would you?"

"Is that like the seven sins?"

"No, but don't feel bad. It was a concept taught by a Persian mystic named Bahá'u'lláh, the founder of the Bahá'í Faith. Long story short, he was actually talking about a pocket dimension on the other side of the veil which he was able to travel. One of those valleys is the valley of knowledge. He describes it as the enlightenment of learning through pain, but things are a bit more literal on this side of the veil."

Wendy skipped in excitement. "Really?"

"Well, when the great war happened and entities from alternate realms began to mingle, it became a campus. A mingling of the great minds throughout history. Most of them are pricks, but it is a popular meeting place for magikal practitioners throughout the realms. There are a few friends there that helped me when I first got here, and they have agreed to help you as well. Ah, here it is."

Makao stopped at a pair of large doors. The wood was decorated with pale dots in two horizontal lines with hand-crafted black door handles in the middle. Makao didn't use his keys, simply pulling on the decorative handles. He bent down as he entered the portal, Wendy following closely behind. Her eyes were blinded against sudden summer-sun on the other side.

Wendy's grandmother lived in outer Greeley, the desert of Colorado. Though the temperature only reaches high forties in Celsius in the dry planes, it was all she had to go off of. She had seen videos of belly dancers in Egypt. Even those videos didn't prepare her for the energy emanating from the deserts of the Middle East; the bustle, the energy.

The magik.

Wendy 's chest constricted as the air was stolen. The climate was such a change from the mountain-winter in Colorado. The hot air shocked her lungs, triggering the familiar struggle for air that she was accustomed to. Thankfully, it was manageable. The wheezes diminished when she extended her stomach through her pursed lips. Instinctively, she patted her pockets, finding the hard plastic in one of her inner coat pockets. A puff and some deep exercises later, she was able to breathe.

"You, okay?" Genuine concern covered Makao's face.

"Oh," Wendy waved in front of her as she caught her breath. "I'm used to it." *breath* "It was the sudden climate change." *breath* "Didn't think I could have one here though."

Makao pointed to his glasses, "My eyes are getting better with every gig I do. Another fifty years and I should have regular eyesight. The more energy you gather on this side, the better your body will be. Give it a few years and you won't have that problem any more."

Breathing easter, Wendy smiled as she put the inhaler back in her pocket. "That's something to look forward to."

Wendy's eyes stared at the shaded-sand by the shadow of the building where the door resided, but also rose to the bright, reflective sand. The sand held a heavy air as the raw beauty of the cavern took her breath away. Beyond, a sand-dune stairs of hardened sand led toward an oasis; a city, carved into a cliff of rocky slabs. The air pulsed from the city in the cliffs. The zapping on her skin indicated a potent power lay ahead of them.

Makao bent down to shade Wendy's eyes. "Are you okay? We can meet them later…"

Wendy straightened her shoulders while brightening her smile. "I can handle it." She sighed, holding her palm up as she put away her inhaler. "Trans-porting, or teleporting, or whatever, is new, but I'll get used to it."

"You know," Makao started, "it's such a day-to-day occurrence. I have forgotten what a shock it is. You know, to travel. Though, I remember being scared of snow."

When Wendy's eyes fell upon him, he continued. "I picked up a woman in northern Russia. The snow was basically covering her windows. It was awful."

Wendy laughed, then sighed. "Yeah, I guess that would be scary. Come on, let's meet those friends of yours."

Makao smiled, lumbering into the smoldering sun. Wendy followed him towards the city. The heat and power of the sun enveloped her as it sizzled into her skin. It was the unease of limb sleep with the comfort of a heavy blanket on a warm day. Though Wendy wanted to complain, she was too mesmerized by her surroundings.

The cavern walls cradled a spring that was ten kilometers in diameters. A fresh sort of water that was surrounded by carts and vendors. Though, these people didn't only delve in drinks and meats. Paper, pens, and external laptop batteries' prices were shouted in the main square. Each vendor hawked their wares to the people bustling right by them. Makao didn't stop either, he made a straight line to the massive doors that seemed to be the epicenter of the commotion.

The pair climbed into a carved-out cavern. Architectural craftsmanship created skylights, pillars, and open corridors. The shade was cool, allowing crowds to mutter by in their groups. It was magnificent, Wendy's eyes bounced completely around her surroundings, excitement and wonder filling her.

Waving out his arms, Makao only spoke. "Welcome to 'The Valley of Knowledge.' The afterlife of libraries. Or rather, the library of the afterlife."

Wendy stared at him, "Really?"

"Yep, most of many lost libraries are here, for example, the accidental burning of the Duchess Anna Amalia Library in Weimar. The destruction of the Library of Alexandria, and Library of Nalanda in India. Any bit of knowledge that has gone missing from the earth, for the most part, survives here."

Wendy looked at the markings on the domed ceilings, and was only able to utter one word. "Amazing..."

Makao patted her shoulder as he pointed with his head. "Stay close. People have been known to get lost in here."

She chuckled as her feet began to move. "Should I ask for how long?"

He tilted his head back in thought, "Well…when you don't have to eat or pee-"

"Okay! I get it." Wendy laughed. "Lead the way, I'll stay close by."

He smiled back before leading her down the cavern. Rooms of books were categorized by culture, or specific libraries. Entire football fields filled with books, behind Jackar doors; it was a beauty and a sense of discovery boiling in Wendy's blood. She was anxious to get lost in the stacks herself. She didn't know how to read the long-dead languages in which the books were written, although at that time, such realizations didn't even cross her mind. Instead, all the thought was of the discovery, the adventure of seeing writing no one living had set eyes on in literally thousands of years! Though she kept to her promise and kept him in sight, which was easy since he stood taller than anyone else around him, the urge to wander remained constant.

Eventually, they made it down the stone stairs to the candle-lit caverns in the depths of the library. It seemed the deeper the stairways traveled into the earth, the smaller the rooms became. Makao traveled down until he stopped in front of a smaller, plain door. The only thing distinguishing it from the rest was a Cthulhu plaque on the front. He pulled the door handle, releasing notes of laughter and idle-chatter.

Taking a confident step in, Makao announced. "Sorry, I'm late everyone!"

"Oh, It is perfectly fine, Makao." A soft Asian voice sung on the other side.

"Ah! Makao, my friend. Come in, come in," a deep, jolly-voice called.

"And close the damn door behind you," a harder voice carried.

Wendy would have stayed behind, wouldn't have willingly interrupted the pure ball-of-yellow radiating from the room; the unbreakable bliss these friends shared when they were together. It was too much. She wanted to wander away from the energy, she wanted the silent adventure awaiting amongst the books, among the solemnity of the books, and to go unnoticed indefinitely. Yet, a childhood shyness twisted her heart as she watched Makao walk in.

She did make a promise, however. Silently, she slipped in the door behind him, trying to mask her energy so as to blend-in with the wall.

Makao saw right through it, grabbing Wendy's arm and dragging her along with him. "I saw the new bar the Nordic's made-up. Seems they even got okolehao."

Three pairs of eyes focused on Wendy as she was shuffled into the middle of the room. Three people sat in wooden chairs around a small, circle-desk covered in books. One was an Asian man in plain monk-robes, his hair in a long ponytail leading down his back. In the middle was a jolly man who could pass for a black-haired Santa. On the opposite end was a goth girl with stunning lines making up her brown skin and dark eyes. All their eyes sparkled as they studied her, just as the god's did previously.

Avoiding her eyes, Wendy raised her hand and waved.

"Oh, who is this, Makao? Is this the teaching project you had today?" The man in the middle's voice danced slightly.

"Yes," Makao's hand, set itself upon Wendy's shoulder. "Everyone meet Hel's new reaper, Wendy."

The three looked stunned as their eyes shuffled from their companions to Wendy. The monk was the first to recover, bowing his head to Wendy. "Please excuse us. We were quite unaware Hel pays attention to the goings-on of the mortal world."

The goth lady snickered, "That's an understatement! You had to have done something big if you got that hermit-god's attention."

"Where are our manners? Welcome, come sit." The jolly man brought his hand out. Across the small table, two chairs formed out of thin air matching the set in which they were already sitting. Makao was unfazed as he took his seat, but Wendy just stood there.

Wendy pointed at the chair, taking a moment to speak the words stuck in her throat. "It just fucking appeared. Can we all do that?"

The man laughed, "If you practice and gather enough energy on this side of the veil, *anything* is possible."

Makao chuckled, "Wendy, let me introduce everyone. The pretty boy is Lee." The monk nodded. "The jolly, happy-man is Venchi and the happy girl is Chayya. They had all been mortal when they joined a god's line."

Venchi's eyes frowned, although his lips pulled, "With exception, my wife would hunt you down if she heard you say that. My soul is my own."

Pointing to Venchi, Makao corrected. "With exception, these are the people who helped me when I first crossed the veil. I've asked him to help you make your diversion amulet."

Dazed, Wendy stared at Makao. "Like… the one that you let me use?"

Makao smiled, "Exactly. You'll need something you won't forget and can wear all the time. Like a ring or a necklace.``

In reflex Wendy touched her neck as if to find something, but it was bare. She did a mental check of her fingers, bringing her mind back to her apartment. "I don't really do jewelry. Left them all with an ex, you know."

"An ex?" Chayya quirked her head. "An ex what?"

Confused, Wendy said in her statement in a questioning tone. "Ex-boyfriend? Like, former boyfriend?"

Her aura changed. Wendy could see the girl's heartbreak. Chayya's eyes gentled as she leaned forward. "You ran?"

"No." Wendy stepped back, her eyes shifting to Makao. "I left him. I wasn't happy so I broke it off with him. Got rid of everything."

Genuinely surprised, Chayya's eyes bulged on Venchi. "How far has the world come?"

Venchi chuckled with storm cloud undertones, "It has come far in many ways, but some realities have stayed the same." He looked at Wendy. "I take it that you are American, yes? Chayya is from seventeenth-century India. Though I have a family that lives in Northern Italy, My family originates from this side and can spend more time in the realms without repercussions."

Wendy felt her heart crack, just as she saw Chayya's aura shatter. The sympathetic empathy that only the tortured could understand. She didn't understand how women could walk away. In the seventeenth-century, the 1600s, for most women, there wasn't any choice.

Wendy gave her warmest smile, making sure to meet eyes with everyone around the table as she finally took her seat. "Well, I'm excited to learn. It's only been my first day and I have already learned so much. It's so completely different. However, I do have a question. How can I understand you?"

The entire table exchanged glances before settling their eyes on Wendy. Lee was the one to ask, "What?"

"Well, I didn't think England invaded India until later in history. I could be wrong but," Wendy waved her arm between her and the group. "Shouldn't there be a language barrier?"

The entire table froze for a moment, all registering the sentence, before the table burst out laughing. Hysterical, from the gut, laughter. Chayya's hand pounding on the books in front of her with the extent of it. Wendy probably should have been insulted. However, the light shining from the group was too pure not to love. Wendy smiled as all the uncomfortable tension dissipated from the space. Wendy was able to breathe as her worry flowed away from her.

"Wow, Makao, she is much sharper than when you first came. Didn't I have to spell out that fact to you in the libraries?" Chayya practically spat over the table.

Venchi wiped a tear from his eye. "Ah, the joys of a new perspective. Such a gift."

"No child, none of us would be able to understand each other on the realm of mortal earth." Lee composed himself, successfully suppressing his features. "Here, we are energetic beings. Technically, your mind is processing the intention of each word as the intention set in that word, meaning that your mind can translate both the written word, and the spoken word of any other being." He paused. "In other words, communication between hearts and minds."

Wendy blinked as she lowered her eyes to the hands resting in her lap. "That's crazy."

Lee reached his hand toward Wendy. "My goddess, Guan Yin, does not judge. As you have said, you are here to learn. What you have said has only reminded us of the joys of rediscovering the realms."

"Precisely." Venchi patted his legs in agreement, "Thank you my dear Wendy for the joyous laughter. Laughter can be among the most powerful of magik in the right circumstances."

"Getting back on task," Chayya said, clearing her throat as she stifled her laughter. "Once you have your talisman, we can help you enchant it with the essence of the void to make you intangible within the physical world."

"Here is a list of ingredients you need to gather, along with the actual amulet." Lee stretched out a piece of paper to Wendy. "You can get them from your goddess and then we can travel to the veil."

"Yeah," Makao cut in. "I was thinking we could all meet back here when Wendy is ready and head over there together."

Wendy took the paper that Lee held. She stared at it for a moment before asking, "Is there a time frame on this? Should I grab the first thing I find or can I actually look for something."

"Ah! Let's call it within twelve mortal hours. The wife will be angry if I don't come back by tomorrow." Venchi proposed, gaining agreement from everyone else at the table.

Wendy nodded even if her stomach nodded. "I bet Hel has something."

"Sounds good to me." Chayya sighed, getting up from her seat. "In the meantime, I think I'll check in with my brother."

Lee reached out, picking up one of the books on the table in front of him. "I'll stay here. I have research to do anyway."

Venchi barked out a laugh, "Hiding out here is better than hiding anywhere else. May as well help a friend in the search."

Makao turned to Wendy. "Want me to walk you to the Nordic realm?"

Wendy softly shook her head, "Nah, I need to possess everything. Plus I need to really think about what I am going to enchant. Sounds like I'll have to wear it until I die after all."

Wendy could see Makao's fist clench, but he still nodded. "I understand. It's been a big day for you after all. No one should mess with you as long as you've got Hel's sigil on your back. If anyone does, don't be afraid to throw her name around."

Wendy sighed as she got up. "Considering how everyone talks about her, I don't think I'll run into any problems."

"She made quite an impression on the other deities during the great war." Chayya muttered as she used her key set in the lock of the small room, giving one more wave goodbye before closing the door behind the hymn of her midnight dress.

With a few more words of encouragement, Wendy followed right behind her, using her own key to travel into the dark hallway of the death doors, silently stepping into the near darkness with the door softly shutting behind her.

For a while, Wendy just stood there, letting the built-up overwhelming experiences of the day wash over and through her. Her mind processed everything she had gone through that day. It was just so much, but she eventually started walking. Her hand gripped her keys, but nothing glowed. She was too uncertain on where she wanted to go. She knew she didn't own any jewelry because of the move to the apartment. She could ask Hel, as she said she would, but she didn't want to return to the Nordic realm at the moment. She wanted her mountains, she wanted familiarity, she wanted a bath; just some time to wrap her head around everything.

She didn't really pay attention as she walked, using the motion to help her meditate. She had just come across the idea to look for some nature to lose herself in when a creak stopped her heart. A door in front of her opened. She was about to hide when a familiar face popped his head in the doorway. Unruly black curls were buzzed close to his chocolate skin, but Wendy could never forget his eyes.

"Gus? Is that you?"

Hel,

You know what's weird about my life? Things just happen, little things that change life forever. My mortuary job started with a slap, my journey towards witchcraft started with a book, and my life with Gus technically started at a playground. Life, adventure, it presents itself in the smallest moments. I'm going to explain it later, but gods! The moment he pulled out that yellow motorcycle...it was like destiny slapped me in the face! At that moment, I knew everything would work out.

Gods, I see why the immortals are so fascinated with the living. Just imagine if we could see the same in ourselves!

Chapter Eighteen: Getting Settled

The two stood frozen in mid-step, stuck in the shock of the moment. As time moved, uncertainty flowed through her. It was dark and she was in an unfamiliar place; no one would blame her if she got it wrong-.

"Wendy?" Gus stepped forward, fully into the hallway. "From High School? Did Theater with Faye?"

"Was Zira's best friend at the time," Wendy responded, taking her own step forward. "Oh my God, is it really you?"

Gus smiled. His entire face bloomed with light as he stepped forward to wrap Wendy in his arms. Lifting her off the ground as he would sometimes do in the hallways. Wendy couldn't help but squeal in delight, hugging the old friend around his neck. Excitement filled her, all the emotions and troubles of the day set aside for a moment.

She smiled at him as he put her back on the ground, her eyes studying the subtle differences in his face. "God damn Gus, I haven't seen you since you graduated. You went to the army, right?"

187

Gus huffed out a half snort through his nose, "Yeah, worst decision of my life, but I did it. What about you? What are you doing here?"

Wendy looked down, trying to grip the fleeting happiness as her previous emotions started slithering up her back. "It's my first day here. Actually, I'm on a break and was thinking of how I was going to go home for a bit. Maybe take a hike to process everything."

His face settled into a mischievous grin as he stepped back. "First day pondering, you say? I know just the place."

Without another word, he grabbed her hand and began to lead her down the hallway. As they walked, he fished out his keys out of a black zip up jacket that he wore above long blue jeans.

Unable to help herself, Wendy giggled. "Where are we going?"

Bringing out his kea, he stopped in front of a blue, heavy metal door. He stuck his key in as his eyes bored into Wendy's. A glint was there Wendy had never seen before. "The same place I always go when I need to think."

As a dramatic asshole, Gus pulled back on the door. Unceremoniously, he pulled Wendy's hand through the portal. The two giggled as they used to. The laughter poured from Wendy as they crossed the threshold into the shaded light. The deep musk of forest-earth mixed with the pine mountain air. The cloak around Wendy made a good barrier among the small snow piles that littered the brush. These were mountains in which Wendy felt at home.

Wendy slipped out of Gus's hand. Stopping to fully absorb her surroundings. "Gus? Are we-?"

"In Colorado?" he finished the sentence with a smug smile. "Yep, right above Idaho Springs, a few miles above the dirt bike track."

Wendy turned and pointed to the metal shack behind them. "Did we just come out of an outhouse?"

He flung his arms out as he couldn't hold his smile. "That's not the point. Now, come on. We have to climb a bit more to get to the lookout."

Wendy chuckled as she followed him up the mountain. She fell a ways behind, the awe of being back home stifling her steps. Uneven bark snagged underneath Wendy's fingertips with every tree they passed. Each of her steps mushed under her feet with every step. Her heart sang as she smiled. She was home.

"Wendy!" Gus called from in front of her. The army obviously made him more fit than she could ever be. "It's right up here."

Without another word, Wendy quickened her pace towards him. As she climbed and broke the tree line, her breath rushed out of her as her eyes caught the town. The pair were on a cliff overlooking the small mountain town, where landmarks looked like toys as Wendy followed the line of cars bustling along the lifted highway. The highway sounds traveled all the way up to the scenic viewpoint.

"Would have taken you to the top of the waterfall, but I have found from personal experience that the forest rangers don't like seeing people up there. Besides, this is way better of a view anyway."

Wendy's head snapped to him. Gus was already sitting on a boulder looking out on the town. She walked over to him, one eyebrow raised. "Personal experience? You saying you lived up here?"

"Yeah, when I was little. When I was in eighth grade, we moved to the city for my mom's job. Didn't I take you and Zira up here once or twice?"

Wendy shook her head as she got comfortable leaning against the boulder. "We adventured up to Evergreen a couple times, but not here. I wish I knew. I used to live up near St. Mary's Glacier."

Gus locked eyes with Wendy as he pointed towards the incline. "Like, right up the hill?"

"Yep, we would drive down to the Safeway at least once a week though."

Gus whistled, "Small world. Speaking of, what are you doing on the dead side of the veil? You have to be connected to the underworlds to be in the hallway."

Wendy turned to show him the back of her cloak, "I'm Hel's newest reaper." She turned back to him. When only seeing a confused expression, she clarified. "The Norse goddess of the underworld?"

His face relaxed, his body leaning back. "Ah, that explains why I have never heard of her."

Wendy waved her hand as she got comfortable again. "Don't worry, she's also known as a hermit-god, so I don't think she gets her name out there."

Gus chuckled, the sound soothing among the silent trees. He let the sound hang for a moment. His voice dropped as he softly asked, "What happened?"

With a sigh, Wendy told him everything. Everything from the mortuary transport job to Will's death. Finally bringing to words the most ridiculous story that no one else alive would believe. By the end she felt a bit lighter, the venting therapy allowed her to process the hectic situation. The view helped with making the words flow out from her without hesitation.

"And now," Wendy finished. "I have to find something that works as a diversion amulet so I can bring souls to Helheim. It was hinted that it should be jewelry of some sort, but I can't even keep track of earrings. What if I lose it?"

Gus laughed, "It doesn't have to be jewelry if that's not your thing. Just anything that you can keep on you." He fished through his pocket and pulled out a little yellow toy motorcycle, the old sports bike's paint worn by time. "I enchanted this little toy my dad gave me, just like my phone and keys; if I don't have it in my pockets then I don't leave the house."

Wendy's eyes bulged at the recognition. The long-ago memory of a child she once met. This type of situation doesn't typically happen to normal people. This encounter was a sign. Wendy jumped after it.

Wendy felt the stir, the flutter, the golden flame. Her magik made itself known through every molecule of her body, jolting her with energy that was not her own, but so much brighter. This was magik, this is destiny.

Un-realizing the moment Wendy was having, Gus continued. "Actually, I think I might have something you can have."

Her attention immediately whiplashed back into the conversation. "Um, what?"

He looked over to her, laughing eyes locked on hers. "Don't get any ideas. Bought it for a bitch that cheated on me, You would be doing me a favor by taking it."

Wendy averted her eyes to the city to hide the sudden heat that settled in her zygomatic tissue. "Well, you definitely don't have to but it would really help out. They only gave me," Wendy made finger quotes, "Twelve mortal hours. Like, how the fuck am I going to keep track of mortal time AND realm time?!"

Gus laughed, jumping down from his perch. "Well, it's actually. It's my room-that I can get to through literally any doorway-meaning that we have twelve hours to kill. I say we don't worry about it for the next few hours. Now, I don't know about you, but I'm hungry, and Main Street sounds amazing right now. If I learned anything, being on the other side can eat away the calories."

Playing on the playful yellow in his aura, Wendy shrugged. "Only if you pay," when he perked an eyebrow up at her, she put her palms up. "I didn't think I'd need my wallet picking up dead souls. I'll get it the next time."

He smiled, making his way over to her with clunky grace. "You better. Remember, I know where you work now."

Wendy giggled as she started to follow him down the steep decline, the two making zigzags to descend safely. "What about you? You can't be dead since we're here."

"Well, no I'm not technically dead. Not technically alive either."

"What do you mean?"

"I'm a conduit for the master of the Haitian underworld, Baron Samedi. Whenever he needs to come to the mortal world, he uses my body to do his thing. It has its perks, but I haven't gotten a straight answer on how long I have to keep this up for."

"Wait, he uses you as a vessel? Like, possessing you?"

He jumped up on a log, putting out a hand to help Wendy up. "Yep, and until he is done with me, I can't die. Was told that I wouldn't age and would have to go on the run when people figure that out. Supposedly, I'm not the only one in this situation, but that doesn't really make me feel better."

Wendy dropped to the other side, turning to watch his face. "Isn't that a good thing? Most people would kill to live forever."

His eyebrows lifted as he leveled his eyes on her. "Did you ever watch Doctor Who?"

Wendy shrugged, "Yeah, with my dad when it was on cable."

"Remember Handsome Jack? Sort of? Then, consider this. I still feel everything, I don't heal any faster than normal people, but I will always heal. Now, what would happen if a government found out? I don't stay in

America, I go to war torn countries all the time. Plus, the fact I will probably live past everyone I know or will know. So..."

Wendy looked at her feet and quietly muttered, "I'm sorry Gus."

Gus let out a sigh, "No. It's not you. I've been in this situation for the past three years. Guess it's made me bitter."

Wendy went quiet, his statement hanging heavy in the quiet forest. The only sounds were the steps in the brush and the distant sound of cars. Though Wendy would have enjoyed the quiet between them, the uncomfortable ending made her mouth move.

"On the bright side, our lives are like an anime. I don't know what type of anime it is yet, but you got to admit that it's cool as shit."

With his chuckle dissipating the air around them, the two continued their hike.

***

It was better than if they had never spent any time apart. There wasn't any dull conversation. The short silence during their meal was light and breezed into the next topic. It wasn't all about the other world. They talked about his mother, her friends, where they both had been. Being around him was therapy. Wendy instantly realized the calming effect he had on her, and the ease they had around each other. There were sparks under the friendly smiles, but there was no pressure. No pretending.

After lunch was done and paid for, the two went to the back door that led to the alleyway. Using his key, Gus opened the door and led Wendy into his room. Honestly, it reminded Wendy of his old basement. There were no windows, only a main room with three doors leading to a bedroom, bath, and laundry room. The main room was fitted with a brown couch and recliner set, a large TV, and a full liquor bar that Wendy started snooping around.

Wendy supported her diaphragm as she yelled to Gus in the other room. "Good God you're an alcoholic. There's stuff in here even I have never even heard of!"

"I prefer the term, 'alcohol enthusiast.' Ah, here it is." Gus came back into the main room, stainless steel glimmering from his fingertips.

He walked over to Wendy and put the metal into her hands. It was a beautiful, clean cylinder, the latch decorated by a five pointed star with a small lock in the middle. Right under the circled star was a loop that swiveled. It was too big for a bracelet, but too small for a belt.

Wendy balanced the unlocked metal by the back hinge on the tip of her pointer finger. "You were going to give your girlfriend a locking collar?"

Gus grinned, "Don't kink shame! This was before I knew she was cheating. Good for you, because it locks, you don't have to worry about losing it. Plus, it's sterling silver so you don't have to take it off in the shower or when you go swimming-"

"Where's the keys?"

"What?"

Wendy repeated slower, "Where are the keys to this collar, Gus?"

Gus looked away as if to look at the floor around him, "I know they came with me when I moved.."

Wendy chuckled, "Wow."

Gus looked back at her, his eyes glittering even if his face was a mask of innocence. "I'm only trying to help."

Rolling her eyes she held it up to study it. Turning the lock to her, she mumbled, "It even has the star..."

"Is that a bad thing?"

"No. no it's actually a good thing." she pointed to the ends, "Fire, earth, air, water, and the top one is spirit. If it were downward facing, it may be satanic or it could be symbolizing the earth, but that's a whole issue in and of itself."

Gus took a step closer, "So... good witchcraft if the star is up and bad if it's down?"

Wendy shrugged, "Witchcraft is almost never black or white, it all lies in intention and the emotions behind it."

Gus let out a breath, "Makes sense. So," Gus walked around Wendy to the back of the small bar. Gliding by so close that her heart subconsciously jumped. He bent down briefly to grab a brown bottle and opened it, holding it out to her. "Wanna celebrate?"

Wendy gaped at him, "Celebrate what?"

He shrugged, "Completing a quest? Finding lost friends? Your first day in the world of the dead?"

Wendy smiled, "Though day-drinking sounds awesome, my quest isn't done yet." Wendy put her free hand into a cloak pocket and pulled out the folded sheet of paper that Lee gave her. She brought it up and unfolded it. "I still need to find… 'Raw Opal stone, raw Cat's Eye stone, Bay leaves, dried Hellebore leaves, Fern seeds, Bracken seeds, Heliotrope oil, and Raven feathers. All items can be substituted, do what feels right to you.' At least they are helpful."

Gus took a quick swig of the opened bottle, "Any idea where to get that stuff?"

"I saw a market place in the Nordic realm, Plus, I bet that Hel will have most, if not all of this stuff. I should probably check in with her anyway."

"Well, you will have to tell me all about it over a drink later."

Wendy leveled her eyes on him with a grin. "Persistent, are we?"

With a smile, he rolled his eyes. "Duh!"

Wendy couldn't help but laugh as she started to put everything in her pockets. "Tell you what, Will's bar is going to open in a week or so. Come to the opening. My treat, I owe you for helping me out today."

He shook his head, "You don't owe me anything, Wendy. It was hard on my first day too. I'm just glad I could help."

Wendy stepped over to him, wrapping her arms around his slender figure, his skin soft and warm as she gave a slight squeeze. "Thank you for kidnapping me for a bit. It helped more than you know."

After a slight hesitation, he hugged her back. "No problem, Wendy."

Wendy pulled back, looking up into his eyes. Then her eyes went up to his hair. "I miss the 'fro. I can't *boing* your curls anymore…"

With a chuckle, Gus playfully pushed her. "Go do your shopping, woman."

Wendy giggled as she waved a final goodbye. Putting her bronze key in the lock and stepped into the dark hallway. As she walked, she was full of energy, full of life. The warm darkness was more comforting now, the environment was less foreign. Without much thought, the energy showed her the way to Hel's door. The other doors disappeared as she reached the large wooden doors with Hel's sigil on it. Wendy practically skipped through the doors and passed the piles until she saw the glowing screens. Hel wore headphones, concentrating on the multiple screens while the mouse and keyboard clicked. As a fellow gamer, Wendy got in the goddess's peripheral and watched as Hel finished her online match.

When victory appeared on the screen, Hel smiled over at her. "I like you more and more every minute. How did everything go?"

"Good, I'm just looking for the stuff for the invisibility amulet and I'll be all set." Wendy pulled out the piece of paper. "Do you have anything on this list?"

Hel took the paper from Wendy and opened it. She took a moment to look it over before she shook her head. "Sad to say that I haven't been out shopping in quite a bit. I don't think I have anything on this list. The market by Yggdrasill should have everything though."

"Want to come with me?"

Hel sucked air through her teeth, leaning back in her chair.

"That requires pants though...How about this-" She bent down, scouring under her desk until she pulled out a leather bag. A hide rope tied it closed at the top. "How about you get double everything on the list, and we'll call this your first job for me."

Wendy held out her hand and took the heavy pouch. A seed of uneasiness settled in Wendy's stomach. She didn't want to go alone.

Seeing the look on Wendy's face, Hel added. "If you can't handle it today-"

"No," Wendy shook her head and put the pouch in one of her pockets. "I can do it."

Concerned, Hel leaned forward. "I know you have been through a lot, especially for a mortal. I don't want you to get too overwhelmed on your first day."

Wendy smiled. "I'm okay. I actually ran into a friend that really helped me out. I'm good for another shock or two."

Hel raised an eyebrow. "Oh, are they cute?"

Wendy felt her heart skip, "Well, yes-"

Hel raised up a hand with one finger extended at her. "No."

"Wh-What?"

"No relationships." Hel waved her finger again. "Friends are okay and even encouraged, but there will be no dating while you are in my employment."

Wendy tilted her head, "What, why?"

"Think about it. You are entering the world of immortals. You will be alive for the next thousand years at least. Mortals change so much in the short time they have, imagine what it's like living for thousands of lifetimes. This isn't high school where you can just break up and never see them again! Plus, immortals are very possessive. Like, start-wars-over-their-failing-relationships, possessive. It would just be better for everyone if you wait a few centuries before you even *think* of dating. Sex is fine, just don't pledge yourself to anyone."

Wendy's eyebrows furrowed, "Shouldn't I worry about getting pregnant?"

Hel waved off the question. "Pregnancy doesn't work like that on *this* side." She sighed somewhat exasperated.

"And don't try to change the subject. Do you understand what I'm trying to say?"

Wendy sighed with her entire body, "I guess it makes sense."

"Good, now." Hel smiled as she waved at Wendy, "Have fun on your quest. You can have the rest of the day off after you get your amulet done. Just come back tomorrow, mortal time, and I'll show you the rest of the ropes."

Wendy nodded. "Thank you."

"No, Wendy. Thank you and welcome to the Helheim staff."

When Hel put on her headphones, Wendy turned to find the kitchen. It took a bit, but Wendy eventually found it, going through the back door into the afternoon chill, and immediately bumping into someone on the other side.

Apology on her lips, the other person spoke first. "Watch where you are going! Don't you know who I am?"

Wendy looked up to see a tall, but lean woman. She looked to be in her forties with subtle white in her brown hair. She was pretty, dressed in a black cloak over a plain brown dress.

"Uh, no. sorry, it's my first day and I was just going to run an errand-"

"Oh!" She stopped Wendy with a roll of her eyes. "You must be that mortal the goddess is infatuated with. I'm glad to hear that the goddess is putting you to work appropriate and fitting to one of your station."

Anger spiked within at the tone of the woman, "What *the fuck* is that supposed to mean?"

The tall woman towered over Wendy in such a way that Wendy could see up her nostrils as they flared and she spoke in hushed screams. "I am Randi, the high priestess of the order of Hel and have been head reaper for my goddess for more than two thousand years! If you were under my reign, as it should have been, I would beat you mercilessly like a slave for addressing me in that tone! However, much to your luck and good fortune, you have infatuated my goddess for some reason and she made other arrangements regarding your training."

Randi straightened, seeming to compose herself. "However, if my goddess is sending you on slave errands, I may have overestimated your influence with her." Randi walked through Wendy, pushing her aside as she entered the room. As she passed a stunned Wendy, she threw a final challenge and a rub over her shoulder. "As long as you remember your status as 'dog of the reapers,' we won't have any issues."

Wendy watched in stunned silence as Randi walked through the kitchen and out of sight. Wendy was furious, but also a bit grateful to Hel. If Wendy had her as a teacher instead of Makao, she would have had such a far-worse first day. With a deep breath and mutterings of what she wished she said to the skinny twat, Randi, she walked out the door

She wandered a bit around the village to cool off before finding the stables. Baldur wasn't there, but another hand helped Wendy find Rune and got her ready to fly. It took a while, but Wendy didn't mind the lesson.

An hour or so later, Wendy was flying through the sky toward the tree which was covering practically the entire Nordic sky. The stunningly fanciful view she more fully appreciated the second time around. She took in more of the view as Ruen flew her over the lush green forests and towards Yggdrasill.

As soon as Wendy landed, she made sure to thank the pegasus, promising to buy it a treat for all her help. With a few strokes of Ruen's muscle, Wendy headed towards the market place. Wendy felt like she was at the Renaissance Festival with the mixture of traditional Viking get-ups and the modern outfits spattered among the crowd. Wendy spotted pointed ears and wings on some of the people as they haggled, the sport of bargaining in open-air markets sparkled the area with a profound energy that Wendy simply adored; a smile making itself at home on her lips.

The trip was almost uneventful, almost soothing.

"All right love," the shopkeeper spoke as she intricately folded the separate herbs and seeds into individual pouches. "With everything altogether it will be three silver coins and one copper."

Wendy immediately pulled out the bag Hel gave her, fishing through it to find the right coins, and barely registering the woman standing next to her until she let loose a long whistle.

"Taking advantage of an obviously naive mortal! Such a for-see-able choice." she chuckled. "However, you might want to rethink that price."

Wendy looked to the voice to find the most stunning woman she had ever seen. She was art come to life. Taller than Wendy in sandal flats attached to some very strong legs. Shorts and an 'I Eat Guys For Breakfast' shirt barely covering her healthy, glowing skin. A tipped pointed ear held her shimmering black locks from her face as her silver eyes looked at the shopkeeper.

Wendy knew her mouth was gaping, but she couldn't snap out of the trance, let alone hope to stop herself.

However the shopkeeper was not as affected. Letting out a sigh, the shopkeeper continued to fold as he spoke. "I thought the Valkyries were done harassing me today, Regin."

Her face furrowed as she tilted her head. "Really? I thought that was tomorrow, or was that yesterday?"

The shopkeeper looked up at the ceiling. "What do I have to give you, at this exact moment, for you to go away." He said somewhat dejectedly.

"Oh, that's simple. Let the wonderful Wendy keep the copper. You honestly don't need the cake you were going to get with that anyway."

"Fine." The shopkeeper quickly shoved all of Wendy's purchases into her arms. "Two silver then, but then you leave me alone." In Wendy's estimation, he was quite happy to negotiate such an arrangement.

Frazzled, Wendy fumbled at first getting out and then handing over the silver coins. When Wendy finally did hand them over, she didn't even register she had bowed as she thanked him.

As Wendy turned to leave, Regin tisked and stage-whispered, "Such a bad sport."

Wendy looked at her, giving a weary smile. "Thank you for your help, I think."

"No need to thank me. It's the least I can do for all the things you will go on to do."

Walking alongside her as she walked, Wendy guessed. "So you can see the future? Is that how you knew my name?"

She stopped, slapping her fingers against her chest. "Oh dear, this is the first time, isn't it? I am Reginleif. Ever knowing, Valkyrie oracle, and badass extraordinaire. And you are the mortal witch Wendy, among the most interesting of mortals with one hell of a right hook."

"Uh, thanks?"

"No thanks needed! I told Brynhild that she would get what's coming to her." Regin clapped her hands, bringing herself to a stop in the middle of the street. "Anyhoo, I'm needed back at the Valk-house. But before I go, for cryptic, oracle-derived reasons, I must reiterate. 'Make your greatest weakness your greatest asset,' and remember to fight like an immortal. Don't be afraid to go for the low blows. That is all. Remember it well. Ciao!"

Not letting Wendy respond, Regin waved as she spun on her heels and disappeared into the crowd. Wendy debated going after her, but simply shook her head, instead turning to find a door for returning to the valley of knowledge.

***

The second time to the valley was better than the first. First off, she didn't have any trouble breathing. Second, she was able to absorb so much more. The details in the architecture from the worn stones, the range of cultural clothing of the readers, and even the lack of clouds in the sky. She was used to mountains and trees obstructing the horizon, but she found it unsettling how far the sands seemed to go.

Wendy stayed inside the building that Makao's room was in, exploring the rooms and shelves as if she was the proverbial child in a candy store. She loved the energy of libraries and this was no different. It's always so calm, but not lethargic. Energy of the mystery that is held in each book, the curiosity of learning, and the excitement of finding out their secrets.

She set out to find anything on the Valkyries or the Nordic realm. When she didn't find anything, she looked for anything on the name Bridget. Eventually, she got distracted by a volume of books filled with Hindu stories about the gods and a tome on Sumerian magik which just so happened to be hidden in a corner and wrapped in a dusty, worn-cloth. Wendy took her treasures down to the room with Cthulhu's sigil on it and slowly opened the door. It was empty, silent, and still. Wendy smiled, sitting down and opening the story book. In the silence, Wendy lost herself, delving into the stories as she had with so many others. Spending hours as her imagination brought the stories to life, and brought the new culture into perspective. When her mind got full, she flipped through the Sumerian magik book. The symbols and diagrams fascinated her naive and virgin mind.

"I see we have found a fellow scholar."

Wendy almost hopped out of her seat, fumbling the book outright at the shock.

A boisterous laugh boomed from the doorway as Venchi fully stepped into the room. "I didn't mean to scare you."

"Usually I don't scare so easily. These books are just so interesting." Wendy chuckled back. "If anthropology didn't pay so poorly I would have loved to spend my life studying other cultures....How others saw magik and viewed the world; the similarities and the differences."

He laughed as he took the seat across from her. "Now you have years to experience them yourself. With access to the underworlds, it is possible for you to see them all."

"What about you? Have you seen them all?"

His head flexed back. "Gods, no. I'm way too young for that and won't live long enough to try. Plus, I don't have access to the underworlds. I'm limited to the pocket dimensions, unfortunately."

Before she could think about her words, Wendy set down the book and focused on Venchi. "How are you able to be here *and* the mortal world if you haven't made a contract? The others made contracts, right?"

The burly man sighed back, his body relaxing back into the chair. "I am a 'special case.' My ancestors were kind practitioners who first made contact and then befriended the *Bl-Jackini*, entities from this side of the veil who helped humans in my homeland. My ancestors gained so much valor with the *Bl-Jackini* that the loyalty became hereditary. No matter how far my family traveled, the *Bl-Jackini* would come to our aid. Visiting us as children and, if deemed worthy, showed us how to travel between worlds."

"That's amazing!"

The old man smiled, his eyes far off. "Yes, but it comes with its own challenges and misunderstandings."

"You said you have a wife, right? Does she know?"

He barked out a laugh, "All secrets are revealed eventually, when you live a married life. She found out shortly after our second son was born. She didn't take it well at first and practically left me. However, her love for me won her over in the end."

"Doesn't your body get sick? Makao warned me that being on this side shortens your mortal life."

Venchi smiled as he shook his head. "No child, one of the gifts that I received from the *Bl-Jackini* is the immunity to the shift. In fact, the energy from this side will actually extend my life in the mortal realm."

Wendy leaned forward. "Really? Can you teach me?"

"I'm glad you are so eager to learn, however this was a gift. Only an entity that can travel the veil can give that gift."

Wendy frowned, "Only the *Bl-Jackini?*"

"No, any still able to cross the veil. Fay, angles, demons; they are all the same entities just appearing to different cultures and being called by different names."

Wendy let out a breath, a small part of her hopeful she could still have a normal life with her father, and Nevaha and Jack; a glimmer of hope she didn't have to leave her world behind.

"But enough about me." Venchi waved. "What, may I ask, grasped your attention so tightly you didn't hear me enter?"

"Oh," Wendy sat up and looked at the open book she still had in her hands. "I'm reading about Kali and the ten Tantric goddesses."

The two talked, rolling into the depths of intellectual conversation about the different gods and realms. The flow of topics they delved into far deeper than any lecture could. In what seemed like minutes, Lee entered the room. Sliding into the conversation as he taught Wendy about the goddess Guan Yin; a compassionate healer and the entity that Lee dedicated his mortal life toward. Soon after, Makao came back, deciding to contact Chayya since Wendy was ready.

Using a small, black cup, Makao filled it with some water he got from one of the upper floors. The room sat in silence as he scried, reaching his mind to tell Chayya to come back. It worked, her curved frame entering the room a half-an-hour later. With everyone gathered, the group made their way into the Hallway of the Dead.

The group walked about two hundred meters until the doors faded into the never-ending darkness. It wasn't the same hallway where Wendy would find Hel's doors at the end. Makao instead led the group to a chasm of stillness. There was nothing, it was not a cave with ceilings nor stones at the end of far-off cliffs. It was a chasm of nothingness. The space between stars; the darkness separating the living from the dead.

As they continued, the darkness became thicker, black mist replacing the familiar gray of adjusted eyes. Chayya reached into a black bag that she had brought with her. With a few minutes of concentration, she lit a small white candle with the focus of her mind and the power around her. Though the light couldn't cut far into the fog, she still passed a lit flame to everyone in the group. When everyone was set with their own candle, the group moved deeper into the veil.

The light from the candles only kissed the holder's face when Venchi stopped them.

"I think this is plenty far enough to make a sturdy altar." Venchi turned to Wendy. "This is your time to shine, Wendy."

Wendy recoiled, "Me? What am I supposed to do?"

"The veil is energy in physical form." Chayya stated. "Manipulate it into a flat surface so you can set all the ingredients on it. Think of it as cotton, mold it into what you need it to be."

After a nod from Makao, Wendy hesitantly walked to the front of the group next to Lee. With a smile, Lee silently offered to hold the candle. Wendy passed the candle over before looking straight into the nothingness. With a long breath, Wendy stuck out her hands in front of her. Stretching them out until she couldn't see her fingertips.

Like cotton? It's mist. It wasn't physical. Neither is energy.

With a curious thought, Wendy pulled back her hands and raised her right palm out in front of her face. She closed her eyes for a moment, opening her chakras and flowing energy to her hand. When her palm became warm and tingly, she slowly pushed it forward. Wendy blinked when her hand hit a wall. It wasn't a physical wall, if she tried she could easily thrust her hand through it. It was like sludge, a thicker version of whatever coated the doors of the magikal hallway. Because it was thicker, Wendy observed that it moved differently. It flowed around her hand, feeling more like the meniscus layer out on a lazy whirlpool.

Wendy beamed, her heart fluttering at the new experience. She brought up her other hand, taking a moment to make the veil tangible under the left hand's fingertips. She glided her hands down until they rested at

218

chest level. As if she was attracting the flow of magik in her body, she pinched the veil toward her, molding the flowing sludge until she had a small, chest-high shelf. Crudely patted together with clumsy veil-hands, it wasn't fully flat and Wendy could swear that it tilted a bit. Nonetheless, despite feeling good at having been able to do it, it did take quite a bit out of her to manipulate the mist.

When satisfied, she smiled back at the group. "Does this work?"

Everyone in the group stared shocked at her, wide eyes not blinking as they moved from Wendy to her shelf.

Wendy's smile faltered, "Did I do something wrong?"

"No. no. Nothing is wrong." One of them eventually managed to reassure her.

"I have never seen anyone be able to actually mold energy like that." Lee marveled, handing Wendy back her candle.

"Neither have I, and I have been present for hundreds of rituals in the veil." Chayya breathed.

Makao huffed. "When I made my amulet, I just *smooshed* the energy until it made a surface somewhat off the ground. Had to sit down for the entire ritual."

A bit self conscious, Wendy brought her candle to her shelf, seeing the small ripples in the black. Softly she muttered, almost to herself, "Oh."

"We are only impressed. Now take this." Wendy turned to Vinchi who held out a blade for her. It was old, the hilt discolored and a bit frayed. It was the blade which allured her; a curved lightning bolt made from a rainbow of colors, the candle-light glinting off the art piece.

Wendy picked it up, carefully studying the piece before looking at Venchi. "What is it for?"

Venchi pointed to her shelf. "You must combine all the ingredients in a cloth made from the veil. This anthem will help you with that."

Wendy looked back at the shelf. Slowly, she put the candle down first, making sure it wouldn't fall. Then she looked straight forward. She lifted the magik dagger toward the nothingness and, as if she was cutting off the wallpaper, Wendy sliced a thin sheet off of the mist. As it separated, it turned into a fabric consistency, the darkness movement felt as Wendy caught the sheet in her left palm. She let out a breath, laying the sheet flat on the table.

From her cloak, she pulled out all the other ingredients along with the metal choker. She placed the choker in the middle of the sheet. Inside the silver unlatched circle, Wendy began placing all the other ingredients. Without prompting or thought, Wendy anointed the collar with the Heliotrope oil. Once it was covered, Wendy sprinkled the bay leaves, dried Hellebore leaves, Fern seeds, and Bracken seeds over the collar; the oil making the herbs linger on the metal. She then wrapped the feathers around the amulet, using three of the ten she'd purchased earlier. Lastly, she set the Opal and the Cat's-Eye in the middle. When finished, she concentrated her magik to flow toward her fingertips, and allowing her to securely wrap the veil cloth.

When she was finished, she turned back to the group. "Now what?"

"Now," Chayya breathed as her eyes lingered on the desk. "We feed energy into it until the veil envelopes it." She brought her eyes to Wendy. "We will just be transferring energy into you. You are the one who has to channel that energy into the amulet."

"Do I have to say anything? A chant or something?"

"Every aura is different, such as everyone's magik is different." Lee smiled. "Do whatever your heart tells you is right."

Wendy nodded, turning back to the bundle. When she did; Makao, Chayya, and Venchi all put their free hands upon Wendy's upper back. Wendy glanced to see that they all had their eyes closed, concentrating on the task. Quickly, Wendy did the same, grounding herself and following the flow of energy through the vessels of her body. It felt different than when she was on earth. Here there was no earth or sky to draw from. She felt power in the mist, but the energy from the others was much more tangible. The hesitant, forest-blue wave, the guarded-tan flow, and the jolly, wise-yellow, all seeped into Wendy, powering her far more directly than only other time when Wendy had practiced by herself. Looking into her heart-space, Wendy opened the door into her soul, into Eabha's energy; the intensity taking control of all the other energies. Wendy lifted her hand to touch the veil pouch, the ripples of the unworldly energy reacting to her own. Wendy directed everything into her contact, the rush of energy shocked her entire arm.

Wendy took a breath, letting the words of her heart flow without restaurant.

"With this enchantment, one shall go unseen,

With this enchantment, one shall be in the in-between.

Dark shroud of the vail, hear my plea

By my word, so mote it be."

Wendy repeated the words, chanting the rhyme as the flow of energy traveled down her arm into the material. The ripples turned into waves. The darkness manifested, storming under her fingertips as it receded; the veil soaking into the metal as if it were a sponge. As the black disappeared, it seemed to take the other materials with it. When everything cleared, the only thing left on the counter was the white candle and the collar.

Wendy picked up the candle and the collar. Turning to the others in triumph, she found them all snickering.

"What the hell's so funny?"

"Oh nothing," Lee smiled. "We just really liked your chant."

"It was very cute." Chayya chuckled. "Very storybook-esque."

"And very cheesy. Did you mean for it to rhyme, or did it just come out that way?"

Wendy gripped the choker and brought her fist to her hip. "Oh, come on! It couldn't have been worse than whatever the hell else you all came up with."

"Nope, because I didn't say anything. I just did it."

Wendy turned to Venchi, "It wasn't *that* cheesy, right?"

The trader only smiled, "What matters is that it worked. Now, we should go back and celebrate this wonderful achievement." With that he turned and started walking.

Wendy threw up her palms in exacerbation. "It wasn't *that bad*!"

"You even used the word 'shall'." Makao laughed. "It's *so cheesy*, it deserves to be in one of my D&D campaigns!"

The group started moving as they laughed. Wendy lightly protested as she followed behind them.

Hel,

Looking back, I have to wonder how much Reginleif knows. What has she seen? What does my future hold? The question should probably keep me up at night, but, honestly, I like sleep way too much.

Chapter Nineteen: Caught

The next few days felt like weeks. Because of the time difference in the veil, Wendy was able to easily transport two-to-four souls in a mortal hour. The rest of the time she worked on moving her apartment to her new home in the underworld. Without help, she slowly dragged and carried her life through a door into a mirror-image of her apartment. When she had down time, she adjusted to her new world by walking around the Norse realm. True, many kept their distance because of the mark on her cloak; but, with a few smiles, the locals warmed up to her. She kicked the ball with Fenrir and the younger souls of the village, learned how to sew hide from one of the elders, and helped out at the stables. Honestly, she was happier than she had been practically since she was a child. Everything was new and exciting. Without realizing it, she had barely spent any time in the mortal world. However, her time on earth wasn't spent in Colorado. Wendy quickly learned that the doors of the dead could take Wendy literally anywhere she wanted to go. Sweden, Hawaii, Canada, and England were just some of the places that lost souls were found synchronizing with the Nordic realm. Some of them actually knew about Helheim, being followers of the Nordic gods who were not chosen by the Valkyries to dine in Valhalla.

The best part of the gig, Wendy decided, was that she could dress however she wanted under the cloak. After work, she teleported to the Texas Renaissance Festival. There, she spent more than she would have liked to on a dark-green dress with bell sleeves, a black corset, and a deep brown belt with a pouch attached to her hip. She would practice her braids when she wasn't working, filling her hair with different chandeliers of braids flowing from her scalp. She was living a fantasy and couldn't be happier.

The only downsides were her run-ins with the other reapers. All of them seemed to share Randi's outright distaste for Wendy. When she asked around about it, she got similar answers.

"Don't mind them," Hel shrugged. "The order never did play well with others, even when they were mortal. Girls were initiated when they were young and would dedicate their entire lives to me in order to secure their place in Helheim. They're just… well, jealous that you didn't have to go through all that. I figured something like this would happen, but don't worry, they will warm up to you eventually."

***

In the comfortable silence, Wendy walked past the different doors of the now-familiar hallway, only one door giving off the energetic light. Wendy felt her own energy changing as she approached, putting the key into the lock on the door handle. The energy on the other side was filled with sorrow and somewhat relieved despair.

Some ghosts are relieved, mostly those on their deathbeds who lived in a sea of pain and drugs. Others worry about those they left behind. Some are crushed by guilt. Guilt of letting the people around them down, guilt of not completing their goals, guilt of finding comforting release from the struggles of life.

As Wendy turned the handle, she prepared herself.

"No! No, don't step on that! It's vinyl, you know!"

As if she still was transporting for the mortal world, Wendy walked into a crime scene. Three officers guarded the apartment door while the coroner took pictures. It must be a busy day, the transport team wasn't here yet. When Wendy was working, she would speed to get to the coroner's cases.

"I know they ransacked my room, but *fuck* have some class!"

Wendy looked at her clearly from the bathroom door. Her face, not yet through the barrier, though Wendy still brought her fingers to her choker, subconsciously making sure no one but Sally could see her. Panicking, the short-haired girl with white tips waved her hands as she screamed at the investigators.

Wendy took a deep breath and stepped through the door. "Sally, Sally! They are not going to hear you."

Sally froze, all of her muscled tightening. She was thin, lean, but not naturally. No. It was the bones of someone who was sick. Either sick of the body, or sick of the mind. She was only in a t-shirt because this was her room, because she was tucked in her bed.

When she didn't come to work, a friend with a key came to check on her, which was five hours after she was tricked into an overdose. The two boys who thought they were going to get lucky, gave her too much. She was a musician who was a bartender when she wasn't practicing the saxophone or the piano. She also had a history of using. To the law, it would be an open-and-shut case.

But none of that was Wendy's concern.

Her concern came from the tears overflowing the girl's terrified eyes. Her voice trembled as she uttered, "W-What?"

Wendy stepped closer, conveying all of her sympathy into her aura. "They can't hear you, but I can. Tell me, what happened here?"

"Zack…and Henry." she started as she fully faced Wendy. "They came over to hang. I-I told them I was a lesbian. Then they…then they."

Wendy stopped her, clasping her hands in hers. Eyes locked as Wendy connected to her wavelength.

"It's over." Wendy let her lips tip. "It's all over. The suffering is over and there is nothing you can do about that."

Sally flinched, more silent tears fell as her eyes locked on Wendy. Wendy took another step closer. She squeezed Sally's hand, "All I can do is take you to a better place. One where you will be accepted and give you the chance to start over."

Sally's breath caught in a chuckle, "I thought lesbians don't go to heaven."

Wendy let her smile grow, "Who said heaven was the only afterlife?"

Her eyebrows knitted, "What?"

"Helheim is a peaceful paradise. In the snowy mountains of the Nordic realm. A place where you can be yourself." Wendy smiled, "We would love to have you."

Sally's head sagged, the fight leaving her body under Wendy's fingertips. "Listen lady." Sally muttered. "I'm not a good person. I've done some shit…"

Wendy's smile never wavered. Her hand softly lifted Sally's chin to lock eyes. Wendy read her, she could see the scars, the hardship Sally went through every day. Wendy reached out with her own energy, an aura of peace. The same message that helped Wendy all those years ago.

"It's okay. I'm here to take you to a place where everyone will accept you for who you are. A place where you won't suffer anymore. A place where you can be free. You could stay here to wallow in the sorrows of your former life or you can start again. What will it be?"

Sally looked struck, slowly turning to watch the government officials take pictures of her corpse. Her eyes absorbed one last look of a life that ended way too soon. After a moment, she nodded, "You're right. It's not the first time I started over." Sally turned back to Wendy, a sad smile on her face. "I don't want to become a wallowing ghost or something."

Wendy smiled brightly, "I'm glad! You made the right choice. If you follow me, we'll be on our way."

Wendy turned, still holding onto Sally's hand as she walked back to the door. Wendy found that if she let the souls dawdle, they would start asking to bring things with them. Wendy fished out her keys, closed the bathroom door, put the key in, and thought of Helheim. When she was sure the link was secure, Wendy turned the key.

The first thing the pair saw when the door opened was a winter wonderland on top of a frozen waterfall. The sun shined off the white blanket that green bristles peeked out from. The sight brought Wendy to tears when she first saw it and found it was a good opener for those who had just died.

"Welcome to Helheim, Sally." The pair turned to see a lovely brunette, the other-worldly former-goddess glowing around the soft snow. "I am here to take you to the main hall, we want to hear your story."

Wendy could hear Sally's breath catch at the sight of the Goddess. Though, Wendy was used to that reaction by now.

"My...Story?" Sally asked before Wendy softly pushed her towards the goddess.

Wendy only smiled, "You'll be fine, I believe in you." Wendy looked at her coworker. "You got it from here Nanna?"

The goddess stepped forward, taking Sally's hand from Wendy. "Yes, I got it from here."

Sally smiled back at Wendy, "Thank you for everything. I'll see you later?"

Wendy smiled, "Definitely, Have a good day, Sally."

Sally waved as Nanna led her away, recording her story to Hel, and getting her officially energetically bound to her afterlife. Wendy stopped watching the spirits off as they walked down the path. Instead, Wendy turned and shut the door. She put her key in and opened the door to the familiar hallway of doors to do the entire thing over again.

Centering her energy, she looked for the next door. Her energy pulled her as the door of the deceased called to her. Once the door was found, Wendy didn't hesitate unlocking it.

This time, Wendy found that the wooden door led to a hospital room. The curtained off room was set by the window with all of the man's belongings. He was a grandfather by the pictures that were taped above his head. Though the body was still tucked under white covers, the spirit was sitting up in his wheelchair, looking out the window.

He had a beard, a full one that didn't match the wispy hairs on his body's chin. He looked tired, worn by the time he had been abandoned here. His family practically forgot about him and only visited on holidays. Just to say they did.

"I suppose you are here to take me away?"

Wendy walked more into the room, bowing her head. "Yes, I am, Aillen. I'm here to take you to the afterlife."

Aillen sighed, "I've been scared of it for a long time. Now that it's here, I don't know what to think."

Wendy brought her eyes to his face. "No one ever does."

The elderly man looked at Wendy, surprise flashing across his face. "Considering how you look, I must be going to heaven."

"A heaven. You are being invited to Helheim, in the Nordic realm. I assure you, it's just as good."

Aillen huffed out a laugh. "All these uptight bitches saying I need to accept the word, not knowing that I would get an invitation to spend my afterlife with Vikings."

Wendy smiled, "Exactly. I assure you it's-"

"Wendy, is that you?"

Wendy froze at the sound of the familiar voice, the hurt-disbelief she had never heard from her friend before. Wendy turned her head to lock eyes with Neveah, dressed in black scrubs standing next to a seemingly confused CNA, the younger girl dressed in maroon scrubs and a messy bun.

"Um, Neveah? Who are you talking to?" The girl hesitantly asked.

When Wendy didn't respond, Neveah put her hands on her hips while never taking her eyes off Wendy. "My sight has gotten a hell of a lot better since the exorcism we did. So don't pull this standing still crap. I can see you."

Wendy held up her palms, "Neveah. I can explain."

She took a closer step toward Wendy. "The hell you better! I barely hear from you since Will died and now I find you apparently invisible, talking with my patient? What the hell is going on Wendy?"

Aillen's eyes jumped from the three women, seemingly entertained by the drama. His hazy aura blurred for Wendy's eyes. Seemed Neveah's sight was better than even Wendy's. Stuttering, Wendy looked Between Neveah, Aillen, and Aillen's body. After a silent moment, Neveah's eyes separated from Wendy's face to look at the two Aillan's, her eyes bulging as she registered what was happening.

"Laia," Neveah whispered. "Get the RN in here. I'm going on my break."

The other girl stammered, looking at Neveah as if she lost her mind. Neveah ignored her as she turned to the door of the room, muttering loud enough for the room to hear. "I need to go on my thirty. If anyone wants to save our friendship, they will meet me out front by my car."

With that she stormed off. The CNA whipped her head between Neveah and Aillen's body. She walked over, putting gloves on that she had stashed in her front pocket. She would try to wake him up, try and do the change herself. Wendy wasn't concerned with that at the moment. She couldn't move her eyes from where Neveah was standing.

"You know that CNA?" The spirit softly asked.

Wendy turned to him as the brick of panic slammed into her, "She's my best friend. I didn't think this would happen. I'm sorry I need to talk to her."

The old man chuckled, "If you let me see how this turns out, I'll let you take me to whatever afterlife you're selling, little girl."

Wendy smiled, "You mean it?"

He shrugged, "Please, I've been stuck in that bed for the last year! I need to see how this shit pans out."

Wendy let a small chuckle fall from her lips. "Guess we better chase after her then."

Aillen gestured to the wheelchair he was sitting in. "You'll have to push me."

Wendy just stopped herself from rolling her eyes. Instead, she grabbed the haze of his hand. Contrasting her energy on her palm so she could Pull him up out of his chair. Without his physical body, his true soul was able to move just fine. Without another word, she dragged him to find her friend.

It was relatively easy to find the front doors in the small retirement home. Once she was outside, she headed to the open car door of Neveah's sedan. Neveah hunched over with her feet dangling outside the vehicle.

Wendy slowed as she approached, the cold energy of betrayal working off her friend. A knife of gilt stabbed Wendy. Of course Neveah is upset, they were coven sisters. It *was* a bitch move to keep something this big away from her.

Neveah's soft voice shattered Wendy's ponderings. "You know-"

Wendy's eyes focused on Neveah's slouched head, elbows supporting the weight on her knees. "I have been so worried about you since Will died. No one has really heard from you since last Saturday. Almost a whole week-and-a-half of unanswered text messages and missed phone calls. Then, when I heard your voice in that room... I couldn't help but feel happy, because you sounded... Happy." Neveah looked up at her, glistening eyes capturing Wendy's. "When you were at the funeral, you barely cried. You helped everyone else, especially his mother, but everyone was worried about you. You acted like... I don't know, Like he was moving to another country. Like he wasn't dead. Now, you're.." Neveah's eyes shifted to behind Wendy. Wendy turned her head to see Aillen, waving back at the sudden attention of the two women. Wendy sighed, her head dropping as she gave in.

"I sold my mortal life to earn Will a decent afterlife. I was given an offer by the Nordic goddess of the underworld. She said she would save him if I gave her a thousand years of service. I am her reaper now."

Wendy's head snapped up when she felt Neveah's fingers constrict around her forearm. "What the fuck you mean, 'Mortal Life!'? I can touch you so you're not dead-"

"No, no." Wendy chuckled, waving with her free arm. "I'm not dead yet. However, I have been warned that my life has probably been shortened by a decade or two."

"Oh," pain dropped from Neveah's eyes. "That's something I guess."

Wendy chuckled nervously, "If it makes you feel better, You're the only one that knows."

Brown, torn-eyes traveled back up toward Wendy's gaze. A small, whispered question was released into the air.

"Why didn't you tell me when everything was happening? Were you going to tell me?"

"I... Well, I wasn't." Wendy's eyes broke off to study the ground. "I messed up your life enough with the exorcism thing. I know your marriage wasn't always good, but-"

Neveah's hand slapped Wendy's arm enough to sting. "My marriage has nothing to do with you. You did nothing wrong!" Nevaeh leveled her eyes on Wendy. "Nick is not your problem and anything he does is not on you. Above that, he will never stop me from helping out my best friend. So, you don't have to deal with it all on your own anymore. Let me help you."

Wendy blinked in shock. She didn't know what to expect, but she didn't expect the raw emotion in Neveah's eyes. The determined love, someone who didn't want to lose Wendy from her life. Wendy could literally feel the aura of concern radiated from Neveah's core. Fuck, she really cared about Wendy, she was someone who truly didn't want to let her go.

Wendy sighed, "When do you get off? I could show you everything then-"

Wendy's words were cut off by a symphony of squeals along with the sharp squeeze around Wendy's chest. Neveah bounced them in glee as her excitement grew. "Yay. I get to see my bestie after work."

Wendy rolled her eyes, but couldn't help but smile back, relieved that it turned out okay, although her head was filled with doubts. It took a lot for Wendy to accept everything, and she honestly wasn't sure how Neveah would process everything.

***

Later that night, after both of their shifts were over, Wendy picked Neveah up from her house. They walked down the street to a gas station, ignoring the other people near the register and heading to the locked restroom. Wendy took out her keys, unlocking the private door. Though, instead of leading into a dingy bathroom, the door opened to Wendy's apartment. Casually, Wendy entered. Neveah hesitated before taking a cautious step in, allowing Wendy to close the door.

"Why is your apartment in a 7-11 bathroom?" Neveah asked as she touched the walls, surprised when they were real.

"I can get to it by any door with a lock. I just didn't want to walk up to a random person's house to do it. That was the best door that won't raise suspicion. Want any tea?" Wendy asked over her shoulder as she headed towards the kitchen.

"I feel like I need a bowl or a shot." Neveah muttered as she followed.

Wendy chuckled, bouncing around the kitchen to make the tea. As the water boiled and the leaves seeped, Wendy told Neveah everything. The second escape of the demon, Hel finding her, and what she did when she found Will's body.

When she was done, Neveah gazed dumbfounded into her teacup. "Damn."

"Right?!" Wendy exclaimed. "Like, for most of it, I barely believed it was happening. A bit of me was convinced it was all in my head."

Neveah pointed with her pinky, "Can we promise that we tell each other everything from now on? No matter how ridiculous it sounds, I promise to believe you."

Wendy took the outstretched pinky into her own. "Promise."

Neveah smiled, unlatching her pinky in the cheesiest way possible. "Anyhoo. When are you going to show me Helheim, or Will's bar?"

Wendy flinched, "Well…"

Neveah's excitement slipped. "What's wrong?"

"Remember when I said that my life expectancy had been shortened? That's because I physically entered the realms, so I can't bring you until you… you know…You don't have a body anymore." Wendy nervously pulled back her hair.

"That's not fair." Neveah pouted back in her seat. "You said you astral traveled to visit Hel the first time. Couldn't I do that too?"

Wendy blinked, gears obviously turning until she threw up her hands. "Fuck. Let's try it."

Clapping her hands, Neveah jumped up from the seat. "Let's do it!"

Wendy set up the living room to give Neveah every advantage Wendy could possibly think of. She set up a salt circle with candle flickers dancing around the room. Wendy set the five candles as if they were points of the star. Wendy burned mugwort and Wormwood and put on a "meditation music 963 hertz". Then Wendy guided Neveah through the process of leaving her body.

To Wendy's near-disbelief and buried annoyance, Neveah figured it out within two hours. It was super easy for her, barely an inconvenience.

Hel,

Now that I think back, She had several things working on her side. Mostly, the whole "my apartment is in a pocket dimension in the thinnest part of the vail" thing. That is probably why she picked it up so fast. I love her and am super happy for her, but damn. Definitely brought me down a notch.

Chapter Twenty : Fight

Wendy learned something very quickly in observation of the preparation for the bar's grand opening. Immortals are easily bored and each entity has their own way to cope. Some created drama with mischief and rumors. Some meddled with the lesser beings in one way or another. Some fought, some fucked, and some were just passing the time. But all of them loved to party.

The pocket dimension expanded with the energy inside of it, meaning the room changed its dimensions according to the amount of people inside it, and also meant that there was no cap on guests. Lilly explained to Wendy that it was more than just a simple bar opening. Since the detaching of the realms after the war, events like this had become more political. Because the greater gods can't leave their realms, they tend to send lesser representatives to scope out the other realms' strengths and weaknesses.

"In this day and age, where smaller lines are fighting to stay out of Nirvana, war has become a constant. Listen sugar, make sure you're wearing your cloak and don't be afraid to throw Hel's name around." Lilly lectured.

Most of the opening preparations consisted of stocking the thousands of kinds of liquors. Since each realm had one or more preferred drinks, all needed to be easily and readily accessible for the small army of bartenders who would be working the event. They were all of lesser lines; fay folk, vampires, succubi, incubi, and even a Japanese Yūrei.

***

Neveah convinced Wendy to take her to the opening, where she was already planning on meeting Lee, Makao, Venchi and Chayya . When Wendy informed them, the group was excited. None ever hearing of a mortal being able to astral project in the realm.

The day of the opening was a spur of double-checking and adding the final touches to a great many projects. Wendy was given permission by Hel to oversee the event since it was her investment. However, Nanna slipped that there was going to be a priestess reaper meeting; meaning Hel was making sure Wendy wasn't around those snooty snobs.

Wendy enjoyed the physical labor and had fun setting everything up. It reminded her of her theater days, spending hours making the sets and costumes, which was now substituted by hanging lights and decorating the two floors. When it was finished, the club looked like a cross between a fairy forest and a new year's eve party. Real diamond beads were braided with flowers that hung from the ceiling. When the lights kissed the stones, the colors would sparkle like a disco ball all around the room. Considering the lights kept changing colors, it was the perfect opening touch. Upstairs was a bit more simple, a few torches to pay patronage to the Viking culture, and small langskip boats were suspended from the ceiling to hold candles. The last finishing touch, TVs with various sports broadcast on them.

It seemed most realms had a favored sport of some type. Modern knowledge enabled each realm to make a sports-type channel of their own. It wasn't thousands of channels that hosted nonstop content, it was more of recordings that were distributed to those who wanted it. For the opening, Will got showings of a week's worth of Valhalla huts.

On top of the world tree, Yggdrasil, is what the mortals recognized as Valhalla, even though it seemed to have different names for each part. The warriors handpicked by Odin or Freya lived and ate in the hall of Glaðsheimr. On shifting clouds, the undead fight each other as they prepare for the final battle, the sun shading the land in gold, where the blood and gore splatter didn't cover. By night, the dead had regenerated so the feast could commence. For the warriors, the occasional trip to the other parts of the realm were more like holidays where they would be treated like royalty. To say that the years being worshiped went to their heads would be a dramatic understatement. Imagine, she thought, of having the stereotypical musician egotistical freak out, but for thousands of years! However, the warriors certainly knew their craft.

The battles were hypnotizing, the warriors so experienced they danced with the strength and finesse that came with hundreds of years of practice. It was still murder, but it was pretty murder; beauteous slaughter.

It was true they all had a choice to go back. Be reincarnated and do their mortal life differently. However, hardly anyone ever did. The loyalty and love made people dedicate their life-energy to the realm. War was different in the future, where lives traded with a pull of the finger. These warriors respected the art of the battle and banned all modern weaponry. In turn, creating the most physically fit magikally empowered humans imaginable. It was both inspiring and threatening all at the same time.

An hour before, Wendy excused herself and got ready. A quick shower, making sure to keep her braided hair dry. When she was done she had transformed into a renaissance festival's dream. Green bell sleeves under a brown corset that sat over a brown and green dancing dress. Her crimped hair sat in a high ponytail with sweeping bangs to drape over the left eye. Just enough makeup to catch the eye and Wendy felt confident.

Smiling, Wendy picked up her phone and dialed Neveah's number. It only took four tones for her to hear her bestie's voice.

"Is it time?"

"Yep!" Wendy responded, "Just astral travel here and we will get going."

"Okay, Nick will be here in an hour and a half so him coming home will wake me out of it."

"Sounds good, but remember that you can leave at any time. I've been warned by Will, a fight is likely going to break out at some point."

Neveah snorted, "I've been in one or two fights, I know how to be smart."

Wendy chuckled, "Fair enough, I'll see you when you get here."

With a click, the call was disconnected. Wendy faced her scrying mirror. Wendy had given Neveah a sigil she had personally made. When the two mirrors had the same symbol enchanted on them, they became energetically connected. The theory was tested with a psychic exercise over the phone. When the friends were predicting what the other was touching with near-ninety percent accuracy, they were confident that it worked.

Within twenty minutes, Wendy began to feel Neveah's energy. It was strong, comforting energy. Her aura manifested in the room around her. Wendy gave one more energetic pull to her form before she could see the beautiful purple and blue energetic flame. When one astral projects, they don't take a mortal form. They look like ghostly-bright energetic mists. Balls of light in a sandstorm of aura clouds. Her collar still held a border of darkness but her excitement bled through with incredible light. It was beautiful.

"Feeling stable?" Wendy asked with a hand on her hip.

Neveah couldn't speak in words. It was more like impressions on the mind. One might not get it word for word, but you would get the overall gist. The only reason Hel could understand was because of her off-the-scales power level. The power of a goddess.

Wendy focused energy to her fingertips. Neveah didn't have a hand, but if Wendy imagined one, she could usually drag Nevaeh along. Taking Neveah's hand, Wendy took out the separate platinum key. Because it was a special day, she was allowed to borrow a key that worked like her house key, taking her directly to the back door of the bar. It was the best for fashionably late people.

Wendy unlocked the door to reveal the upstairs in full swing. Cheers and laughter thundered through the wood. Wendy sent a boost of energy to her grip in Neveah as she entered the room. Thankfully, Wendy had coordinated with the group and reserved a rounded table. Will would be their personal bartender when he wasn't making the rounds and greeting everyone he needed to show respect to. No matter how silly and inappropriate he truly was, he'd always been good at first impressions. Calm, professional, and likable. No one would ever guess his phone was filled with anime girls with tails under their skirts.

Honestly, Wendy was proud. Will gave a bigger smile as he toasted them from across the bar after seeing Wendy and Neveah take their corner table. Once the girls were settled down Wendy let go of Neveah.

"So, what do you see?" Wendy asked looking out among the crowd.

"God, it's like a mesh of different watercolor splatters. The colors are so bright, I can barely tell them apart." Neveah let out a breath. "You may have been understating things just a little bit."

"Don't worry, I made sure that this seat was magikally reserved. Only people I allow will feel comfortable here."

"Like a spell?" Neveah asked.

Wendy shrugged, "Put my energy on it when the room was growing earlier. It was a trip to witness."

"Yeah, I can't wait to actually see it. Instead of through rainbow blob vision." Neveah seemed to sit back in the seat.

"There isn't any rush. Oh! There they are." Wendy began to wave as she got the group's attention.

All dressed up for the occasion, Venchi, Chayya, Lee, and Makao walked up to the table. Venchi and Makao wore button up shirts and groomed appearances, while Lee and Chayya were stunning in elaborate makeup and flowing dresses. Lee especially was only recognizable by the aura around them. Every one had a wondrous expression as they laid eyes on Neveah's energetic form.

"I take this to be the living you were telling us about. That is fascinating." Chayya muttered as she got close to the table.

Wendy smiled and nodded. "Yep! Everyone, this is my bestie and my coven sister, Neveah. She is astral projecting all the way from the mortal world. Neveah these are my friends on this side of the vail; Chayya, Venchi, Lee, and Makao."

"Nice to meet you, even though I can't actually see you." Neveah projected.

The group blinked as they processed her mode of talking.

Venchi cleared his throat. "I apologize, it's just a surprise. You have to realize that it is extremely rare to see one of the mortal realm freely move among us."

"I do admit, I had my doubts." Chayya smiled, holding her forefinger and thumb slightly apart in front of her face. "Just a little though. Neveah, I have to say that your aura is beautiful and I'm glad you came."

Her aura rippled with light "Well…thank you."

The group moved into the booth making small talk as everyone settled with each other. With too much energy to sit, Wendy trusted her best friend to her teachers' care and went out looking for Will. It wasn't too hard finding him, she just had to follow the laughter.

On the other side of the bar was a line of bulls-eyes where daggers, axes, and other 'light' attacks could be shot at. Thankfully, the extra energy that was used in the bar only strengthened the integrity. So they could shoot as much as they wanted.

On one of the four-man tables sat two tankards whose handles were clutched by laughing men. One was Will and the other was definitely a lesser god. Compared to the other guests, Wendy could distinctly see his aura. It was earthy, always changing. It was as if all the seasons lived in his aura. The colors of fall. The warm laughter of summer. The flowers in summer. Though the dominant was the snowfall of winter, and the loneliness of being stranded under piles of snow.

Wendy decided not to acknowledge it as she came up to the table. Since they didn't see her, she signaled her approach.

"Ooy!" she called an extended cry as she hopped over.

Will looked over and with a raised tankard, he full on anime moaned back. Making everyone around him uncomfortable but made Wendy laugh.

Until Wendy saw the snake.

He was beautiful. The light sparkled green against the underbrush scales of a seven foot snake, Wendy hadn't noticed him, thinking that the snake was the god's armor. On top of his boa shaped head, were two swirling brown horns. The best part, the beauty was resting on the horns that sprouted from the scalp of the god. That was so *cool*.

"Heyo, beautiful!" Wendy greeted the magnificent entity; then her eyes lowered.

He was shocked. His swirling green eyes fixed on Wendy. His slender face was covered by a thin beard, his jaw creaked a bit open. All of his hair was a deep red that was accentuated by the firelight.

His stiff form leaned a bit forward, "Bríg?"

Wendy brushed it off with a smile. "Nope! Though you're not the only one to say I have a look-a-like. My name is Wendy, the goddess Hel's newest reaper."

It was just a flash, but his eyes gave a glimpse of true loss. The loss that she had seen in the eyes of family members. It was quickly covered by a welcoming smile. "Well, my apologies Wendy. It is very nice to meet you; I am Cernunnos and up there is Adharcach."

Wendy's eyes sparkled as her eyes moved back up. "May I say, Adharcach, you are magnificent."

"Oh yeah, didn't you want a snake in middle school?" Will muttered before he took another sip.

Without taking her eyes off Adharcach, Wendy nodded her head. "Yeah, but Dad is scared of them. I had a whole summer where I read a bunch of books on them."

The boa's head stretched toward Wendy. Most would be scared but she outstretched her hand. Giggling when the tongue tickled it. When it was clear that he wouldn't go any further, Wendy dropped her hand and smiled at Will. "Anywho, I just wanted to let you know that the group is all here."

Though his lips muttered, "Sounds like a personal problem." His body moved to stand. He lifted his tankard to Cernunnos and Adharcach. "I'll buy you a round next time you come by."

Cernunnos raised his tankard back, "I'll hold you to that."

The two only made it a few yards when Wendy began to drift to the left. The music that drifted from the stairs called to her. Flutes, bassoons, drums, and stringed instruments played an energetic jig making her entire body react.

A heavy sigh came from next to her. "You wanna go dance, don't you?" Wendy pouted out her lower lip as she turned back to him to nod. Will retorted with an eye-roll. "What do you want? I'll go get your guys' drinks."

Wendy jumped for joy. With practiced efficiency, Wendy removed her corset and handed her corset over to him. "Surprise me, but I'll be back after one song."

He pointed at her. "You better. Sai is down there so go to him if you need to."

With a two finger salute from her brow, Wendy headed down the stairs. As she descended the stairs, it wasn't a Cinderella moment. No one looked at her or cared about her existence. Her excitement accelerated in her torso at the amount of entities in the club level. No more than ten booths scattered on the dancefloor, the others were floating in the air. The chandeliers were such a good idea, lighting the dancefloor just enough to not see. With a clear breath, Wendy made her way down the stairs. Soon she found a bit of space near the wall where she closed her eyes.

Breath in.

Breath out.

The allegro folk song called for a pony step on the balls of her feet. Her hips pumping twice at every lean step. Her upper half stayed still as her arms did their best to flow in small twists. The longer she danced, the more she lost herself. It could be considered a meditative state; her body only concerned with and consumed by the music. Her only thought was how good it was to smile. Swaying shimmies, exposed belly rolls and alternating snake arms manifested to the dancer four and one quarter count. It was raw, unplanned and a bit chaotic. However, just as if she were on a stage, she had forgotten they were there.

Way too soon, the song had changed. If it were just Will waiting for her, she would have stayed for another song. Sadly, it wasn't just him and she didn't want to leave Neveah alone for too long. So, without looking at the people around her, she made her way back up the stairs.

Wendy sighed when the upstairs seemed to be cooler. It didn't take her long to serpentine her way through the crowd to the booth. Everyone was smiling and Neveah's fire was bright. That made Wendy smile.

"Took you long enough!" Makao yelled across the table.

Wendy shrugged, a grin on her face. "I got sidetracked. Did he bring back my corset?"

"Will said that he was hiding it." Neveah offered.

Wendy groaned, her shoulder slumping. "Guess I'll annoy the info out of him later. So, what is in the glass?"

Each person had a half goblet in front of them. The goblet was made from dark horn, making it hard to see the color.

Chayya raised her horn, "It's called Mahua. It is a sacred liquor from India. Since no one else had tried it, I got everyone a taste."

Wendy gripped the glass and lifted it to the table. "To new experiences?"

Everyone lifted their own cups. "To new experiences!"

Everyone sipped in toast. Wendy gave a surprise yip of joy as she took a healthy swig. It was a sweet, floral taste that was smooth going down.

By the look of everyone, they all enjoyed it too. Even Neveah had been able to tip the glass a bit to drink some. Wendy's mind wandered to when she first went to Hel's kitchen and she served her the mead. Would Wendy have looked like that?

"And to think that I figured this would be a waste of time."

Wendy jumped. Spinning completely around to face a gaggle of girls. All of them beautiful and physically strong, but it was the slightly too-perfect skin that made Wendy on edge. Especially when she recognized one of them.

Regin was standing to the side of the gaggle. Holding a basket of tater-tots and popping them in her mouth like popcorn. Whatever was happening here, she was only a spectator. Wendy focused at the front. The pointed ear Valkyrie wore only a backless tube top and tight jeans, but her chest allowed her to pull it off. She had boots that matched the punk aesthetic of her braided mohawk. Also, Wendy had never seen perky Cs before, but this woman was obviously not wearing a bra. By the way she stood, she knew she was heart stopping; making her have the energy of a preppy mean girl. Not all the women gave off that vibe, but the obvious

leader was.

With a nasty smile, the woman gave a sarcastic smile. "Hi, you must

be Hel's newest delivery grunt. We were already warned that you were

going to be trouble and I was stupid enough to not believe it. I mean, she

isn't even a year in. What could she have done with so little time?"

"I'm sorry, who are you?" Wendy interrupted, which made the entire

energy around the group freeze.

The brunette gave a single chuckle. Her eyes darkened as she slowly

took some steps in. "I'm Brynhild. Third in command of the Valkyries and a

bitch you don't want to mess with."

Worked up from being interrupted from her still frame moment with

her friends, Wendy threw her hands out before her hands clapped her skirt.

"And what did I do that was so bad?"

Brynhild pointed behind Wendy, "If I'm not mistaken: that is a

living, unaffiliated mortal. You brought a spy here."

Anger flew through Wendy, "That is by best friend. So what if she's

alive?"

The Valkyrie let out a harsh snort. "You think every mortal can pull a projection that well off? They have to be a spy."

"I am a witch. I'm not just another mortal." Neveah defended.

As the one on the end, Chayya stood next to Wendy. "This party is neutral ground. Everyone here will vouch for her-"

Without warning, Brynhild struck out. Latching her fingertips around Chayya's throat. A smile of a killer on her face as she spit through her teeth. "This is my territory, rat!"

It was a fireball of energy. A burning wave that brought with it a familiar energy. A darkness. An energy that shadowed her own and made her lust for violence. Wendy couldn't form a thought as Eabha's energy screamed.

Her legs crouched on the balls of her feet. A painful lightning bolt of energy burned her fingertips. Her first reaction was to feel the skin of the cow's neck beneath her claws. But she worried about the grip on Chayya.

The energy started at the bottom of the spine. Red anger zapped to the balls of her feet and to her right fist. Jumping up, Wendy put all of her energy on the spot on her left lower jaw, nicking the Mandibular nerve.

With the impact, Brynhild flew. Blacking out long enough to let Chayya go. She flew unto the wall, leaving splintered wood as she collapsed to the ground.

Wendy didn't notice her choking friend or the cheering comments the Valkyries made. She was too far gone. She was giggling in a voice that wasn't her own, panting with the lust for violence. She knew the brain dead twat would give a good fight, but would she scream? A crooked toothy smile filled Wendy's face as she crouched down again. Her nails growing in anticipation of the attack.

"WENDY MYER! You stop RIGHT NOW or I'm CALLING DAD!"

A snarl was ripped from her lips as she turned to the sound of Will's voice, but her body froze when she registered. He had a black brick in his hand. Raising it up in front of his leveled eyes.

He's bluffing. He has to be.

Wendy's phone worked in her apartment even if it was spotty service. If this place was close enough to the veil...

Will gestured with the phone again. "I'll call him right the fuck now if you don't stop it with this shit."

Wendy could only growl, showing the same teeth that tore through skin.

"Shut it down!"

Growl.

"I'm warning you Wendy!"

Snarl.

Will only raised an eyebrow, turning the phone towards his face. "I'm telling."

Wendy felt Eabha give up control as her back straightened. The burn of the power still branded her chest, but she was in control again. She put her hands up, rolling her eyes. "You win."

Silence. Dead silence.

Wendy looked around to see every eye on her. Even the Valkyries who were bent down to help their sister stared dumb founded. Everyone looked in either fascination or fear as Wendy went entirely cold.

"I-"

"Her energy is just like Nirvana, The All Mother. She's touched by Nirvana."

Wendy's heart dropped as the muttering started. She looked back, her eyes pleading as she whispered to Neveah to leave. She didn't see her leave, her head snapping back at the sound of someone jumping in front of her, protecting her from the crowd. This action caused the group of Valkyries to start moving. Unhooking weapons and getting ready for a fight.

Cernunnos with Adharcach posed to strike from above laughed over his shoulder at Wendy. "You really haven't changed, making trouble wherever you go."

Wendy pointed at the Valkyrie on the floor. "She started it!"

With a chuckle, Cernunnos widened his stance, "Adharcach, get the pup to the nearest door. I'll watch your back."

As Adharcach slid off the gods' tight but formidable frame, Wendy narrowly dodged a small knife that grazed her cheek. Panting as she hid behind him, she muttered. "Thank you both. I owe you one."

"Buy us a beer next time and we'll call it even. Now get out of here before that berserker gets up and tries to take a piece out of you."

With an apologetic wave to her friends, Wendy started running, following the path to the back door that Adharcach cleared for her. The Valkyries charged with battle screams, axes and knives just narrowly missing Wendy's body. One pinned her skirt to the wall, forcing Wendy to rip it, and the force from which almost making her fall. In a panic-induced haze, Wendy pulled out her keys from her bra and put the platinum kea to her room in the tavern lock. With one last thank you to her snake friend, she closed the door.

Her wheezes sounded deafening in the quiet room until a buzzing from her altar took priority. Wendy walked over, answering when the display read 'Neveah'.

"You got out of there okay?" She greeted Wendy.

Wendy bent at the waist, trying to slow her breathing. "Yeah, I'm back home."

"What the fuck was that about?"

"I don't know. I'm going to ask Hel tomorrow."

"You think that's the end of it?"

Wendy snorted, wrapping her arms across her chest. "Doubt it."

"I'm sorry-"

"Don't you dare apologize. This is that bigoted bitch's fault, not yours."

Neveah sighed, "You sure you're all right? It looked like you exploded back there. Your energy completely changed."

"I lost control for a sec. Anyone who was in my situation would go a little crazy."

"As long as you're sure."

"Yeah, I'm okay. I'm just going to take a bath and go to bed. I'll deal with everything else tomorrow."

Wendy heard Neveah shuffle on the other side of the phone, "That sounds like a good idea. The boys won't be back for another forty five or so, I also have time for a bath."

"Sounds good. Talk to you tomorrow?"

"Update me then, sleep well Wendy."

"Sleep well."

Silence. Post panic silence. Instead of giving it power, Wendy filled the silence with music. Happy, fast music that she knew every word to. A nice bath and some pizza pockets later, Wendy was calm enough to go to bed. For that one night, she let herself block out everything as she tried to hurry toward the refuge of her dreams, and giving herself one last peaceful rest before she dealt with her problems tomorrow.

Hel,

When I was little, I accidentally dated a gang member. Says something about my taste in guys, right? My home school mind didn't register the signs that he was trouble and said I would go on a date. He went to the youth group and we hung out one afternoon on a weekend and he considered it as proof we were dating. After that date, I didn't go to the youth group or really leave my house except to go to the Christian school that was a good twenty minutes away. I figured he would get disinterested and forget about me by then. After three weeks, him and his older brother came over to confront me and I had my dad open the door.

Needless to say, we never heard from them again.

Now, I don't know what I was thinking. That if I just went home after I punched a Valkyrie, that it would go away after a few days? That if I kept my head down for a certain amount of time that it would all blow over? Thinking about it now makes me realize how stupid that was. However, I didn't know everything back then. Gods, I didn't know shit back then.

It's times like these that I can't deny that I'm just a silly little mortal. Thank you for dealing with me.

Chapter Twenty One: Level Up

MEET ME IN THE THRONE ROOM, *RIGHT NOW*!

Wendy bolted up in bed, panting as a cold sweat dripped down her spine. She immediately started getting ready, throwing on a black sundress and her cloak. Not even stopping to eat breakfast. She just ran out the door. Entering the hall of doors and following her gut to Hel's domain. The doors seemed to flee as the large wooden door loomed in front her. She wasn't even close when the doors opened, making the weight in her stomach flip and dive into the dirt.

Wendy couldn't stop walking, fear actively turning her winded-crank as she walked past the spoils of history. It all served as yet another reminder of how out of place she was.

Instead of only a computer light and small candles to light the hall, there were torches. Large, rawring torches the size of Wendy.

In the massive hall leading up to the throne were the same robes Wendy wore. A total of seventeen priestesses stood around. They all let the disdain paint their faces as Wendy walked by. One even spat upon her as she walked past.

She must have royally fucked up.

Feeling as though it was what she ought to do, Wendy knelt in front of the throne. She stayed silent as she kept her eyes fixed to the floor and her concentration on the pulsing, hostile goddess in front of her.

"Are you just *STUPID*?"

Hel's words sounded genuine as she let her words hang in the air. After a moment, she continued. "Seriously, because I want to know *exactly* what a worm-infested cur thinks!" She paused allowing the piercing silence to emanate like sharpening blades in an echoing chamber. .

"Not only did you blindside one of the poodles of Odin and Freya, but you ran afterwards. That's the most coward horse-shit stunt I have seen in a *very long* fucking time! Did you even think of the friends you left behind? Did you care about the fight that took over the upper floor after you left?"

Wendy's breath left her from the harsh stab in her gut amidst the deafening silence. She forced herself to think back about whether she had abandoned her compatriots. No…she waved at them and they looked okay. Well, they looked more stunned. Everyone looked at her like she had just revealed she had a bomb.

"It took me Erecting an Impenetrable Shield of the Forsaken to get those fuckers to leave me alone. One that not even *MY GRANDFATHER* could get through! I moved my lands to the snowy mountains instead of under the roots of Yggdrasil to get those *fuckers* off my back! I also had to stand trial on the battlefield to get everyone off my back. Then here you are, fucking all of that up just as soon as you get here. Practically starting a war, and then you go to *where*?" She again paused to allow the silence to cut away like invisible stabs tormenting Wendy.

"You go to *bed*, not a care in the world! I just want to know what the fuck you were thinking. Huh!?"

An earthquake shattered the ground as a foot the size of an eighteen wheeler crashed next to her. Slowly, Wendy looked to her left… then above her.

Hel looked nothing like the Hel Wendy knew. Instead of a two-meter-tall woman with white hair and a long cloak, there was a monster instead. Dead, rotten skin hung off bones, filthy black, stringy hair that couldn't hide her burning eyes, and literal flames carrying purple in her pupils cut into Wendy, whilst dressed in full-armor. Wendy was suffocated by fear.

"*What the FUCK were you thinking!?*" Hel yelled down at her.

"I was scared."

It was over a mutter, but it sounded like a whisper. Once Wendy started talking, however, she couldn't stop herself.

"I remember thinking, 'oh my god, I want to kill someone.' I lost control and, if Will wasn't there, I was going to go for her throat. I was scared of how I giggled at the opportunity. Then I couldn't stop thinking of the last time. I though… 'I was probably going to try and eat her'…" Wendy trailed off. Taking another deep breath as she closed her eyes, "I thought of college. Of people that used to be my best friends who I will never see again, of people I wish I got closer with…Wondering if I'm ready for all this, if I'm actually good enough for all this-"

"Okay, okay. I see the spiral, so let's cut this off before you dive." Hel interjected, her form slowly shrank and morphed. "I get it. It is only your first week, so I get how it could have been a little much for you."

"What!"

Everyone turned to Randi. In the corner, she had already put her hand over her mouth at her own action.

"Have something to say?" Hel prompted.

Randi dropped her hand. "Pardon me, my Goddess, but why are you letting her off so easily? She tarnished your name with her actions, at an opening party no less."

Wendy stifled the flare of anger, though it was unusually difficult. Hel must have felt it because her attention snapped back to Wendy. Wendy averted her gaze, bowing low in what she hoped was perceived as apologetic.

When Hel let out her breath, Wendy looked back up, somewhat cowering as she watched as her now retransformed three-meter, half-zombie form, began lecturing.

"In the beginning there was life. All the life of the dimensions and galaxies existed in one being. The egg of the universe. Then it hatched. The egg became balls of essence exploding with the rupture of energy. Thus, the galaxies were made. Stars, so powerful as to sustain planets around them. As the mortal side of the veil changed and grew, so too did the immortal side of the veil. As the minds and the needs of the mortal world evolved, so too then did the Gods. They took on the form the worshipers wanted and gained power from belief. Long-forgetting the time when they couldn't think like the humans do, only a handful of the oldest gods have seen God in the sun. The essence of the sun allowed all of us to have life. It was foretold that her magik is fire that ripples like water. Pure balance and the one whom all gods return to in Nirvana."

Now back to her normal look, Hel flicked her hand out at Wendy, "Wendy, please let the side you're hiding out."

Wendy recoiled. "Wel-l I-"

"She is part of you, yet you put her in a cage where she *has to* over-react to break her shackles. Let her out Wendy. It's about time I met her."

Wendy sighed as she felt the heat spread in her torso. Infiltrated power sprouted as Wendy took up her chair. Giving her body over to all of her hate, her anger, and her bloodlust.

Her body straitened and stretched, then she put her arms in a stretch in front of her. She could see her aura. It was angrier than the collected ripples on the Holy Spirit 's, but she did see it on the aura that turned into distinct claws from her fingertips.

A chuckle formed from deep in Eabha's gut. "I'm surprised it took you so goddamn long to ask for me."

The priestesses took a collective step back at the transformation. A move Eabha basked in.

"I got hints of you, but I do say." Hel looked fascinated as she whistled at Eabha. "She must have you buried deep to keep you so well hidden. Go on, introduce yourself."

Eabha raised her eyebrow. "The backseat driver."

Hel put her hands on her hips and leaned forward. "You have no idea, do you? Where do you come from or what type of entity you are? Who made you?"

"I was given the title of Wendy's protector by the Holy Spirit . I'm the one who devoured the demon. Ripping him apart. Bite…by…bite."

One of the priestesses gagged, making Eabha grin wider.

Hel clicked her teeth. "You're completely useless, aren't yuh?"

Eabha snarled, crouching down as her anger flared. Hel only flicked her fingers and Hel forced Eabha back in her cage. Leaving Wendy to pick up herself from the floor.

Hel tilted her head, "Damn, that is actually worse than the lockdown on Fenrir. I must admit I'm a bit impressed."

Wendy took a second to look at the gawking faces before she turned back to Hel. She only waved her over as she turned and started walking away. Only Wendy followed as she followed Hel to the kitchen. Telling the relaxing Blue Heeler to follow, Hel led them all out the back door and through the snow. When the silence stretched to the outside of the town, Wendy couldn't take it anymore.

"I'm sorry. I'm so sorry."

Hel cast a confused look over her shoulder at Wendy. "Why?"

"I fucked up. I made a mess and ran. That was a shitty thing to do. I'm sorry."

"Oh," she looked back to where she was walking. "Show how sorry you are by your actions. Your words really do mean nothing to me."

Wendy's eyes began to sting as she focused on Fenrir's footprints in front of her. Letting out a breath of despair.

"On the other hand, I'm used to it. You have to remember I come from a God who gave birth to an eight-legged horse because he, 'wanted to fully enjoy the experience of motherhood'. After everything that he has pulled, your drama is a breath of fresh air. Plus, I guess I should have warned about the 'always fight back' rule of the Nordic realm. I thought you would have picked up on that because….Vikings, but you'll have to make up for it in the arena."

Wendy's eyes bulged as her head snapped up. Her body felt cold for the first time in the realm. "What?"

Hel walked up the last hump of the steep hike, stopping at the top and looking back at Wendy as she climbed. "Since you let the Valkyrie leave without much of a delay, Odin was the first to hear of your transformation. Because my grandfather is paranoid and war-crazy, he wants you under his wing. To train you in Asgard to fight on the last of days with his other warriors."

"Did you tell him I was working for you?" Wendy asked as she had to use her hands to climb up.

"Oh, I'll get my thousand years no matter what. Your mortality is the only thing on the line."

Wendy's footing slipped a bit, but she quickly recovered. "My mortality?"

"Yep! Half your time would be fetching souls for me, the rest would be spent at Asgard, learning to fight with the best of them. Immortality with no time to enjoy it. No more technology or friends. Plus, because you're not in the vail, your mortal form will deteriorate faster. Within months, you won't be able to go back. So, I suggested a fight for your freedom."

Wendy steadied her feet on the ridge. She bent over to catch her breath before looking back up at Hel. "I'm guessing I'm going to be the one fighting?"

The Goddess cringed back, "You're the one who outed yourself. Sure, I figured it would come up eventually. One, two hundred years before I had to deal with the 'mysterious energy' that would so obviously slip out on occasion." She lifted her palms and rolled her eyes. "But noooo, we had to do everything in the same mortal month. Like you're trying to make a name for yourself or something."

"I'm really not."

"Shush. Anywho, that's why we have a week to power you up."

Wendy sighed and stretched. Petting Fenrir as she did so. "So, will I be fighting that Valkyrie I punched. Brynhild was it?"

"You think a WARRIOR God would let a chance to fight someone who may have the power of the creator of gods go to some Valkyrie? No, he is going to fight for your freedom himself."

Her breath caught, making her choke on her saliva. "I'm what?"

Hel waved her off, "Don't worry, I'm not giving you up that easily. That's why we're going to Alfheim to make an alliance with the elves."

Wendy looked out off the cliff they stood on to the vast trapeze of branches. Each trunk suspended dizzily over kilometers of air. The twisting conglomeration intertwined with another branch of Yggdrasil. On the other side was a bulb of forests and mountains that rested in the tree's palm. It was beautiful, if it weren't clear that Hel wanted Wendy to cross to it.

Without her eyes leaving the drop, Wendy muttered. "Why the elves? Do they hate Odin?"

Hel followed Wendy's eyes. "Odin is the one who took Freya away from them. Freya never forgave him for that."

The sadness in her voice snapped Wendy from her fixation. Her eyes caught Hel as she began to walk across the limbs. Not wanting to be left behind, Fenrir and Wendy followed. It was daunting, thankfully Wendy's times hiking in the woods and off the beaten path gave her the balance to not fall. Almost dancing as she put one foot in front of the other. Wendy quickly got into a zone, allowing her to quickly follow Hel across the drop.

As Wendy stepped onto Alfheim soil, a wave of true serenity filled her. It was the same feeling that filled her every time she found a new trail. When she was surrounded by mountains and rivers with no other humans for kilometers. When she was alone, but surrounded by life. It was a feeling that warmed her smile.

"Thought you would like it here, but we can't go further until you dance." At Wendy's confused look, Hel only shrugged. "I don't make the rules. You have to earn their trust if you want their help."

Wendy let out a breath. "Do you have a drum or something or am I supposed to dance to the sound of the forest?"

The goddess smiled, pulling out a small rectangle from her pocket. "I have something better."

With a giggle, the two searched through the music player until Wendy found a flowing melody with drums that her hips could easily accentuate. Her arms artfully swayed as she spun and hopped. Flute picked up the pace, calling for leaps and kicks in the dance. It wasn't until the music lulled that Wendy noticed the audience.

They were all swirling with energy. It wasn't like the embers Wendy was used to, it was of the earth. Some held the energy of light, their aura smelling of flowers, grass, and trees. Some held darker energies, auras of fresh soil and stone. All of them were unsure but intrigued as if judging her performance, her sincerity?

Wendy closed her eyes again. She focused on her magik, the essence she was giving out. It was nervous, unsure. So she brought a different attitude into herself. Yellow-golden light. Delight of the dance, happiness of the day, and joy of meeting something in a culture as amazing as the elves. The closer they got, the easier it was to feel the shocks of energy as they scoped her out. She let herself dip into a meditation as her body was held captive by the dance.

A touch on Wendy's forearm shocked her out of her mind. She jumped back, flinching in surprise. She was smaller, dark-skin contrasted with her white hair. The flora energy in her aura harmonized with the sunlight in Wendy's own. The elf was holding out her hand, smiling as she jerked her head at the dancing crowd of elves behind her. Hand-in-hand, the elves made circles of dancing patterns as if they had been practicing for years. This one elf was inviting her to dance with them.

Wendy beamed, taking the beauty's hand and joined in the dance. Something you don't get with modern dancing is the community of the dance, she thought. Putting hands together as the group did to sway in harmony. The connection of everyone's energy playing with each other was an experience she would never forget.

It was an unseen signal, one that made the elves stop in their tracks. A halt that shook Wendy to comply and face him.

It was a giant of a man with brown and red dreadlocks in his beard and hair, his clothes made of twigs and leaves. If the elves were the flowers, this entity would be the bush that held them together. On the safe side, Wendy bowed.

A thunderous laugh rang across the clearing, "Oh, I do like this human you brought me. Humble, with a fae core."

"Do you like her enough to help her? She is fighting Odin for her freedom soon." Hel called from near the branches.

He looked behind Wendy towards the voice, "Oh? And what makes her so special?" After a moment, he looked back at Wendy with a curious expression. "A bit of an introduction then. I am Freyr, brother of Freya and King of the Alfheim realm."

Wendy bowed low again, "Pleasure to be in your presence. I am Wendy, Hel's newest reaper."

Freyr queried an eyebrow, "What does Odin want with a mortal reaper?"

"That's a bit why we are here." Hel called out. "Mind opening her up?"

A shock of panic rushed to her toes as she swiveled to look at the Goddess.

"No, no…it's nothing like that."

Wendy swiveled back to look at Freyr as he bent down to attempt to be at Wendy's height. "As an elder god of the realm, I can unravel locked energies better than Hel can. It may be a bit… abrasive. So I would like your permission before I begin."

Still a bit uneasy, Wendy gave a half smile. "If it will help me against fighting freaking Odin, bring it on."

Imagine the last time one was sick. The emptiness the body feels after expelling itself completely. The cold, the shuttering, and the grimy feeling. Imagine that feeling in your soul. Everything purged from the body on display for every entity to see. Wendy could see it too, but it only looked like a mesh of blobs to her.

Whatever Freyr saw made him study the blobs more closely. "Well this is a chaotic bundle, isn't it?"

"Well?" Hel prompted.

Stroking his beard, the god seemed to spread out the contents. A feeling that made Wendy shiver. "There seem to be four distinctly different energies in her. One is definitely of the fae, but not of this realm. It is woven tightly with the mortal soul that controls the body. Then there is the dark curse energy.-"

Wendy wasn't able to speak, but her entire body tensed. Seeing her reaction, Freyr straightened. "Oh! Don't worry mortal. The curse has been broken, if not recently. However, it is powerful. Probably a generational curse. Gaining power with every person who it has attached itself to."

"And the fourth energy is the creator's energy?" Hel inquired.

He nodded his head. "Most definitely. Holding the entire mess together. It is truly remarkable. Both the forest energy and the darker energy are powerful. I would say the power of a lesser god, just small enough to squeeze through the veil. That, combined with the creator's blessing, will put the mortal on fighting ground with the war mongrel."

Wendy gasped at the rush she got when Freyr returned all of her essences back into her body. The cold shutters made her kneel on the ground. Fenrir came over to her, licking her hand and comforting her with the touch of his fur.

Hel didn't seem to care. Clapping her hands together as she walked up to Freyr. "Good, so you will train her?"

The god smiled. It was as if all the beauty around him brightened at the simple gesture. If Wendy wasn't already recovering her breath, that smile would have taken it away. "One, she does a soul bonding to combine all of her fragments, Yes."

"Soul bonding?" Wendy panted out. "Like a marriage ritual?"

"I think you're thinking of a hand-fastening." Hel shrugged.

Freyr held up a finger, "No, those of true love have been known to do soul bondings before. However, the concept is still the same. Unity of one's self is the key to strengthening the soul. Once you are truly one, then I will be able to teach you to harness the entire being of yourself."

Wendy had just stood when Hel nudged her back into a bow. "She will have it done as soon as she is able. Then I will send her to you for training."

He gave that bright, warm smile as he began to walk back into the forest. "I hold my breath for your return."

With a few waves from the elves, they all followed him into the forest.

 Once they had all left, Hel patted Wendy's arm. "Hope those friends of yours don't hold anything against you for abandoning them. Spells like the one you'll need to pull off take some serious firepower."

Wendy sighed, "Yeah... can't go asking the priestesses, can I?"

"Don't hold it against them too much. You should have seen the fit they threw after I started letting non-clan-members into Helheim. Took them hundreds of years to get over it." The goddess snorted. "They still go haywire whenever I bring in new technology. It's kind of funny actually."

Wendy followed Hel and Fenrir as they headed back to the mess of branches. "So, they just hate me because I'm not Nordic?"

Hel shrugged, "Its bigoted and outdated, but they will get over it. They were raised to serve the clans. The only reason the Vikings survived for so long is their loyalty to the clans and their willingness to kill anyone who wasn't one of the clans. No matter if you win or lose, I have a feeling that they will warm up to you soon."

"Why?"

"Well," The goddess grunted and jumped to another branch. "If you become Odin's war dog, it means you are worthy enough for Asgard. Making you, technically, a member of the clan. If you end up winning this shindig somehow, they will have to respect you for your power and basically leave you alone."

Wendy let out a breath as she did her best to keep up with her. "So no chance of winning them over with my amazing personality?"

Hel just laughed as they made their way back to the snow-covered mountain top.

The bar was quiet compared to the night before. On the club level, only a dozen or so entities in small groups spread out across the floor.

Though eyes followed her movements, she didn't look back at them. Her eyes were locked on the concerned smile Sai cast her from behind the bar.

He gave a small bow of his head, "I'm glad to see you're safe."

Wendy rubbed the back of her neck as she leaned the other against the counter, "Was it bad after I left?"

"It was eventful." Sai sighed. "However, it was expected that a fight would break out anyway, so it was dealt with efficiently."

Wendy let out a breath, "That's good."

He smiled, "Plus, it has been great for business. Everyone is sharing the story of how the Nirvana's power was found in a mortal fox who got away after punching a warrior of Odin."

She groaned, let her head bend and shoulders drop with the action.

Sai pointed up the stairs, "Go tell your brother that you're okay. He's been worried all night."

"I'm going, I'm going. Thanks for everything Sai."

Taking a moment to look around at the evading eyes watching her, Wendy climbed the stairs. As she entered the bar floor, it seemed that the entire room quieted. The patrons, taking notice of her presence, while the staff…

"Wendy! Oh, my gods!" Lilly rushed around the bar and pounced on Wendy. Rapping her arms around the mortal and squeezed all the air out. Realizing this, she took a step back. Eyes fretting over Wendy. "You aright darlin'? When that fight broke out, someone said you made it out but-"

"Whoa!" Wendy held up her palms out in front of her. "How bad did it get?"

The succubus bit her lip in a way that was so natural that it took everyone's focus. "Sweetums, Gods don't fight like dem mortals you're used to. There was several decapitations and disembodied piles cleaned up at the end of the night." She suddenly looked around. Not liking what she saw, she pulled Wendy to the back room behind the bar. When safe, Lilly leaned back on a barrel and smiled. "Once the word got downstairs that a redhead mortal had shown a blessing of power from Nirvana, it went crazy. Supposedly you made quite an impression with your dance earlier. Good job on that by the way."

A shock through her body left a burning in Wendy's cheeks. "Was anyone on staff hurt? Is Will okay?"

Lilly flicked her hand down. "Oh, Yah. Sai was on top of things. Your running away gave a good cover for your friends to defend themselves so they turned out fine... in fact... everyone who got beheaded... they'll be up and walken around today..." She took a movement to close her eyes and breathe deeply. "Everyone was worried that you died. Then we heard the announcement and we've all been worried sick."

Wendy froze, "What ... announcement?"

The blond hair draped over her pectorals mJackor as she cocked her head. "You fighten Odin, of course. What other announcement did-ja think I meant?"

Wendy's eyes bulged as she released her breath. "Everyone knows?"

"Hun, it's going to be broadcast live. Well...not like mortal world technology...but everyone in every realm is going to see how it turns out."

"Other realms are going to send a representative?"

Lilly shrugged, "A bit more complicated than that. but yeah."

Wendy stepped so she could lean against her own large container of liquor. "So...I'm fighting Odin because this is all a big political stunt? He wants to show off to the other realms?"

The succubus rolled her eyes, "You better wrap your head around how big this situation is, sugar. You are proof the old ones aren't lying. You are proof the stories of the old ones are true. Some are even predicting it's a sign of the end times."

Wendy blinked, "Huh?"

"Yes, it's that big of a deal. When the war was happening, lots of the oldest of us called out to the one they remembered. The one they considered to be their mother. When Lucifer had used the catholic church to destroy all other beliefs in the mortal world... well, most of us stopped believing in her..." Lilly leveled her eyes in a way that showed how serious all of this was. "Whoever controls you, controls the creator's blessing. Meaning that you just became a kind of celebrity on this side of the veil. So... that's fun, right?"

After Wendy's mouth hit the floor, she let out all the curse words that she had heard her father and his biker friends use when they were working on their project vehicles, and every insult she ever read from the internet. She only stopped after Will entered and reminded her that everyone could hear her.

Once she calmed down, she got down to what she came there for. "Do you guys know how I can get ahold of the people I was with at the opening? I need their help and I need to apologize."

"Oh, I forgot." Will reached in his deep pocket and pulled out a small black mirror the size of a makeup mirror. "I was told to give you. I figured you knew what it was."

Wendy smiled, "A scrying mirror! This is exactly what I need."

"Good. With that settled, I better get out there." Lilly brushed her hand on Wendy's arm. "We're rooting for you."

Wendy smiled in response then moved her eyes to Will, "You okay?"

Will snapped like a preppy highschooler, his hip sticking out and everything, "Girl, You know I can take care of myself."

She rolled her eyes, "I know, but I heard the fight was pretty bad. You weren't hurt, were you?"

"Oh, I'm fine. Just a finger and a half lighter." He held up his other hand and, sure enough, his pointer finger and a bit of his middle finger was missing.

Wendy jumped up and immediately examined the wound. She ran her hands over the skin over the nubs of the fingers. "These are healed…"

"Yeah, it was my bad too. My grip on the sword was shitty-"

"No, idiot! It looks like it happened years ago, not just last night. It should still be bleeding."

"If I were alive maybe." Will shrugged. "But since I'm not alive, it should grow back in a few days. That bitch of a horse cracked my ribs on the second day here, and those took a day and half to heal."

Wendy looked back at his hand, lost in thought. "Wow."

"Right, so you should be careful because I don't think your limbs will grow back if you get hurt." he said, taking back his hand.

A bit dazed, she nodded. "I'll do my best."

Will ruffled her hair with a smile, "I know you will. Go tell your friends that you're okay."

Then he was gone, back out to his waiting customers. Wendy took a moment to absorb the newest information, and let it sink in how drastically things had changed in one night. However, she couldn't change the circumstances. With that fact in the forefront of her mind, she cleared her mind and began to scry into the mirror.

She took long deep breaths, her eyes lost in the dark background as she entered the meditative state. She felt the energy inside her body activate as she directed it to her third eye. Through her third eye, she pictured Makao. His energy, his face, and his voice filled her thoughts as she tried to connect to him through the mirror. She felt a click as her energy connected to Makao. When this happened, she sent mental images of the library room in the valley of knowledge. A mental image of all of them meeting around the wooden table. After she sent the message, she felt the connection break. She was a bit unsure if he got it, but there was one way to find out. She went to the back door and headed to the library.

***

She was beginning to think that the mirror didn't work. She hadn't been waiting long, but the wait was killing her. A book sat in front of

Wendy but her eyes didn't read the words. Her leg bounced as all of her focus was locked on the wooden door. The air seemed too dry in the buried library room, and the high ceiling windows the only source of light. Lastly, her mind wouldn't stop running in circles.

What would she do if they refused to help? Honestly, she hadn't known any of them for long and she left them after starting a bar fight. It was a possibility that Wendy would have to find other people to help her. Neveah would definitely help and she could possibly ask Gus, but they didn't have the experience Makao and the others had.

Then there was the distinct possibility Wendy's scrying skills sucked.

The hinges squeaked as the door opened. Wendy's eyes shot up to meet with Chayya's surprised dark eyes. There was a moment of silence as the girls registered the other. However, the silence was too much for Wendy.

"I'm so sorry for running off."

Chayya blinked, "What?"

Wendy studied the ground, "I just ran. I was scared and I ran. It was a coward's thing to do and I'm sorry."

Another moment of silence held its breath before Chayya dispelled it with laughter. Light, uncontrollable laughter having her doubled-over the books in her hands. The sudden release of the tension made the sound contagious.

Waving her hand, Chayya took in a breath as she tried to speak through the giggles. "That's what you're worried about? Out of everything that happened, that is the first thing you say. What were you thinking anyway?"

"I wasn't." Wendy admitted. "When the Valkyrie put her hand around your neck, I snapped. That never happened to me before."

The black-haired beauty immediately stopped laughing. Her expression was replaced with confused shock. "Wait, you legitimately didn't know about Nirvana's gift?"

"Sort of." she shrugged. "I wasn't really sure if it was real I guess."

Chayya walked over and set her books down to grasp Wendy's pale fingers within her own. "Thank you."

Again, Wendy shrugged. "For losing control?"

"For protecting me." She leaned back. "Only my brother and the rats have ever stood up for me. It made me happy that you reacted so fast."

Wendy leaned back in her own chair and huffed. "Oh please. Will would trip all over himself to protect a goth hottie like yourself."

Her eyebrows knitted, "goth?"

"Duh, of course you wouldn't know that word. It's a bit complicated, but it's someone who wears lots of black."

She glanced down at herself, "I wear black to represent the black rats of the Karni Mata Temple that gave my brother and I refuge from the mortal world."

"Rats? Like actual rats?"

She grinned, "That's a story for another day. What I am trying to say is that I am grateful, and you did absolutely nothing wrong."

"Well, it definitely wasn't expected." The two girls turned towards the door to see Lee, Venchi and Makao walking through it. They all put their books down while Venchi continued. "We probably should have known, what with the way you were able to manipulate the veil, but none of us expected you had the blessing of Nirvana up your sleeve."

Wendy held up her palms, "I was just as surprised as you were."

Lee put their hands on their hips, his nails still manicured even if he had removed the makeup. "Are you saying you did not know you held Nirvana's Power?"

Wendy shied away a bit, "I mean…yes and no. I didn't know it was a big deal so I never mentioned it."

Makao groaned, "Please tell me you have a plan of defeating Odin. Maybe another mystery power or something?"

She perked up, "Actually, Hel found me a trainer and as soon as we mend my chaotic soul, he'll train me."

"Mend?" Lee asked.

"Like soul bonding? Not the marriage type but like solidifying the energies…inside me."

Makao sliced through the air in front of him. "You have to know how that sounded."

Wendy slapped the outstretched hand. "Anywho, long story short, for some unknown reason my soul is in four pieces and I have to be whole in order for Freyr to train me to fight Odin, because that is my life right now, and I came to you guys to ask for help. I know I have put you guys through a lot, but please help me."

Chayya held up her hands, "Why do you think we are all here?"

Lee shot a look to Chayya before turning to Wendy. "We met here as soon as we heard the announcement. We have been looking for a way to assist you without you... becoming a permanent resident of this side of the vail."

"Or ethical." Venchi spit. "Some of these rituals from the darker times make me sick to even read."

Wendy let out a breath. "Thank you. All of you have helped me out so much and know that I'll repay you-"

Chayya snorted, "We're not only helping you. These are the types of things this side of the veil thrives on."

"It definitely has been a bit dull the last hundred years or so." Lee sighed.

"Plus, you can't put a price on the chance to see a fight like the one you're getting into." Makao chuckled. "How many times per existence do you get the chance to see someone like Odin fight? I can't wait to see how the ruler of the Nordic realm will fight you."

Wendy fake swooned. "Aww, guys. I'm so touched."

Venchi walked over and patted Wendy on the shoulder. "If it is a soul mending you need, A soul mending you shall have. You, however, need to find more people." He smiled, "Call Neveah and any other friends you have. We'll all meet at your residence because it is so close to the veil. That will be a good spot to do the ritual. Leave the research to us and Makao will take us to you when we have it planned out. "

Looking each one in the eye, Wendy thanked them before turning and leaving to find Gus. rushing down the dark hallway of doors. With the memory of his man-cave in the forefront of her mind, she was able to find his door within a few meters. Her pulse pounded in her ears as she waited, hoping he was home.

Nervous, she knocked again. This time receiving an answer.

"Let me put some pants on."

Wendy sighed in relief, now able to hear his footsteps as he approached. The first glance of his face looked groggy until his eyes registered it was Wendy. His eyes bulged, "Wendy! What happened last night?"

Wendy sighed, "You saw what happened?"

"No, just the part where the scariest woman I've ever met was throwing axes at you while you ran away with a monster of a snake." He moved to guide her inside. "Then I hear that you threw the first punch."

Wendy walked into the room with a grone. "She put her hands on a friend, then I snapped, then everything spun out of control."

"It's not that big of a deal." He tried to sooth, "I mean, they are Vikings. Fighting is what they do right?"

"But I'm not a Viking. Now I have to fight their leader and-"

"Whoa, their leader? What do you mean?"

Wendy sighed, making her way over to the couch and plopping herself down on the cushions. "I guess I have power belonging to the god of gods." She tossed up her hands, "Because somehow that's a thing. Now I have to beat Odin in combat or I lose my entire afterlife to training in Asgard."

"Hold on," Gus walked over and sat next to her. "Odin? You have to fight Odin? Shouldn't Hel fight him, she owns your contract, right?"

Wendy let out a dramatic sigh, "I think she is mad at me for making so much trouble for her. She was assured that she would get her thousand years of service, no matter what, so she doesn't have a reason to fight. Plus, I think it's also a political move. If Odin conquers the power of Nirvana, then he'll have more sway over the other realms, or something like that."

He put his elbows on his knees, leaning forward as he let out a breath. "So what's the next step? Do you have a plan?"

"Well, my senpais are researching a spell right now to," she held up her fingers to resemble quotation marks, "'mend my fractured soul'. After you agree to help me I probably should go to the bar to recruit Will and the others. Then we are all meeting at my house since it is close to the veil."

"Hold on," Gus looked over, casting an amused grin. "Who said I would help you? You haven't even asked."

Wendy smiled back, "Come on? We're friends, aren't we? Friends help friends when they are about to get their ass kicked, right?"

He chuckled, "You're right, but I'm adding another drink to the tab you're racking up."

With a heave, Wendy slunk to her feet. Turning to him with her hand outstretched. "For this, I'll get you your own bottle of the best mead you'll ever have."

His eyes sparkled. He stood, grabbing her hand only to pull her into his arms. With a squeak at the moment, she looked up into his stunning smile. "Deal, as long as you drink it with me."

Wendy felt her cheeks tingle as they warmed, her heart skipping a beat at the obvious invitation. Though her mind took the opportunity to slip out the back door, her mouth tried to work but only stammering tripped out. Her betraying body couldn't help but push into his warm chest.

Seeing her difficulty, Gus let her go as he let out a laugh. Throwing over his shoulder as he went to the other room, "Don't worry. It won't be until after all this has blown over."

Wendy watched him go, stunned. When her brain went back to its post she yelled, "You're a jerk!"

"I know!"

***

Gus tagged along to go to Will's bar. Sai stayed behind to watch the bar so Lilly and Will could go to Wendy's place. Her apartment wasn't dirty, however there was some clutter and dishes that needed to be picked up. While Wendy was doing that, Will and Gus caught up. Turns out that they had a few classes together in high school and were excited that they had a kindred spirit on this side of the veil. Once everything was cleaned up, the small amount of furniture was pushed to the walls. Leaving the living room open for the ritual. Wendy called Neveah over, convincing her to Astral project even if she couldn't help. Soon after, Lee, Venchi, Makao, and Chayya showed up and began setting up the ritual space.

The living room was carpet, meaning that Wendy's plain comforter was sacrificed to serve as the drawing mat. Using an ink infused with dragon's blood, vervain, acacia, barberry, and eucalyptus; Venchi began drawing a complex sigil. The border had symbols that wrapped around the circle. Inside the border, seven triangles pointed outward with seven longer triangles pointed inward. In the middle was a circle with more symbols Wendy recognized as planetary sigils. Once completed, stones such as angelite and black salt were set to surround the mat to close it in. A home mix of incense filled the room with a haze of magikal power as everyone took their positions. Wendy was designated to lay in the middle of the mat while everyone surrounded her. With everyone in place, the ritual started.

Chayya led the grounding meditation, allowing Wendy to focus on entering the deep cavern into her mind. She seemed to hop down the mental staircase, entering the same small room where she met Eabha before.

Just like before, Eabha was waiting for her. A smug smile on her face. "You sure about this? Fusing with me?"

Wendy shrugged, "As sure as I'll ever be."

"You do realize what this means if we do this? You won't be able to hide me any more, I won't be able to be locked away any more."

"I know."

Eabha stepped closer, "You have to know that you won't be the same. My energy will change you from the goody-two-shoes you try your best to be into something else. Are you prepared for that?"

Wendy took a deep breath, "Yes, I know."

The mirror image raised an eyebrow, "Aren't you scared?"

"Yes." she replied instantly. "I'm frightened. Your savage brutality scares me. The lust you have for violence scares me to my bones. Scares me so much that I unintentionally locked you up, but now is not the time for fear. I don't want to give up this adventure and you don't want to be controlled. Working together is the only chance we have of defeating him or anything else that tries to go after us. That is why I'm doing this. What about you?"

She blinked, "What?"

"Are you ready?"

A toothy grin ripped across her face, "Oh, little Wendy, I've been ready to get out of here for years."

The two clasped hands, making the world turn blank. It was not white as if going to the light at the end of a tunnel, nor was it dark like the moments before sleep. It was almost as if it had been in Florida.

Auras of color radiated around her. Though her eyes were closed, she could feel every person that was surrounding her just based on their aura. What captured her attention though, was the light protruding from her own body. Dark and light swirls surrounded the flowing ember that Wendy was now so used to. As the others put more energy into compressing all of her energies together, the faster the ribbons moved. Up until the flames consumed them all.

Hel,

I passed out after that. Of course everyone was worried and forced me to take a break. Gus brought me food from the mortal world and the whole thing evolved into a bit of a party. A hangout with friends before I left to train with Freyr. I think some of them believed that this would be the last time they would see me. I was going up against Odin afterall, it wasn't a leap to think I would lose (even though I technically did). It was nice though. To look around the room and see everyone who supported me in this new life. It gave me the strength I needed to face the next day.

What about you, Hel? Of course you have your priestesses, Bauldur, Nana, and the people of Helheim, but do you realize that? I know you have a habit of focusing on who is against you, such as your family. When was the last time you focused on those who support you? Appreciate you? Just something to think about.

Chapter Twenty Two: Training Montage

Fenrir was the only one to go with Wendy to Alfheim. Wendy tried to get ahold of Hel, but she kept running into the priestesses. Some were nicer, some avoided their eyes, and some were just plane mean. Though, they were always mean, so it wasn't much of a change from before. Even though they knew she wasn't just another human now.

Wendy decided not to think about it. Instead, she took the same path that Hel showed her. Made her way across the branches as she followed the dog's little leaps across. Once on Alfheim soil, she realized there were elves already waiting for her. Without a word, they led her into the forest.

Any description of this forest would never do it justice. Each tree had its own life force, and its own aura. Each animal, flower, and blade of grass sung in harmonious pitch with those around it. The animals and elves respected the home they were given, dancing on the balls of their feet to dodge the delicate foliage in their path. The forest was different than the forest she was used to, she reflected. There was more moss and more wildlife in general. Wendy felt light, excited to be surrounded in such a magikal place.

The elves lead her to a dirt clearing, the soft soil surrounded by trees and brush that the onlookers clearly hid behind. In the middle of the circle was Freyr petting a giant golden boar. This boar was almost as tall as her, as its back reached the god's waist. Once she entered the circle, Freyr turned to her with the heart-stopping smile all gods seemed to have.

Giving the golden boar one last pat, he walked to meet her and Fenrir. "I can already see the difference. Your aura isn't as blindly chaotic as it once was."

Wendy scratched her scalp, "You can tell? Because, I've got to tell you I don't feel any different."

"Trust me, young mortal, it will make all the difference." Patting her on the back, he started leading her to the middle of the circle. "Now, we have to start at the foundation. Please, take a seat."

Doing what she was ordered, she sat criss-cross in the dirt. It was soft soil, like right out of a flowerbed bag. She mindlessly dug her hands through it as she listened to Freyr speak.

"Now, Odin hasn't fought in the open in years. Some said he was saving his energy for Ragnarok but that's obviously not true. Though, you shouldn't think of him as rusty or frail. After all, he has the power of an entire realm at his disposal; but I don't think he will call upon it. It may be an unfair fight, but he will want an honorable fight. I highly doubt that he will even use a weapon, though doesn't mean he'll be unarmed. He hung himself on the world tree in order to know the power of the runic spells and plucked out his own eye to drink from the waters of wisdom. Even his voice is said to make those do his will. He will be using any charm in his arsenal to get you to surrender."

Wendy's shoulders slumped. "Even his voice is charmed?"

"That's not the worst; he also has teleportation, and telekinesis on his side, along with his shapeshifting."

"Shapeshifting?"

Freyr held out a palm, "Though the favor lies with him, I promise to give you a fighting chance. Now," he held out his hand, his earth energy surging up his arm to make a flower physically float in his hand. "Gods who are connected to their realms may draw power from them. Of course, that energy comes easier to those who have worshipers, making Odin the most connected to this realm's power. His only rivals would be Thor and Loki, though Thor would never make a move on his father and Loki has a portion of himself locked up with acid forever dipping on him."

Wendy raised her hand. With a confused smirk, Freyr gestured to her. "Where does Hel fit?"

"Ah, Hel is a rather special case." He flicked the flower into the air, spinning and falling as a real flower would. "She has access to her own underworld she has been syphoning from ever since she was given the role. She did this secretly until Baldur and Nanna were killed. When they entered her realm, she made an alliance with me and moved Helheim closer to my realm. Our alliance was enough to make those in Asgard abandon their pursuit."

"So she was able to make a shield that Odin couldn't get through because she had her own magik pool?"

The god smiled, "Her father's trickery didn't skip a generation. Combined with her mother's wit, she became a force in the Nordic realm. Thankfully, she is a recluse and has no interest in competing with her grandfather. Instead, she fixates on the progress of the mortal world. However, I am getting off topic." He crushed the flower in his hand, opening his palm to reveal a decorated knife. "You possess a connection to Nirvana. The maker of the realms and the true entity of the sun. This means that you may be able to connect to the unclaimed energy of Nirvana and harness it as the gods do."

Wendy's eyes bugged as she pointed to the knife. "You're saying, I can do that."

He laughed, "You can do much more than that, mere mortal. Through the visualization of your mind, you should be able to mold your energy into whatever you need it to be." the knife changed into a bird, flying away as it added its song to the forest. "Though, we have to start with the basics, manipulating mana." He sat down across from her. He was only wearing a cloth skirt making Wendy's eyes fix on his face as he did so. "Hold out your palm and concentrate your energy there."

With an inner smirk, Wendy closed her eyes. She began breathing in her four count rhythm, connecting to the flame resting in her inner self. As she connected, she realized that it did feel different. She couldn't exactly tell what the differences were, but the flames felt more solid. Instead of a candle, it felt like a hearth-fire that couldn't be easily blown out. This made it easy to connect to, sending the connection through her root chakra into an earth that pulsed with magik. Once connected, she mentally went through the rest of her chakras. Each one bursting with energy as soon as she focused on it. Then she connected to the sky, to Nirvana. It was not like anything she had ever felt. It was as if it was crowded.

Too crowded.

Thousands of tones connected with her, snapping the rubber band on her momentum. Internal fail-safes immediately severed the connection. Her hands clutched her head to keep the splitting pieces together. Her nerves vibrated as the adrenaline pumped her heart at record speed. Her deep breaths didn't contain wheezes but still labored as if she climbed a mountain.

"Mortal!"

The voice was muffled, but she knew it to be Freyr's. She could sense that she was laying down on the ground, her side making contact with the cool soil. It was the timid, wet licks from Fenrir that grounded her. The dog's concerned response snapped her back into reality. She opened her eyes slowly. The light was a harsh adjustment that she had to ease into.

She sat with one hand still cradling her skull, "What happened?"

Freyr gave her back the space she lost when she collapsed, "I ask you the same thing, what did you tap into?"

"I-I don't know. I did everything I normally do, but when I connected to spirit… I didn't think of the Holy Spirit … I thought of Nirvana…guess that wasn't the right answer."

He took a moment to blink before letting out a boisterous bark of laughter, "I like your enthusiasm, mortal. You definitely reach for the stars, but I wouldn't suggest connecting to Nirvana. At least not until you are fully in this realm. Even then, you may want to approach it with caution."

Not having the mental capacity to continue the compensation, she gave a thumb up as she moved back into her criss-cross position. Seeing her pain Freyr sighed, "Change of plans, we will teach you how to shield first. Making it with sound is the least difficult so we will do that. The goal is to make a sphere with kinetic energy to protect us from the energy we don't want to let in." Closing her eyes to check that her connection to the earth was still intact, she nodded. Seeing this, he took a deep breath. "Start by activating the center. While focusing on your own energy, hum out the English letter M." Closing her lips, Wendy hummed the frequency. As it went on, she could feel the flame inside her dance. The ripples bouncing like raindrops. After a moment he continued.

"Now to make the dome. On the exhale, puff out on a high note." He demonstrated with a puff like air being released from a ball. Wendy copied until she could feel the umbrella of light above her.

"Now below." Freyr mimicked the buzzing of a bumble bee. As Wendy's nasal passages vibrated, Wendy could feel the space underneath her fill with motion, and all of the hairs on her legs were drawn to the almost electric current.

"To the east." He began to extend the letter E with his entire breath.

"To the west." He circled his lips to lengthen his Oh's.

"And, to the south." He used his entire breath to speak the letter I.

"Lastly, the north." He let out a calm sigh, like he said 'Ah'.

"Open your eyes"

At his request, she did. All around her was a slightly permeable shield of power. She couldn't describe the look of the energy as it popped with flame as it also flowed like water. If she concentrated, she could make certain parts thicker and swirl the energy with her mind. When comfortable, she thought only of the Holy Spirit . The calmer light flowed into Wendy, soothing her mind a bit as it entered her sacred space. When she was ready, Wendy outstretched her palm and directed the flow of energy up her shoulder and down her arm. She imagined pink cherry-blossom blooms and, just as Freyr's flower did, the rippling embers emerged into her palm as a soft, small blossom.

Wendy looked up at the god with a huge grin on her face as she breathed. "I did it." her eyes watered in victory. "I see it."

He nodded, a grin expanding his own face. "Finally, draw it into yourself. Shrink it to surround your heart to be brought out when needed."

Wendy closed her eyes again, bringing the sphere in and encasing her light in it. When done, she opened her eyes again. "That was awesome!"

Freyr's smile deepened, "Seems like you're ready for combat training."

"What?"

***

Combat training it was, throwing her into the deep-end with a barrage of psychic attacks. They ranged from feelings of depression and anger to images taken right out of a horror movie. As soon as she got used to protecting from one type, he would switch with another. The mental strain Wendy experienced in nursing school couldn't hold a candle to the exhaustion Wendy felt after these exercises. When it got too much from her, the magik of the elves put her to sleep. Then they would wake her a few hours later to do the exercise over again until Wendy could seamlessly transition between attacks. It was strenuously relentless.

***

At night, Wendy went over breathing techniques. Her meditations focused on the movement of magik through her body, getting used to moving the power from one limb to another to the shield that surrounded her, and concentrating on the warm-shock sensation she felt as it followed her commands. Though she ended up falling in and out of sleep as she meditated, she could see demonstrable progress during her sparring sessions.

***

When she could defend a good number of Freyr's attacks, they started offensive training.

"Just as you made the flower, bring your energy to where you need it in the body. Forming it into what you need,"

Wendy closed her eyes as she directed energy to her fingertips. Opening her eyes, she could see the transformation into claws. The firing energy extended to make the knives cover her digits. Out of curiosity, she recondensed the energy in her palm and created a kunai. She tossed it up in the air, and was surprised when it separated from her. When it was back in her hand, she lengthened it to the size of a thin, short sword.

She lightly gripped it in her hand, and muttered under her breath.

"Fuck, I'm a magikal Green Lantern."

Freyr's eyebrows furrowed. "What?"

Wendy waved it off, "Never mind, but *how* is this going to work? Do I get a target or a dummy to practice?"

"The best way to practice is to actually do it."

"What?"

Wendy was blindsided with an impact in her stomach that sent her flying across the valley. Barely giving her any time to recover, Wendy had to roll to dodge the next fist coming at her. And thus started her hand-to-hand combat training.

Because of her years as a catcher on her childhood softball team, her legs were able to hold her close to the ground. Though her glutes and adductor magnus screamed at her, she was able to dodge the taller god's attacks. By redirecting her magik flow to her legs, she learned that she could jump as if she was on a trampoline. Able to bounce around and do flips with half the effort it would have taken on Earth. Seeing this, Freyr suggested that she fight the golden boar.

If one had never seen a boar in person, just know they are scary as hell. They're quick, with horns as big and long as an arm and sharpened at the tip. Red gashes indicated the times where Wendy wasn't quick enough. Additionally, it was partnered with a snarl that sent shivers down to her toes. Wendy did try to fight back. She mainly used claws and spikes of magikal energy. Incorporating any battle tactics she had seen from years of watching drawn and programmed characters fight. By the end of the week, he didn't have to hold back much with her. Though they both knew it would likely take a miracle for her to win.

"Why are you fighting so hard, little mortal?" Freyr asked as he sat across from her. The fire lit the forest night. "Many have faced armies to fight by Odin's side. Yet I have never seen anyone push themselves so hard to reject his offer. Why?"

Wendy opened her eyes. Finding a small ball of light resting near her nose. They looked like lightning bugs, but were actually small fay creatures. If it weren't for their playful movements, they would look like stars that lit up the night sky. A sky unhindered by the atmosphere of the mortal world.

Wendy smiled at the little creature, poking it and giggling as it scampered away. "I don't want to be a fighter."

"Oh? But you catch on quickly. It wouldn't take more than a few hundred years for you to be feared on the battleground of Asgard."

Wendy let out a breath, letting her shoulders slump. "Honestly, that's it. I don't want to fight. I would be lying if I said I hate fighting, there is a part of me that loves it…a bit too much for my comfort, but I don't want it to be my life. There is so much that I don't know, so much that I want to find out, and so many mysteries I haven't solved yet." She looked at him with a strained smile. "Imagine getting your wildest dream. Something you never thought possible given to you like a gift. Then to have one stupid mistake take all of it away. That is why I'm fighting so hard."

A small smirk played on Freyr's lips. "Not the answer I expected. Most fight their hardest for someone they love."

Wendy shrugged, leaning back on her arms planted behind her. "I'm doing that too. I don't want my dad to worry about me. To him, I would have disappeared. Neveah knows and I bet that she would find a way to visit me. My dad would never have a clue…"

Wendy trailed off, her stomach turned at the despairing thought. He has no one left. Without Wendy...

"No reason to dwell on the consequences of what has yet to come. The important thing is that you have considered them." He chuckled. "You are definitely an unexpected one, little mortal."

She chuckled back. "Just tell me straight, How much of a chance do you think I have?"

He shrugged, "Like I have said, you have a talent for providing the unexpected. I just hope that your talent can fool the wisest in the realm."

The night tapered into silence. Both of them lost in their own thoughts. Wendy realized when she slept, she didn't dream. The entire time she was in Alfheim, sleep seemed to be only a dark place of rest. She was so preoccupied, she had barely noticed. When she did, the thought cascaded. Her outlandish fantasies had been her escape for so long that the absence of it worried her. What else would she lose if she became stuck here? How much of herself would she lose? She chanted to herself that everyone changes, but that didn't replace the loss. It didn't stop the fear.

"Hey. Wake up. Waaakkeee uuppp." Wendy woke up to hands jostling her back and forth. She opened her eyes to see the white-haired goddess above her. When they made eye contact, the goddess grinned. "Good morning, little human. Today is the day!"

Wendy groaned, rolling back over away from her. "Five more minutes."

Hel let out a huff. "Rude! I apologize for the mortal. Hopefully she wasn't like this the entire time."

Freyr laughed. "No, just right before she gets up. She kept asking for a drink of energy, but not the tea of the elves."

"It tasted like dirt and sadness," Wendy muttered from her place on the ground. However, she did start to stir.

Hel faced her, hands firmly placed on her hips. "The more time you waste getting up, the less time you have to get ready. I hate to say, but we are in a bit of a time crunch. We've still got to get you dressed and shit."

With a groan that encompassed all of the aches and pains throughout her body, Wendy stirred. "Is it really that time already?"

The goddess rolled her eyes, "Really, not a morning person, are you?"

"No, working the night-shift killed my love for the mornings." Wendy yawned, taking her time to stand up. "I guess I'm as ready as I'll ever be though."

"You are glowing with confidence." She motioned her hands in the direction of Helheim. "Let's move out."

"Just a second." Wendy groggily walked up to Freyr and hugged him. "Win or lose. Thank you for teaching me."

Wendy felt his hand pat her back, "Of course, little Wendy. Keep your focus at all times."

"I will." Wendy released him and turned to the giant golden boar. Giving him a pet on his head. "Thank you, too." It snorted, nudging back at her hand in response. Wendy giggled before waving at all the elves in the surrounding forest. "Thank you all. I promise I'll come back to dance again soon."

The elves cheered, the forest erupting in song as their response. Wendy nodded, turning back to Hel. The goddess just stared, her eyes darting from Freyr to the forest back to Wendy. After a moment she shrugged and started walking.

"Fenrir said that you were doing well; all things considered."

Wendy sighed, keeping her eyes on her footing as they traveled across the branches. "All I can do is my best. Not really sure how my best will stack up, but I'll at least make a spectacle out of it."

"That's pretty much all you can do." the goddess shrugged, "I've done everything I can on my end. Enchanted your armor, talked to Freya so she could talk to Odin, got your name out there as much as I could. If anything, everyone at the bar is rooting for you."

Wendy let the confusion hide her embarrassment. "So they don't boo me as soon as I walk out there?"

"That and if enough of the bigger gods sympathize with you, they might do something stupid to help you. Everyone will be watching me and my father, Loki, to make sure we don't help you cheat. If someone else helps you, it might be the distraction you need to win." She slowed just enough to put her hand on Wendy's shoulder. "However, I wouldn't count on it."

Wendy's shoulders deflated, but she smiled at Hel. "Thank you. Thank you so much for everything."

Hel rolled her eyes, giving Wendy a healthy pat on the back. "Enough of the dramatics. Just do your best and try not to give me this much trouble in the future. Do that and we will call it even."

The pair started making their way down the mountain. The sounds of their steps in the snow needed to fill the quiet forest. Wendy enjoyed the distracting serenity up until the wooden-structures came into sight. Then the unmistakable figure waiting for them made Wendy throw up all of her guards.

"Randi! Good, take Wendy to get ready. We'll meet in the throne room when everyone is good to go."

Randi bowed, "Yes, my goddess." With a sideways glance at Wendy, she began following.

Resigned to her fate, Wendy stalked behind as she was led silently through the main street to Hel's fortress. Wendy stood tall even though she hadn't showered in almost a week, her only bathing coming from a stream in the forest. There were rips on her baggy shirt and running tights from the golden boar, her body bruised, and her half-ponytail in a rat's nest in her hair. She didn't mind before, but now that she was around people she couldn't help but wish Randi would walk faster.

They walked through Hel's kitchen door, going through the open doorway and into a maze of doors behind the throne room. Seemingly at random, Randi stopped and held the heavy wooden door open for Wendy. Without making eye contact, Wendy entered and quickly scanned the room.

It was small, made from wood and boulders as most of the fortress was. A wooden table-set sat neatly in the corner with a pile of clothes on it. The room lacked a bed but made up for it with a large wooden basin containing steaming water. It wasn't a shower, but Wendy was still giddy to see it.

The door closed behind her. "Undress so we can get you clean. You smell like pig droppings."

Wendy turned to see that Randi didn't leave. In fact, she was getting comfortable, even removing her cloak. "I can take it from here, you definitely don't have to stay."

She huffed, "You are not going to meet your mortal friends. You are meeting gods. I am here to make sure you get it right along with checking the enchantments on your clothing. Now hurry, we have no time for your childishness."

Not able to argue, Wendy started discarding her clothes.

***

When Wendy was working as a CNA, she prided in making the patient feel safe, but also had some sort of privacy when available. If the patient could, Wendy would let them clean themselves while she stayed in the same room but looked away. If they couldn't, she would try to make it like a spa experience. Massaging the shampoo in the hair, scrubbing every inch of the feet, and rubbing the patient's back with the wash rag.

Randi was nothing like that. It was as if a warden gave a bath to a prisoner. Rough and unforgiving. She scraped the rough soap over every bruise, dunked her under the water without warning, and seemed to rip Wendy's hair out of her head any chance she got. Especially when she started braiding her hair. Wendy's eyes watered as she silently suffered while Randi pulled the war braids in her hair. Wendy's hands often reflexed instinctively to cover her sore scalp, only to be smacked away.

Randi huffed. "Just as I begin to see why you were chosen, you start acting like a baby. You will never join the clans if you cry from a little hair pulling."

Wendy bit back a growl. "Oh, you think I'm worthy now?"

"No, but children of slaves are given the chance to earn their place in the clans, and you will be given the same."

Wendy couldn't help but laugh. "Did they all have to fight gods?"

"No, they fought the clan's enemies. Proving themselves in the battlefield to earn their place. You will earn your place with how useful your power is to the realm."

Wendy felt it harder than it had ever been to hold back her anger. The fantasy of punching the cow were only held back by the fact she still held Wendy's hair. Instead she grated through gritted teeth. "Great to hear."

"Almost done, whelp. Then we can place your garments on."

***

An hour-and-a-half in total and Wendy was ready. Of course, there were no mirrors for Wendy to see how her torture turned out. Instead, Wendy was quickly shoved out the door and told to meet Hel in the throne room while Randi cleaned up. Wendy tried not to smile as she left, but the image of Randi cleaning up after her was a small achievement. As Wendy walked to the throne room, she let herself dwell on the thought until a plushy smacked her in the face. As she reeled, Will's laughter chimed through the air. Wendy focused on the sound, seeing him by the entry to the throne room.

"Will, what the fuck?"

He only shrugged as he snickered, "Should've been paying attention."

With a sigh and a light smack on his arm, Wendy smiled. "Aren't you going to wish me luck? Or give me a small pep-talk before I go get myself killed?"

"Oh, is that what I'm doing?"

"It better fucking be. I'm in this mess because of you."

His face animated as he brought his fingers up to his chest. "Ooohhh okay, I'm the one who went Super Saiyan and started a bar fight."

Wendy snorted, "Bitch. Your bar, your fault."

"Enough! Or I'll send you both to time out."

Hel's booming voice echoed in the hall. Like Wendy, she was also dressed in furs and armor, a decorative helmet covering the top half of her stern face. Both Will and Wendy stopped immediately and faced her.

Obviously amused, Hel waved at Will. "So? Aren't you going to give her a pep talk?"

Will turned his body to Wendy and slapped his hand on Wendy's shoulder. With a big smile, he declared. "Don't fuck it up, we are all watching you."

Wendy rolled her eyes but she smiled warmly. "Tthhhaaannnkkssssss."

Hel clapped her hands together, "Super compelling, now let's hit the road. We're going to pass fashionably late if we don't get going."

Wendy started to follow Hel's retreating form when Will's hand stopped her. She turned to him, his face not holding the smile it once did. He looked worried. Wendy smiled, patting his arm. "Even if I lose. You won't get rid of me. I'll still visit you at the bar."

He let his hand fall off Wendy's shoulder. "But I know what losing would do to you. Just do your best and whatever happens, happens. Okay?"

Wendy nodded. Giving one last wave as she jogged to catch up to the Goddess as she walked to the darkness. At first, Wendy was confused. She figured that, since Asgard was on top of the world tree, they would just ride a pegasus up. Instead, they went out the great doors. Traveling in the darkness until they approached a warped stone door with no handle. The door opened without Hel touching it, the scratching of stone against stone making Wendy flinch. It opened to a gray chilly sky. As they both cleared the door, it closed. Leaving only a boulder in its place.

Wendy took a moment to look around at the breathtaking view. Stone cliffs hugged a broad river. The green of the brush splotted the grays of stones that were only a few shades darker than the sky. It was a painting Wendy hung in her memory to enjoy for the rest of her life.

"Where are we?" Wendy asked as she turned in circles.

"Norway. We have to cross Bilröst to get into Asgard."

Wendy stopped spinning and crooked her head at Hel. "You mean the rainbow bridge? It's in Norway?"

Hel gave her a sideways glance, "Yeah, where else would it be?"

"Well Asgard is on top of the world tree. Why are we on earth if it's just another part of the Nordic realm?"

"Oh. Well the short answer is wars. It's harder to get into Asgard if you have to take the long way around. Though there is a backdoor in Yggdrasill, since this is an official visit we have to go through the official entrance." She waved her hand, "It's just for show nowadays because it's getting harder and harder for Heimdallr to open the portal."

Wendy nodded, "Makes sense."

"Now when we get there, just don't talk unless you are asked something. Most of my family have charms and shit in their voices. The only time you need to speak is when grandpa asks you to join his ranks. Other than that, it's better for you to just follow my lead."

Wendy thrust out her thumb pointing upwards with an enthusiastic grin.

"Smart-ass," Hel chuckled. "By the way, your armor is enchanted to prevent breaking in the body. As long as you keep it on, you are safe from breaking any bones or snapping any ligaments from attacks. It will still hurt like a bitch, but at least you can still keep fighting. The bands that Randi put in your hair should raise your wisdom capabilities and your quick thinking skills a bit. It won't be anything close to Odin's, but anything helps."

Wendy touched the leather band Randi put in her hair to hold the braids back. "Thank you."

She shrugged, "Show me with your actions. The bridge is up ahead."

It was a cliff extending out to a platform, the stone dangling precariously over the massive drop to the river. Near the edge sat an old man. His hair was white and his skin reflected a great many years in the sun. He looked homeless, if Wendy were being honest. His clothes looked warm but worn. He also had a gray blanket wrapped over his shoulders.

At their approach, he stood to greet them. He gave a short bow before smiling warmly at them. "God dag gudinne Hel. Ansiktet ditt skinner av skjønnhet denne dagen."

"Guess you didn't get the message." Hel pointed back at Wendy with her thumb. "Sadly, she is American. Mind speaking English?"

He fixed his eyes upon Wendy. They seemed to be as gray as the stone they were standing on with the indicative shimmering movement all the gods seemed to possess. The part making Wendy stare, however, was that his pupils were elongated. Not quite as extreme as a goat's, but enough to draw the eye.

He held out his hand and gave a more formal bow. "My mother made sure I could never be impolite to a lady. Especially not to one as yourself. May I introduce myself as Heimdallr, guardian of Bilröst."

Feeling like it was the right thing to do, Wendy took his hand and did a smaller curtsy back. "An honor, great god Heimdallr. I am Wendy, reaper for goddess Hel."

Heimdallr hesitated for a brief moment before letting his hand fall. His eyes bore into her as if intrigued as he muttered, "Not what I expected."

"Sorry to do this but..." Hel circled her hand at the space behind him.

"Oh, Of course,"

With a wave of his hand the stone began to glow the primary colors. Like smoke from an incense, the colors bled into the air. As the colors crossed, the colors briefly meld into the cross colors. The image of all colors of the rainbow swaying among the variants in a never-ending dance expanded as the area across the cliff became hazy. An unnatural shimmer started fogging the space in front of them, which was only about a meter or so in front of them. This was also where the rainbow bridge stopped. The great rainbow bridge, only about a car length wide and a meter long.

"That's it?" The words flew out of her mouth before Wendy could stop them. The sentence gaining her looks from both the gods, making her immediately panic. "I'm sorry. I'm sorry, ignore me."

Hel looked at her in the way you look at a really stupid person, or else someone who had done something incredibly stupid. "Yes. What were you expecting?"

Wendy blushed furiously, "Nothing, nothing. Hollywood just lied about how big it was, that's all."

Hel grabbed the back of Wendy's shirt-collar, and man-handled her across the bridge and into the portal. All the while, Heimdallr bent over at the waist as he laughed hysterically behind them.

***

Wendy's breath caught when the fog cleared on the other side. From the short section of the rainbow bridge, Wendy could see most of Yggdrasill's reach. From the base to the mountains where Helhime was, to the suspended Alfheim. She was also able to glance at the places she had never been, her heart jumping at the prospect of visiting them. Though, she wasn't able to stare for long. Hel pushed her through large wooden gates into the bustling courtyard. The sound of the wood planks under her feet creaked as she let Wendy go.

Imagine a castle, within a bustling Nordic kingdom. Now, combine that image with the craftsmanship of a professionally built tree house. That is Asgard. Branches artfully protruded the floorboards, but no one had fear of the place falling around them. The craftsmanship was no less than the carving on Hel's door and the architecture was damn impressive. Did Wendy get to admire it? No. She was too busy catching up with Hel and making sure she didn't get lost.

On the other side of the city was the great castle. A feat of engineering that was decorated to the nines. The massive building was connected to Glaðsheimr, meaning that the main rooms were wide open areas as they made their way to the back of the building. They diverted to the right, avoiding the massive open doors that seemed to lead into an ocean of clouds, and headed to a smaller set of doors. They lead into a type of hallway serving as a mini armory with an array of knives, swords, axes, and shields displayed on sturdy racks.

Hel turned on Wendy, placing her hands palm up to Wendy. "Stay."

Wendy's eyebrows knitted, "But-"

The goddess emphasized by pointing at her, then at the ground, "Stay." She walked a few steps, looked back at her for a moment, then slowly turned to walk into the sunshine.

Wendy took a breath, decompressing as she let out her breath, the silence hitting her like a freight train. The first time alone she'd had that day. She despised it. The thoughts and anxiety banging at the door of her mind, the prickles of doubt slithering up her skin. Worst, there was no one out there, only Hel to cheer her on. Gus came to mind, sending another surge of panic through her. If she lost, she would lose him too.

"Wow, I can almost see the energy with how much you're freaking out. Little hint, panicking does the opposite of helping."

Wendy jumped around to see Regin. The oracle was dressed in a shirt that read, 'Ready to Rumble' this time. Her hand full with a pretzel and a large fountain drink that she took a large sip out of while Wendy recovered from her scare.

Wendy took some deep breaths, "Oh, it's you, Regin."

She shrugged, "I knew you would be here."

"Oh, right. The seeing-the-future thing. Any chance you can tell me if I win or not?"

She shook her head, "No spoilers. Plus the future is so wibbly-wobbly that if I told you, it might rip a hole in the universe or something."

Wendy sighed as she leaned on a clear section of the wall. "Fair enough. Then why are you here?"

"To see how you're doing, silly!" She smiled brightly. "I told you that we're friends. You hide it well, but you always freak out before a big fight. I wanted to make sure you weren't overthinking." She waved her soda as she shifted her weight, "As always, I was right."

Wendy chuckled, "You got me. I got some training but I'm up against a god. I don't see how a fucking week of jumping around can prepare me to beat him."

She snorted a laugh, "Oh mortal witch, even if you trained for hundreds of years you would never beat him. Especially in his own house. You can surprise him though."

Wendy's head snapped up, "Surprise him?"

Regin took a long drab of her soda and shrugged. "Sure, he is the god of wisdom. Nothing surprises him anymore. If you catch him off guard, bet he would give you a break."

"So, impress him with my skills?" Wendy guessed.

She held up a finger, "Only one hint per playthrough. I can't be a good crazy-oracle character if I give you all the answers! Anywho, the show is about to start so I better get my seat-."

"Wait." Wendy only just stopped herself from lunging forward. "Will I be happy? With how all of this turns out, I mean, will I end up okay in the end?"

Regin stilled. Her eyes softened as her smile became soft. "Little witch, you always find happiness. It doesn't matter what situation you're in or who is around you, you find it. Even when things happen that make you sad, you never stay down for long. Like moths to their god lamp, it's why people love you. Now go out there and face your destiny." She walked a few steps before turning back around. "Oh, we have margarita nights every other Wednesday. If you don't show up we will have to black bag you. Don't worry, I'll show you where it's at after our first training session. It is a simpi's job after all. See you then, toodles."

Wendy watched her go. She was a bit stunned, unable to process the compliment at that time. She stayed frozen until Hel came back and got her. Leading her to the battle ground and her destiny.

Hel,

What's more important; how others see you or how you see yourself?

On one hand, you are the only one who has. They're the one who has to live in their own thoughts. When a person dies, they only have themselves to blame on where they end up. They made the decisions and they are the one who has to deal with themselves at the end of the day.

On the other hand, others can see what you've become accustomed to. They see how hard or not hard the person is working. They see the actions and can point out flaws or strengths of that person. Of course, some people are just dicks. Throwing out negativity for one reason or another, but fuck those people.

Everyone sees me as a kind, fairly happy-go-lucky person. That's partially because that is the energy I want to put into the world. It's also because I have honed my self control. There are days I want to kill. I want to destroy the body and spirit of someone who has gotten in my way or gives me a nasty look. I want to be like one of the Valkyries and start a fight out of the blue. There are also days I hate myself. The depression screams that I don't do enough. That I'm not good enough for the gifts I have been given.

So what is more important; that others see me as an entity of light or the fact that there are days I can't live with myself?

In my eyes, you're comfortable with yourself and you don't give a fuck what anyone else thinks. However, I don't know what you think of yourself. Plus the fact you are WAY older then me, so you have probably been through enough shit that you have lost all fucks. I don't know, just my random thoughts.

Chapter Twenty Three: Greatest Weakness

Hel led her through the door to an arena pit. The wooden pin was surrounded by elevated bleachers filled to the brim with human and non-humanoid creatures. Wendy realized some of the patron's eyes were glowing, and reasoned it must be how they are sharing the fight with the outside worlds. At a fancy box seat on the far end of the arena sat two filled thrones. One was obviously Freya, her face structure similar to Freyr with flowing strawberry blond hair instead of the red and brown dreads. Next to her was Odin, an older man with a long white beard and an eyepatch. He wasn't in armor; only in a long royal tunic, pants, and a fur-lined cloak. His throne was flanked by two black birds watching everything expectedly. The entire atmosphere made Wendy's hands sweat.

Wendy stopped when Hel halted and copied her formal bow. After a moment of silence, Odin spoke.

"Daughter of Loki, what is this you have brought me?"

Hel gestured her hand toward Wendy. "The reaper Wendy, still mortal under my employ."

He took a moment to study Wendy. "This is the one with the mana? She, who has the blessing of Nirvana?"

Is he serious? Wendy's eyebrows furrowed as she internally questioned everything she ever thought of Odin. However, she did feel his power. She took a moment to strengthen the sphere of protection she had around herself. Mentally making the sounds to block out the influence he was already projecting.

"She seems to be All Father," the goddess responded.

Odin's eye moved to Wendy. "Power like that will do quite nicely. I invite you to join my army. To live in Asgard and join us in battles and feasts. To train with the best to fight the end-time beasts."

Wendy squared her shoulders. She felt it, her lips about to tell him anything he wanted to hear. She directed more energy to her shield as her mind resorted to her theater stage mindset. Projecting with her diaphragm she answered clearly. "I am greatly honored, All Father, but I respectfully decline."

The crowd erupted in murmurs, all surprised by her answer. Only Odin and Freya seemed to be expecting this. Wendy continued to maintain eye contact, not backing down.

"Not one has ever declined my offer to join the great hall. Perhaps a battle to see which one will have it all?" The old man stood. He was leener then Wendy expected, but it was his aura that made Wendy struggle to not take a step away from him. As if it was a short jump, he gracefully landed from his ten foot perch. The clouds on the ground puffing as he took a few steps towards Hel and Wendy. "Your bravery is also one to be admired, I believe a challenge is required. A challenge of skill will decide your fate. On the battlefield, you shall be the first to correlate."

Continuing to crutch on her theatrical mindset, Wendy let her mouth run without really thinking about it. "To ensure an honorable duel, I ask that I decide the rules."

Both Hel and Odin's eyebrows jumped to their scalps. They exchanged a look before Odin addressed Wendy again. "Speak."

"Considering you're a god and I am a mortal. If I can make you bleed before my body fails me in the match, then I win. If I pass out or can't fight anymore, I will join you in Asgard. Sound fair?"

The god erupted in a boisterous laugh sounding like thunder during a storm. Wendy shook from the sheer power of it, but forced her eyes to stay fixed.

"A challenge you were careful to not misstep, what am I to do other than accept? To give the mortal some slack, I shan't even use my axe. A battle of magik it will be. Before the feast, the winner will be called by Skadi."

A large, bulky woman with blond hair who wore all white furs, stood. She was so pale that she would have almost blended into the clouds if she weren't on the elevated platform. Appearing to be the strong, silent type, she walked to the edge of the bleachers and nodded.

"Then it's decided." Hel gave a short bow. "I'll make my way to my seat." Before she did, she gave a reassuring squeeze to Wendy's arm before disappearing right in front of her eyes.

Wendy blinked before Skadi pulled out a horn from a pack on her waist. Without much of a warning, she blew it, a trumpet barreling through the arena.

On reflex, Wendy jumped back as far as she could and immediately started channeling energy into her body. As she did, she watched the old man grow. Black fur started replacing his tunic as he morphed into a massive black bear, roaring as he began his charge. She did the only thing she could think of at the time, she ran.

He was the size of a grizzly, even though black bears were supposed to be smaller. With that big of an animal, the best way to defeat it would be to get behind it. The arena was in more of an oval shape, so she ran to the apex. If she could use the wall to jump behind him-

Wendy began jumping, trying to get behind him as she had done with the boar in the tree-filled forest. However, the bear had one thing the bore didn't. He reached out, slashing at her and nicked her side. Wendy sucked in a breath at the pain, but kept moving. Running while making sure that the cut wasn't too deep. It hurt, but the adrenaline kept Wendy moving. She stayed close to the ground, weaving and jumping off the walls to avoid the claws and teeth of the snarling monster. He could run fast. Standing to quickly change directions but his slashes missed Wendy's wily battle tactics.

On a lucky break, she made two quick jumps off adjoining walls to get on his back. Before she could even raise her hand, he flopped back. Landing on his back to crush her. She jumped off his tough hide. Clouds puffed from the impact as she landed. Wendy used the moment to run. Changing tactics, she began making throwing stars out of her blazing energy. She only had to make him bleed after all, she was confident that these would stick. Using a wall jump to change her direction, she threw them overhand as she would a throwing-axe. Though her training was not used to practice her aim, only one of the four stars got close. He changed directions, avoiding the spikes poking up from the white fluff. Wendy ran the opposite way, realizing that the stars disappeared as soon as her concentration was broken.

Wendy hissed at herself. There was so much working against her at the moment. If she had more time, if she tried a bit harder, if she could just think. Only one thing rang through her mind. A phrase that Regin had said long ago.

"...and remember to fight like an immortal."

How did she fight like an immortal? Fight without fear of death?

Wendy's head snapped at the sound of a booming roar, her eyes catching the shake of the jowls as the massive one-eyed bear prepared for another charge.

Wait! Something that size should have a hard time stopping. She smirked at the ridiculousness of her own idea. Changing her course to meet him head on. In her hands, she created as many caltrops as she could hold. When her mind calculated the right time to strike, she jumped as high as her legs would let her. As she front flipped in the air she dropped the caltrops on either side, trapping him in. As she exited her flip, she extended her leg, creating a knife on the back of her heel. Her calculations were right.. By both of their trajectories, even if he kept running she would still hit him in his back. Wendy's heart leapt as her heel descended towards his fur.

Right before the knife touched his skin, he disappeared. A large raven maneuvering around the extended leg to miss the trap entirely.

Wendy, clumsily landed; everything disappearing with the impact of her fall. Wendy panted as she got back to her feet a small sound making her heart stop. A whistle that made her sweat run cold.

Fuck, not now. It was only a slight wheeze but she could begin to feel the tightening in her chest. She didn't have her inhaler, she hadn't needed it until now. No, this couldn't be happening.

A howl ripped Wendy from her internal struggle. She whipped around to see a black wolf with one eye. It was massive, its head sitting as tall as Wendy's. From reflex, Wendy made a two-handed sword with her power. The blaze crackled brightly with Wendy's determination as she braced to dodge. She couldn't run, as the asthma and the obvious agility of the wolf form made running irrelevant. Instead she faced the beast as it ran up on her, its teeth glistening in the sunlight. Her mind panicking, she swung at the wolf's chest like a baseball bat.

He twisted his body unto hind legs to miss the swing. Using the time Wendy had to waste following through, he latched his jaws into and through Wendy's bicep and deltoid. Wendy screamed as the heat coupled with blinding pain focused in Wendy's arm. He began rattling her, separating her shoulder joint. Wendy reflexively poured her power into her free hand, making a dagger before she swung to dig it into his neck. Knowing, he let go. She would have missed him if she hadn't extended the blade point, nicking him in his shoulder. Wendy smiled, but it faded when a light shone on Odin's back. A complex rune, but one she recognized as a sigil for protection. The cut was small but the sigil was keeping it from bleeding.

"You cheating bastard!" Wendy screamed. Unable to move her dislocated arm, she swung with her good arm. Throwing the sword straight and true right at the fucker's face. He danced around the throw, using the momentum to lunge at Wendy. She tried to roll, but the pain in her arm made her falter. He used that opportunity, ripping his teeth into her other arm. She shrieked at the new pain. Unable to fight as he shook her like a stuffed animal before throwing her. Her breath rushing out as her back slammed against the wall.

Stars filled her vision for a moment until she realized she couldn't breath. She bent over, fighting to get air through the sludge forming in her chest. Each of her arms pulsated with heat as it felt like the teeth were still embedded in her.

"What is that noise that her lungs make? Could it be her body about to break?"

Wendy opened her eyes to the pool of blood that was forming underneath her. She tried to move, but everything seemed so heavy. When she strained over the weight, the stabs of pain forced her to abandon her quest. Instead, she steeled herself against the pain, gathering magikal energy inside herself. If she could just move.

She couldn't move the energy. Her head was starting to feel light as her lungs strained in musical rhythm. She couldn't focus enough to send the energy anywhere.

"Seems your body has failed you. However proud you should feel too. Your skills are promising for a newly-hatched mortal. I believe this spar has been nothing more than cordial. A worthy opponent you do make, though defeat has always been your fate."

Wendy closed her eyes. No, she couldn't go down like this. If she just got up she could... kick him or something. Bite him at least.

"Grandpa!" Hel's voice rang across the pit, "You have to heal her. Heal her right now."

"Why? To heal her before she has surrendered would be wry. It would be more honorable to let her die." Odin sounded puzzled.

"I don't own her soul. If she dies like this, her soul might not come back here."

Wendy tried to focus. Trying one last time to move, resulting in a scream of pain. She bent her leg trying to use the wall to stand but her foot slipped on her own blood, her crash-landing making another pulse of pain wrench through her upper torso.

Everything went black for what seemed like hours. She saw everyone she loved. Then she saw only those who she would be leaving behind. Her grandparents, her cousins, and most of all, her father. They all would have no idea what happened to her. They all would die wondering. Wendy saw her fathers face smile. His bushy beard expanded as he told Wendy he loved her. Words she would never hear again.

She felt someone in her personal bubble. The now human god bending down to crouch next to her.

Please! Wendy called with her mind to anyone who would listen. Screaming as panic made her wheezes race. *Please, help me, Holy Spirit! God! Anyone, I beg you. Nirvana, save me!*

***

A long time ago, Wendy felt in danger and called for help. A small little girl screaming in her mind for someone to save her from something she didn't want to do. Her saving grace came in the form of shadow figures, showing up to scare away the situation. Wendy forgot about the incident, since she made it out unscathed. As Wendy's fear of losing her loved ones fueled this call, she felt the air become thick in a way she had only felt once before. Using the last of her strength, she poured all of her magikal energy into her mouth to make points to her teeth. Like a snake, she struck.

She didn't see the shadows appear on the battlefield. She didn't know that two of the dark figures had restrained the baffled god just in time for Wendy to strike. She didn't see the face of her long-dead dog, Kitty, protector materialize, protecting her master one last time. To her, she only knew she bit him when her tongue tasted the material of his shirt. The resistance of her jagged teeth piercing his muscled breast. She twisted, the figures helping her pin him to the ground. In a frenzy she ripped upwards, her eyes unable to open as everything she had came down into another vicious bite. Demonic growls tasseled with the wheezes as Wendy gnashed at whatever she could get her teeth onto, the adrenaline from fear numbing her mind. Her only thought was to hurt him until she could taste the metallic iron of blood. She needed to keep going till she tasted blood. This wasn't over until he was bleeding.

A laugh from behind her finally snapped her eyes open. She was still sitting in a pool of her own blood, bent over at the waist. A turn revealing that her hearing had not failed her. In his throne, was an unscathed Odin. Clapping with a smile on his face. There was no red, there was no bite. He must have teleported away.

She lost. All her will dissipated; the figures disappeared. As she lost consciousness on the heavenly floor, tears leaked from her eyes. Her last thought before the darkness was of her father. A worried face as he called out to her.

Her heart broke as everything went black.

***

"She's healing fast for a mortal. I was expecting a lot more work."

"Know when she is going to wake up, Eir?" Hel's voice almost whispered.

"She is awake now," the other voice mentioned. "Let me hold off the other Valkyries so you two can have a moment."

Forcing her eyes to rip open, Wendy adjusted to the bright light of the room she was in. She was on a bed, tucked in with bandages covering her arms. She met eyes with the smiling goddess.

"Well, look who is full of surprises. Have a good nap, sleepyhead?"

Wendy took a long experimental breath, the hiss of wheezing completely gone from her lungs. She also tested her fingers. It hurt to move, but they were able to.

Wendy looked away. "I lost. After everything, he didn't bleed. I'm stuck here… I'm never going to see them again." She was wracked with despair, guilt, frustration, and worst of all, a horrendous feeling of having let down not only herself, but also everybody she ever cared about.

Hel's eyebrows furrowed, "What are you talking about? You won."

Wendy's breath caught, her heartbeat pounding in her ears. "What?"

"Your last attack. It was amazing. These long dead souls appeared out of nowhere and distracted grandpa enough for your ghost dog to bite him. The spirit dog bit his entire nipple off before he successfully transported himself away. After you passed out, he even made a whole speech about you being a true warrior and all that shit."

"That you are, I say with credibility now we've sparred, though your skills have the ability to go far." Wendy's heart froze. She looked behind Hel to see Odin. Looking healthy with a grin stretched on his face. "For the first time in my existence, I didn't realize how you had assistance. My ego lost me this match. For the first time I was surprised when the dog's teeth did latch."

Wendy blinked, unable to process. "What?"

"He's saying you won your freedom. Your big power move caught him off guard and he admitted defeat. You won't be forced to move to Asgard. It's all over."

Wendy's vision began to blur, a hot tear running down her cheek. "Really?"

"Though I do detest, I do have one request." Odin folded his arms. "In your leisure let me hone your skills. It would be an honor, as long as you hold no ills."

"Grandpa," Hel interjected. "Can we not do this now?"

With a huff, Odin relented. "I must go to the feast. Mortal, think about my offer at least."

With that, he walked out the door. All eyes watched as he silently left.

"He really likes you." Hel added. "You basically humiliated him and he still wants to teach you. But I can't blame him. You didn't give up even when he rendered your arms useless." She looked back at Wendy, one eyebrow raised. "Any chance you can tell me what happened?"

Wendy shook her head. "I don't know. I just acted."

The goddess sighed, "Well, you made quite the impression. You're the talk of all the realms now. You're practically a celebrity."

Wendy chuckled, "Is that a bad thing?"

"You're recognizable now and not all gods will have good intentions." She shrugged, "However, I think we have some time before we have to worry about it. Though I'd consider taking grand-pop up on his offer. It probably won't be him teaching you personally, anyway, he'll probably push you off on one of the Valkyrie."

"I definitely will as soon as my arms heal."

"Sure." Hel smiled, "How long do you want? Like, two days?"

Wendy rolled her eyes. "Hel, I was mauled. I know you guys can apparently heal by teleporting, but I'll need months to recover."

The goddesses eyebrows furrowed, "What are you talking about? Eir said you would be well enough to join the feast. She just said not to fight till late tomorrow."

Wendy sputtered. "Did she do a spell on me or something?"

Hel flailed her hands, "How would I know? Here, let me go get her. I want to get some of the food downstairs anyway."

Wendy laid back against the soft pillow. She wanted relief to wave through her, but it never came. Only a hard rock sat in her stomach. A feeling that everything was about to backfire. That something was going to go horribly wrong.

Hel,

No one but the human best friend and Eir knows how bad it is.

Thankfully, it's not too bad yet. I just can't drive. Not a big loss, especially

because I can walk anywhere the doors can't take me. Because of this

development, I'm going to try to stay in the mortal world more. I want to

at least be there for the besty's son to graduate. The kid loves me.

Though, I'm not sure how long I can keep this from dad.

In the mortal world, it would be diagnosed as a type of cataract.

Specifically, the same degenerative eye disease one would find in a ninety

year old patent. It would also seem that I am developing arthritis. The

experience on the other side of the veil drained my mortal body quite a

bit. The worst part is that I feel perfect in my apartment, but as soon as I

step out...

I'm not ready to leave the mortal world, so I'll have to learn how

to live with it I guess. I don't see what else I can do. I'm not ready to lose

them yet....

Epilogue

"Not like you could understand…"

I closed the book. Compared to when it had originally been given to me, the leather was now scratched and worn. I sat in my apartment, housed in my own little pocket dimension. At one time, I was giddy from that simple fact. The reality of my situation. Now, my heart was heavy with the knowledge.

I stood, grabbed my cloak and the book. Taking a moment, I fished out my enchanted keys and used them to find the now all-too-familiar door among the mazes. Armed with a big calming breath, I stepped through the veil barrier. Activating my choker, I walked out of the post office electrical door. It was located in the back of the building, only being accessed by authorized personnel so I never had to worry of someone running into me. Though, as soon as my eyes passed through the veil, my entire vision filtered through static. It was hard to see, but I had been taking this path for quite some time now.

Walk three gray fences down, walk two crosswalks, then turn down the back road until I reach the park. There I sat on the watercolor bench. As I took my seat, I took a moment to soak all of it in.

The thing was, not all my vision was gone. Though the lifeless dirt and inanimate objects were hard to see, I had gained the power to see auras. People, animals, and plants exploded with the aura of their hearts. The colors of their moods and secrets they held. That stuff, I can see clearly. In the big cities, I barely have an issue because there is so much energy around. In Nebraska though, I only get a glimpse here or there.

Except on this bench. From this bench, I could see the most important aura. The deep blue aura of my father as he sat in his house, sleeping on his favorite recliner while Sponge Bob played on his TV. He didn't know I was there but what would he say if I just showed up. There would be so many questions that I didn't know how to answer. Plus, I have no way for him to believe me.

I rubbed my hand over the leather. Letting my fingers feel Hel's sigil before I opened it to the last page. I took the ballpoint pin from my cloak pocket and wrote two more sentences.

I don't know how to tell you, Dad. How do I tell you that I'm going to die?